COSMOS AND COMMITMENT

Girlfriends of Gotham - Book Three

DELANCEY STEWART

COSMOS AND COMMITMENT

Girlfriends of Gotham
Book Three

by Delancey Stewart

For my family – the one I was born into, and the one I chose. And to the real Girlfriends of Gotham - Jenny, Josi, Colleen, Michelle, and Marisol.

CONTENTS

Chapter One

A COUGAR ON THE PROWL

Natalie

"YOU ARE the coolest girl I've ever known." CJ's warm hand slid across my stomach as we lay side by side in his bed, staring up at the ceiling of his bedroom. One jagged crack ran from corner to corner. On my worst days, I imagined it would cave in and we'd be suffocated under the weight of someone else's bed, someone else's life crashing down on us. CJ always laughed when I mentioned this fear.

I turned to look at him. "I've never been cool. I think I've spent most of my life trying to figure out how to blend in and not make a jackass of myself."

That slow sexy grin spread across his full lips as his brown eyes danced. It both honored and irritated me that he found my confession amusing. "You should never try to blend in. You're amazing, Natalie." CJ rolled toward me and kissed me gently on the lips. Not a suggestive kiss, just a sweet reminder that he was mine and I was his. That we were finally together.

"Thanks." I kissed him back, letting myself lean into his warmth for a few seconds, and then rolled out of bed, excusing myself to the bathroom. I took in my reflection with appraising eyes. Blue eyes, maybe too close together, and blond hair, long and straight. Ears that were slightly asymmetrical, and front teeth that I'd always thought were too big. Was I the coolest girl in the world? Definitely not. I was twenty-five, living in New York City, and just trying to figure out how to get from day to day without dropping one of the balls I felt like I was always juggling.

CJ's assessment of me certainly stroked my ego, but even after a year in New York, I didn't have much confidence in myself. I had great luck, as it turned out. I'd stumbled into a position as marketing director at a start-up Internet company, and I'd convinced the greatest guy I'd ever met that I was somehow worthy of him. As I stared in the mirror, all I could feel was that I somehow didn't deserve any of it. I was sick of that feeling. I was sick of being a pushover, sick of waiting on luck and the whims of others to decide my destiny. 1999 was going to be the year of Natalie Pepper. Sure, it was already late September, but a lot could be accomplished in a few months. If these two months went well, I might just declare myself to be destined for greatness in the next millennium too.

I brushed my teeth and hair and splashed some cold water on my face before wandering back into the bedroom, a plan forming. There were ways people worked on themselves, professionals who could help get to a person's true essence, right? I was going to find one of those.

CJ had turned the television on and was intently watching some financial news show. The man could find investment news at any time of day or night. He ate it up like the girls and I devoured *Friends* or *Sex and the City*.

I settled onto the bed next to him and leaned over,

blocking his view of the television. "I'm gonna head out. Meeting the girls for brunch."

His dark eyes sparked. "You sure? We could just stay here in bed all day..." His voice was low, and his fingers traced up my arm. My stomach tightened as my skin heated under his touch. CJ was the one thing I couldn't resist in the world. I'd wanted him for so long that sometimes I still couldn't believe he was mine.

I was about to give in when his phone rang, breaking the moment. "You get that," I said, standing up. "I'm gonna sneak out."

"I'll call you later." He rolled to pick up the handset out of the base station.

I glanced at the phone as I left the room and wished I hadn't. The caller ID displayed the name Irene Halliday. Not a name I enjoyed hearing or seeing, but one that didn't seem to want to go away. I lingered in the living room, putting my shoes on and gathering my things slowly while CJ talked. I wasn't really eavesdropping. I just hadn't left yet.

"I understand, Irene," he was saying. He sounded exasperated, and that made me feel better. "I just don't think it's the right time. Even if it is in the city."

I took my time latching my watch, which had been abandoned on the breakfast bar.

"Well, I'm not exactly qualified, for one thing," CJ said. "It'd be a pretty big jump for me."

Irene must have been making her point for quite some time, because CJ was silent. It was awkward just standing in the living room, so when CJ said nothing else, I picked up my bag and headed for the door. I pulled it open, and as the door swung shut behind me, I thought I heard CJ say, "Fine. We can meet to discuss it. I'm free tomorrow."

My happy mood dissipated as I rode the elevator to the lobby of CJ's Upper West Side building. By the time I'd reached the sidewalk, any giddy elation I'd been feeling had evaporated in the face of the ever-present Irene. What the hell did she want? She'd tried unsuccessfully to lure CJ back to Buffalo, and now she was here in the city. She was way too old for him. I hoped they both knew that. I poked around at the discomfort that always bloomed inside when Irene's name came up. Did I really think CJ would do anything to jeopardize the relationship we'd fought so hard for? Not really. But Irene's presence made me uncomfortable all the same. The sooner she was back in Buffalo and out of his life, the better.

I got on the southbound subway at 72nd Street and hoped mimosas with the girls would help lighten my mood.

———

By now, the staff at Cafeteria knew to expect us most Sunday mornings. Not everyone made it each week, and sometimes boyfriends or even straggling remnants of what would become one-night or weekend flings joined us. But as often as we could, we had brunch together, and it was one of my favorite things. Brunch gave us a chance to catch up, to recap what had happened each week. Lately it felt like everyone was getting busier, and those occasional Sundays were the one day we could all take to slow down and spend some time catching up, pulling our little group back together. This week, Candace had come solo, but Lulu and Andrew were both there. I got to the door at the same time as Tamara, and we wandered over arm in arm as Lulu continued her monologue. Tamara and I sat down at the round table.

"I know you had planned to move, Candace, but Brooklyn? Why not just move to New Jersey? Or Queens?" Lulu sounded disgusted at the thought, and while her words were nearly venomous, her intentions were not. Lulu was hard to understand sometimes, but I'd gotten to know her well. She was an exaggerated personality, and she often made off-the-wall proclamations and completely judgmental pronouncements. She wasn't intentionally argumentative, just passionate. "We'll never see you." She pouted, the full lower lip pushing out as she pushed her long dark hair off her shoulders.

Andrew, Lulu's boyfriend, put an arm around her and smiled. "I think we can manage the subway out to Brooklyn, Lu."

"Seriously," Candace huffed. "If you can find me fifteen hundred square feet on two floors and a garden in the city, we'll move back."

"You have a garden?" Lulu sat up straighter. "You're a gardener now?"

Candace rolled her eyes. "I'm not a farmer, Lulu. It's a green space. Somewhere to sit outside."

"I'm just glad you got it." Tamara pulled a roll apart. "I had like six other couples come in the same day you applied." She was in real estate and had found my apartment for me. Now she'd helped Candace and Gregoire find theirs. "You guys had the best credit profile by far, though."

"Of course we did." Candace sipped her mimosa. "Gregoire has the best everything." She winked, but then her gaze fell on Andrew. "I mean, no offense Andrew. I'm sure your… assets are impressive."

Andrew blushed.

"So, hi, by the way," I cut in.

"Sorry, honey," Lulu leaped up, nearly knocking down a passing waiter as she rushed to my chair to hug me. People at nearby tables turned at the commotion, and the waiter looked offended, moving around Lu to another table. "How are you? How's CJ? How's work?" She stopped to hug Tamara on her way back to her chair.

"Everything is good," I answered. "I think."

"You think?" Tamara looked skeptical, and her blue eyes flashed. "That means something is not good. What is it? Wait, is it breakfast-appropriate?"

"Lulu's here, so we've already veered into inappropriate. No worries there." Candace smiled.

"You're the one who wants to know about my boyfriend's penis size!" Lulu pointed across the table.

Andrew pulled Lulu's pointing hand back into her lap. "It's okay, Lu. They're kidding."

Lulu sniffed and took another sip of her drink.

"What's wrong, Pepper?" Candace put on her problem-solving face. She had a way of seeing the world that made it easy for her to blow through obstacles, but she wasn't exactly subtle. She went after what she wanted like a linebacker, which wasn't my style.

"Remember how I told you about Irene? The woman in Buffalo who offered CJ the job last year?"

"The old lady?" Tamara said.

"She's not that old. Maybe forty."

"That's pretty old." Tamara nodded at her own proclamation.

"Well, she's older than us, for sure."

"What's going on? Is the cougar on the prowl again?" Candace leaned in. "Someone should put that old cat down."

I shrugged. "I'm not sure. She called CJ this morning as I was leaving. He said something about meeting her."

Lulu sat up straighter. "Oh, honey. I'm so sorry."

Andrew raised his eyebrows, a puzzled expression pulling one side of his mouth up. "It's a phone call. What are you sorry for? He's not cheating, if that's what you're thinking."

"How do you know?" Lulu asked him.

CJ and Andrew had been hanging out for the last few months, since Lulu and I spent a lot of time together. They'd developed kind of a bromance, and they always seemed to have the other's back when issues came up, like they'd signed some kind of man pact.

"CJ's a good guy." His expression was serious. "Like a *really* good guy. He's not the cheating kind. Plus..." He looked at me. "He's head over heels in love with you, Pepper. He'd never screw it up on purpose."

A blush crept up my neck as my heart warmed just a bit. Andrew was right. If CJ had told Andrew how he felt about me, then it was certainly true. "Thanks. That makes me feel better." I looked up as my waffles were placed in front of me and thanked the waitress who delivered them. "I still don't like it, though."

Tamara shook her head. "I wouldn't either. *This* is why I don't get involved in relationships. Too much potential for confusion. Too much drama. Too much everything." She was the only one at the table not involved in a serious relationship. She dated. A lot. Like really a lot. But she didn't seem to fall for any of the guys she went out with. I hadn't quite figured her out.

"You just haven't met the right guy," Andrew said. "Let me set you up. There's a guy at the hospital—"

"Wait," Lulu interrupted. "Who is this guy? Why are you saying 'guy'? If he was a doctor, you'd say, 'there's this doctor at the hospital.' Is he a janitor or something? Tam won't date a janitor."

"There is nothing wrong with the custodial arts," I volunteered, feeling protective of the janitors of the world for no discernable reason.

"I'm just saying. If Andrew's setting Tam up, it should be with someone impressive." Lulu sniffed.

"Janitors can be impressive," Andrew said. "Like, what if he's a janitor who goes home and studies opera in his spare time? Or is dabbling in the custodial arts while he's finishing his doctorate in theology? Or what if he's the best damned janitor there is—like if janitoring is his calling?"

"Is he a doctor or not?" Lulu said.

"He's not a doctor," Andrew said. "He's actually a nurse."

Candace spit out her coffee then looked around apologetically. "Sorry," she said, wiping her mouth with a napkin. "I was just picturing a dude in one of those little white hats, with the squeaky shoes and the white skirt."

Andrew squinted and pursed his lips in irritation. "It's 1999, Candace. Men are nurses, too, and we all just wear scrubs." His face cleared, and he turned back to Tamara. "He's a really awesome guy. He plays rugby, is part-owner of a bar in Soho, and he's pretty handsome, according to all the girls at work. You interested?"

"Why is this incredible man-nurse still single?" Lulu asked.

"Why is Tamara still single?" Andrew returned.

"Hmm. You touched me." Lulu leaned back in her chair as everyone at the table began to giggle. She looked around blushing, and demanded, "What?"

"I think you're looking for 'touché,'" I suggested.

Andrew was practically crying, he was laughing so hard.

Lulu stared at him, her eyes squinting slightly like she was trying to decide whether to be angry at him for making fun of her. Finally, she shrugged and turned to Tamara. "Tamara? Why *are* you still single?"

Tamara's wide smile made her blue eyes gleam and then sipped her lemonade, shaking her head slowly. She wasn't talking.

Lulu shrugged again and turned her attention back to her food.

We ate and enjoyed the zinging atmosphere around us as New York City woke up and stretched, recovering from its Saturday night pursuits in the brightening Sunday afternoon.

Traffic picked up out on Seventh Avenue, and from our table near the window, we could see people heading out for runs and shopping outings, dressed in shorts and T-shirts as summer's warmth lingered into the last sultry days of September.

Chapter Two

ALONG CAME A SPIDER

Tamara

CANDACE SEEMED determined to spend the day with me Sunday, despite the fact that I'd planned to head home, get a workout in, and begin work on plans for the week. I had several open houses and a few clients I was pretty sure were ready to pull the trigger on the next good thing I found for them. It was shaping up to be a good month, and I had been expecting to get a jump today and keep it rolling.

"So what are you going to do?" Candace asked as we strode up Seventh Avenue.

"I was going to get some work done..."

"No. About the man-nurse." Candace stopped walking and grabbed my arm, tugging me into a bodega where she continued talking as she pulled water from a refrigerated case and grabbed a pack of gum. "I think men can be nurses. There's nothing wrong with that, of course. And if he's hot, well, that obviously makes up for a lot..." She gave me a mischievous gleaming look and began digging in her purse.

"I don't care if the guy's a friggin' manicurist."

She turned to me and raised an eyebrow.

"Okay, well, that might be a stretch, actually."

She nodded and turned back to pay, her dark bob shining under the fluorescent lights.

"The point is that I'm not looking, Candace. I know you and Lu have found love and Natalie and CJ are finally together, and you all think the world is romance and roses, stinky cheese, and champagne, but there's more to life." I knew that implying career-focused Candace was becoming distracted from her high-powered career by her boyfriend would stir up her ire, and then she'd get busy defending herself and quit harassing me. "I'm twenty-four. I'm not looking to settle down. I could've done that in Indiana."

Candace steered me out of the bodega, and we were walking again, side by side up the busy avenue as horns blared, children wailed, and life of all stripes beat on around us. "First of all," she began. "I'm not exactly laser-focused on my love life to the point that I'm ignoring my career. Or my friends." She raised her eyebrows at me over her large dark glasses. "But when the opportunity presents itself—in any part of your life—you go after it."

"Right."

"Right." She was staring at me. "So?"

"So I don't need to go chasing down men at hospitals trying to create opportunities, either."

"But if someone knows someone who might be a great fit..."

"Andrew was just pulling this nurse guy out of his butt because Lulu was pressuring him. It isn't like he's been at work thinking, 'This guy right here, this scrub-wearing man-nurse, he'd be perfect for Tamara.'"

"Hmm. I guess you have a point."

"I do." I tilted my chin up slightly. People didn't often win in debates with Candace.

"I'm just saying don't ignore opportunities."

"And I'm saying I won't." I was the last person on Earth to miss an opportunity, but Candace had no idea that just my being here—in New York City on my own, healthy and alive—was the perfect illustration of me taking an opportunity by the balls.

She smiled at me, leaned in, and gave me a quick hug. "I'm gonna head back uptown then. I've got boxes to pack, thanks to you."

"Sounds fun!"

"Not really, but we get the keys next weekend, so I guess I'd better be ready." She stepped to the curb and shot a hand out, hailing a cab that stopped suddenly with a grinding of gears. "See you later!"

The cab pulled away, and I continued a strolling pace back to my own apartment. As I fitted the key into the outer door, I thought about what she'd said. I knew I wasn't missing opportunities. I was doing the opposite of that. For a long time, my life seemed like it was going to be devoid of opportunities altogether, filled instead with bleak pronouncements and family who refused to let me do anything for myself. And it wasn't like I hadn't been in relationships. I'd even been in really long, really serious relationships. Now I was ready for other things.

I threw my keys on the side table as I let myself into my apartment. Home. I always breathed a sigh of relief on returning to my own space, my own refuge, a normal reaction to finally having a place to call your own after growing up with four brothers. This apartment, small though it was, was my own. In every way. The exposed brick held a painting that I'd done in junior high school, a scene of Lake Michigan that captured the winter's lonely grays with a reflection of hopeful sunlight off the sand at the water's edge. The mantel held my collection of bright, clear glass boats—something I'd been hanging onto since I was a tiny girl. To me, they had always represented the chance to move on, to get away.

I flopped down on the bed against the far wall, my hands rubbing against the muted colors spread, my head on the few bright pillows. My closet was open, the clothes inside mimicking my bed's hues. Staples of individuality. A predictable constancy with small deviations. That was me.

I flopped down on the bed and stared out the window for a few minutes. Was there something wrong with me? Why wasn't I excited by the prospect of being set up with some manly rugby-playing nurse Andrew swore was hot? It wasn't as if I never got excited about the prospect of meeting men. I liked men, no doubts about that. I liked them tall, broad and lean. I liked them in my bed, and I liked them to leave in the morning. I always set the agenda where men were concerned. Being in control left little room for misunderstandings, for anyone to believe that something was possible when, really, nothing could happen at all. At this point, I wasn't interested in the back and forth necessary for a long-term relationship. Not yet, maybe not ever again. I definitely wasn't interested enough to distract me from all the other things that demanded focus. Work, friends, family, and just looking after myself kept me plenty occupied.

A light flashed at me, so I pushed the button on my answering machine. Two messages.

"Hey, sissy. It's Hal." My brother. Hal was two years older than me, and we'd been more like twins than siblings. He was having a rough time, which meant I was having a rough time. "Just calling to, uh... check in, I guess. Things are... well, they're okay. Clarissa left today." His wife. "And before she went, she told me some stuff. I guess I'm going to be a daddy..." Hal coughed, and I couldn't hear the rest of the message because it sounded like he moved his mouth away from the phone. My head spun as I replayed it. She was leaving? And she was pregnant? Oh, God, poor Hal.

The second message was even less expected. "Hey, Tam. It's Spider. Hal told me how to reach you. Hope you don't mind me calling. Hey, I'm gonna be in the city. I'll look you up."

My blood froze in my veins. Spider. In the city. Looking me up. I pushed down the agitation that began as a swirl of excitement in my gut and then spread out through my limbs in the form of a thrumming pulse of anticipation I had always felt when Gaige Spydell was anywhere nearby.

I squeezed my eyes shut and wished I'd never heard either message. I sat down and flipped open my laptop. I could at least pretend I hadn't heard them. I could pretend for a few hours. Maybe a day or two.

Work and coffee became my best friends for the next eight hours.

Chapter Three

THERAPEUTIC FINGERING

Natalie

CJ SPENT Sunday night at my apartment. We ordered in from the Italian place on Eighth and played SSX on the Playstation 2 he'd given me for my birthday. Sometimes, I felt like a kid again with CJ. We spent a lot of time together just screwing around. We kicked a soccer ball in the park, played video games, listened to music while staring at the ceiling, and often just pretended that we weren't actual adults with real responsibilities. We did more adult things, too, of course, but I think part of what drew me to CJ was his ability to look at the world as it really was and to take each day as an opportunity and an event. If left to my own devices, the universe felt like some interwoven web to me, some complex structure full of meanings and requirements, something to figure out. CJ took it at face value, and it was so much more fun that way. So much less stressful.

"Check out these moves, Cassidy James!" My fingers flew

randomly over the controller buttons. I had no idea how to actually pull off any of the snowboarding tricks in SSX; I knew only that if I pushed all the buttons as fast as possible, my avatar did incredible things and I could win. CJ was more methodical and refused to throw his chances to fate. So he lost. Repeatedly.

"Seriously?" His voice was a hilarious whine. "How the hell do you keep doing that? And don't call me Cassidy." His dark eyes were on my face as he delivered the last part, and his voice grew serious. He hated his name, but I had no idea why.

"Don't be a sore loser, Cass."

"I'm serious, Natalie."

"You're seriously losing." I didn't push the name again.

"I don't mind losing to you. You're cute when you gloat." He dropped his controller on the coffee table and pulled me into his lap. I held my controller and continued flying down the mountain, accumulating points and hooting.

"I'm planning to gloat a whole bunch here in a sec, hang on." My hands were flying over the controller buttons when CJ pulled it out of my grasp. "Hey!"

He leaned down until I was forced to look up into his face. I couldn't help but smile up at him. CJ was the embodiment of every guy I'd ever wanted. He was the all-American football guy, big and broad and strong. I ran my fingers through his close-cropped blond hair, and his dark eyes danced with fun, like they did every time they caught mine.

"Hey." His full lips delivered the word and made my stomach jump with the memory of everything else those lips could do.

"Hey." He had my attention now.

But CJ had something on his mind. He was silent, and a siren blared as it flew down the Avenue beyond 15th Street, where I lived. "I need to talk to you."

I stared up at him.

"Irene called this morning."

"I heard. I was just leaving."

"Right." He ran a hand over the back of his neck as his gaze moved to the walls of my apartment, scanning around us before he looked back into my eyes. "Well, I'm meeting her tomorrow morning for coffee before work."

"Why?" I tried to sound neutral, like I wasn't freaking out. Irene had offered CJ a job last spring, and he had almost gone back to Buffalo, ending any chances we'd had to be together before I'd gotten brave enough to take a chance at all. Things had been quiet since then.

"She's opening a branch of the firm in the city."

I waited for more.

"She wants me to run it."

"Is she moving here?" I sat up. Irene's actual presence was what concerned me. A job was just a job.

"Maybe for a bit, to get it set up, but she doesn't want to live here. That's why she wants me to take it on." CJ shifted his weight, looking uncomfortable.

"Why you?"

"I guess she trusts me."

"Because you have... a history." Irene had given CJ his first job out of business school. I had the sense she'd given him some other things, too, but CJ had never confirmed or denied it, and I'd never actually asked straight out.

"We do." He squinted as if there was a code to decipher written in my eyes. "The thing is, it's a huge opportunity for me."

I tried to read the hesitation in his face. "So what's to consider?"

"It's also a huge risk." CJ looked down, breaking our gaze. "I'm not qualified."

"Sure you are."

He sighed and took my hand. "I love that you think that, but the fact is that I'm twenty-seven. I've been working outside of finance at All Night for two years now. I'd love to get back into it, use my degree and the experience I got right out of school, but jumping into a new venture as VP—taking on the responsibility that would come with a whole new office—it's probably more than I can fake."

"Doesn't Irene realize that?" This revelation had made me even more suspicious of her. "What exactly are her intentions?" When CJ didn't answer immediately, the question I'd been dying to ask flew from my lips before I could stop it. "Did you two have a relationship in Buffalo?"

CJ's eyes widened. "No!"

"Then what's her fascination with you?"

"We worked together, that's all. She thinks I'm smart and that I have a good head for finance." CJ's tone took on a sharper quality.

I raised an eyebrow. "Doesn't she have a good head for finance? It's her firm. Don't you think she might be interested in something besides your financial intuition?"

CJ dropped my hand. "Is it so hard to believe that someone might want to give me a shot without being interested in sleeping with me?"

I shook my head slowly. None of that had come out quite right. "Of course not. That's not what I meant. You said yourself that you're not qualified."

"Maybe I am." A fire burned in his eyes that I hadn't seen for a while. CJ was angry with me. Crap.

"I'm sorry, CJ. I didn't mean anything. So what do you think will happen tomorrow when you meet with her?" I asked, trying to move the conversation away from my belief in him, or lack thereof.

He gave me a skeptical look, an eyebrow raised as he

seemed to ponder whether to even continue our dialogue. "She lays out the terms."

"And you accept?"

"And I think about it."

I nodded. "Okay."

"I can't work for All Night forever, Natalie. If I'm going to stay in the city, I've got to move up. David might be willing to promote me eventually, but there's nowhere for me to go All Night." David was the CEO at All Night Media, the company I had also worked for until recently. That was where I met CJ. "I just wanted to tell you what was going on."

I smiled, but something in the atmosphere between us had changed. The fun had been chased from the room by the questions I'd thrown at him. "Thanks."

"I'm tired. I think I'll sleep at my place tonight." CJ slid off the couch and picked up his bag. "I'll call you tomorrow, Nat."

"Okay." All the cheer rushed out of me, replaced by something that felt like heavy dark sludge.

He leaned down and gave me a quick kiss before leaving the apartment. The sound of door slamming behind him felt final somehow, and a knot of uneasiness pulled itself tight in my stomach. Irene was bad news. There was something going on there, I just didn't know what it was. And if CJ knew, he wasn't telling me.

———

I didn't hear from CJ Monday, even though I hoped it would be him each time the phone at my desk rang. When I left the office, I called him as I walked to the subway, but the call went straight to voicemail. He called later that night.

"Do you want to come up?" Something in his voice told me he wanted to be alone.

"No. I've got a lot going on at work this week. I'll prob-ably just stay here." I hated the idea of not seeing him all week, so I suggested, "Should we have lunch tomorrow?"

"Wednesday instead? I need to make up for not being there this morning."

"Right. Okay." I paused. He'd met with Irene, and now he didn't want to see me. My mind raced with possibilities, and though I knew I should leave it alone, I couldn't. "How did it go this morning?"

"I'll fill you in when I see you." His voice was friendly, straightforward.

"Okay. Talk to you later?"

"Sounds good."

"Okay. Have a good night."

"You too, babe."

CJ calling me "babe" made me feel a tiny bit better. It was silly, but just hearing the term of affection from him warmed the icy corners of my mind, the ones that were harboring suspicions about Irene, the ones that had begun to freeze over after he'd left Sunday. Things didn't feel right, exactly, but they felt better. We'd gone without seeing each other for a few days at a time before. This was not a big deal, although it bothered me that CJ was grappling with a big decision and it didn't feel like he needed or wanted my input.

As I let my mind turn circles around all the possible downfalls of my relationship with CJ and Irene's certainly nefarious intentions, I knew I needed to stop. This. This was what I wanted to change about me. My life couldn't be dictated by anyone else, even CJ.

The plan I'd made Sunday at CJ's resurfaced. It was time to recruit some help. I pulled out the phone book I kept stashed in my television cabinet and flipped through the yellow pages to "therapists." It was trendy to be in therapy these days, I told myself, and spending time working on your self was never time wasted. I scanned the names, wishing I knew what to look for. Most of them sounded pretty intimidating. Dr. Elliott Anders, Dr. Anders Ellicott, Dr. Ellie Cott... How was a person supposed to choose? I was only looking to improve myself, but if I started asking people to recommend a therapist, they might not see it that way.

The scientific approach to selecting the right therapist for me, the one who would be able to help me articulate my goals and desires and formulate a plan for reaching them would work best here. I closed my eyes, dropped a finger on the page, and circled the finger around several times—all part of the scientific process. Then I held my hand still and opened my eyes. Perfect! I'd selected Veronica Chase, LF, LFMT, MA. I had no idea what all those letters after her name meant, but I was pretty sure they meant that she'd be really extraordinarily helpful.

As I got ready for bed that night, I imagined myself and Dr. Chase becoming friends, sure she'd let me call her Veronica, or maybe Ronnie. I envisioned her being impressed with my ascension to marketing director of Adtrack, the company I'd just moved to, and imagined our sessions would be more like gossiping than therapy.

That was because I had no idea what therapy actually was.

Chapter Four

URBAN COWBOY

Tamara

MONDAY WAS A WHIRLWIND. I was out of the office most of the morning with clients, and when I came rushing back in, my right foot aching in the new patent burgundy pumps I'd worn all morning, I blasted through the front lobby without a glance around. To my surprise, two voices called me back as I took my first aching steps down the hall toward my office.

One voice was female. The receptionist. "Miss Hunt? I have messages for you."

The other voice, the one that had me frozen in the middle of the office hallway, my heart doing double-time in my chest, was masculine. It was the definition of masculine, at least to my way of thinking. It was deep, rich, and low, and it sounded like a summer rainstorm drubbing lazily against the roof of a barn. It turned up images in my head of tractors and horses, boots and long lean muscles attached to the best smile I'd ever known.

"Hey, Tam." Gaige Spydell was in my office. In New York City.

I took a deep breath and turned around, not sure what to expect. Would Gaige be sitting there in Wranglers and boots, lounging the way he did in every vision I'd had of him since I'd left Indiana? The idea of him in the city... well, it was incongruous to say the least.

I walked to the reception desk, keeping a dark form in the corner of my vision, not quite ready to face him. I thanked the receptionist for the stack of little papers she handed me and turned around slowly to face the couches.

Gaige, or Spider as I'd called him ever since I was little, sat on the leather couch, looking uncomfortable, like the thing was made of concrete. His long back was stiff and straight, and his knees were at awkward angles as he leaned forward. He was tall enough to make the couch look miniature, and I smiled at the image before covering my reaction with an ambivalent gaze. He stood, looking grateful for an excuse to get up, and I was struck by the sheer size of him. Spider wore gray slacks, shiny black shoes, and a black polo shirt tucked in with a belt. He looked like a businessman on a casual day, not like a cowboy out of place in the big city.

When I let myself look up at his face, my breath caught in my throat. There he was. The Spider I'd always remember, with those penetrating blue eyes and that perfect cleft in his chin, the stubble around his jaw just begging me to scrape my fingers across it. I swallowed and shoved those memories away. That was before. That was the past.

"Gaige," I said, trying to keep my voice neutral. "Nice to see you."

He squinted an eye at me as he cocked his head. I could almost hear the thought go through his mind. *Okay, we're gonna play it formal. Have it your way.* "Well, it's nice to see you too. Did you get my message?"

"Come on back, Gaige." I nodded, turned, and walked toward my office, conscious of the fact that he was right behind me. I imagined I could feel those penetrating eyes on me, seeing everything, tracing my body.

———

I opened the door to my office and ushered Spider inside. He waited until I sat in the tall leather chair behind my desk to settle himself across from me. The lazy half-smile on his face had always turned my insides to Jello. For a long minute, neither of us said anything. We just stared at each other across the hard surface of my desk, the tall windows behind me filled with steel and glass—a screaming reminder that we were nowhere near Indiana, not anymore. What was my brother's best friend, my first kiss—hell, my first everything—doing in New York City?

"You look good, Tamara. Not that I expected anything different."

I raised an eyebrow at him. "Thanks."

I was torn between warring emotions. It was confusing and even irritating to find this visceral reminder of my past sitting here squarely in my present. Yet, when the sound of his low honeyed voice rolled through me, I had to fight the urge to get up and climb into his lap. Spider had been my protector for long enough that letting him shield me from the world was practically habit. Between him and my brother Hal, I'd never have seen or done anything if I hadn't left Indiana.

This staring contest needed to end. If those crystal eyes watched my face any longer, I was sure I'd dissolve into a puddle. I cleared my throat. "Spider, what are you doing here?"

"I need an excuse to visit you?"

I shrugged and looked around my office. "Yeah, actually you kind of do. I'm in the middle of a workday. I can't just stop for an old times chat right now. What's going on? Why are you in New York? Is everything okay?"

A shadow of doubt crossed Spider's face, his lids dipping for just a second as his smile faded. His cowboy bravado covered it quickly, replacing the genuine expression with a cocky grin. I knew every expression the man had, and this was the one that always appeared right before he uttered something infuriating. "Came to bring you back home."

I sat up straighter. "You've gotta be kidding me." A small twang crept back into my voice as the words escaped my lips.

Spider heard it too. "You're a country girl. And I didn't like the way we left things. Plus, I'm worried about you. And about your brother when you're not around."

"Just because I was born in a hayseed town doesn't mean I'm a country girl, and Hal is two years older than I am. He can take care of himself." I leaned back in my chair. This conversation wasn't one I wanted to have here in my office and not in the middle of a busy day, but I doubted Spider would just turn around and get back on a plane without actually talking about whatever he'd come to say. "I can't really have this conversation right now. I need to get back to work." I stood, and so did Spider.

"Have dinner with me, Tam." He didn't move, a mountain of man blocking my path to the door, blocking the path back to the life I'd very deliberately chosen. A scent wafted around him, something familiar and masculine, sweet and comforting. Damn it, but Gaige Spydell smelled like home, and I had to fight off the urge to walk into those big arms and surrender.

"Fine, dinner. Tonight?"

"I, uh, I've got plans tonight. Tomorrow?"

Surprise made me drop my guard. What plans could

Spider have in New York City on a Monday night? If he had plans, then it wasn't true that he'd come here just to convince me to come home. Something close to disappointment chilled my expression, and my face slackened before I recovered. Why would that disappoint me? That would just make it easier to turn him down. "Tomorrow works. Were do you want to meet?"

"I'll pick you up." He still hadn't moved.

I found myself staring up at him. That heady smell of his swept around me, pushed at me by the vent over his head. Cinnamon and rain, leather and a faint hint of whiskey.

"You know where I live?"

"Tam, I know everything about you. Just like forever." He winked at me.

"Just like forever," I repeated. We used to say it to each other. A silly promise that didn't mean anything, especially now. "You're gonna have to move, Spider."

"I know." He took a step back. "Just wanted to pretend for a second that you might let me hug you."

The vulnerability on his face melded with every memory I had of being inside the safe circle of those big arms, and I couldn't stop myself from stepping in quickly and putting my arms around him. "It's good to see you, Spider," I said, my voice a hoarser whisper than I'd intended.

My cheek felt the beating of his heart through the warmth of his chest, and the arms that pulled me close brought back everything I'd left behind at home. It was heady and overwhelming and way, way too much. Being in Spider's embrace made me feel vulnerable, weak, and in need of someone to protect me. I moved back, wishing I'd kept my distance as the sheer proximity of the man before me threatened to undo every decision I'd made in the past two years.

He watched me for a beat longer, those eyes seeing every

emotion I was trying to cover before he stepped back and turned toward the door. "Show me the way out, Ms. Hunt."

The twang in his voice nearly killed me, and as I delivered him back to the reception area, the sight of his broad back moving away actually brought tears to my eyes. Spider was home; he was family; he was open sky and the smell of cut grass and bluebells. He was everything I'd chosen to leave, everything I used to be. The receptionist was eyeing me with interest, so I turned quickly and walked back down the hallway, wiping my eyes with the back of my hand as I went.

Chapter Five

BROADWAY BABY

Natalie

I ARRIVED at work Tuesday morning with my new therapist bestie's name tucked into my bag. As soon as I'd settled in with my coffee and keyboard behind closed doors, I picked up the phone to give her a call.

"Veronica Chase."

Ooh, she answered her own phone. She was clearly down to earth. I liked her already. "Yes, hi there. I'm hoping to make an appointment."

"Are you an existing client?"

"No." Why did I feel disappointed having to say no? "I'd be new."

"I have two slots available for new clients." Her voice was sharp and punchy. She sounded like she was sure about every-thing and probably wore very shiny assertive shoes. I could tell I would learn a lot from Ms. Chase. "Today at noon or next Monday at nine a.m."

I was supposed to have lunch with CJ today, and I didn't really want to miss that. Although I really wanted to meet my new friend and confidante as soon as possible, Monday would have to do. "Monday is good."

"Bring your insurance information, please. Do you know where my office is?"

It was right there on the phone book page. "Are you still on Maiden Lane?"

"That's right. Take the local to Rector Street, or you can walk down from Chambers if you take the express. What is your name?"

"Natalie Pepper."

"See you Monday at nine, Natalie."

I hung up and stared out the window for just a moment, poking at some newly uncovered territory within myself. I was excited but also suddenly worried. Did I really need therapy? What would I talk about? What if my new friend Veronica thought I was completely beyond redemption? No, I was directionless and maybe a little hapless, but I certainly couldn't be the worst she'd seen. It was time to look forward to making a positive change in my life, so I turned back to my desk, ready to face the day, a more self-confident Natalie Pepper.

"Hey, Natalie, I need a favor." I'd barely been working for an hour when Bennett Reed appeared in my doorway, looking slightly disheveled and wrinkled, his light hair sticking up and about two days' of stubble on his chin.

Despite the fact that he sometimes looked a little worse for the wear, I really liked Bennett. He had a lost puppy kind of appeal. "What's up, Bennett?"

Bennett walked into my office and pulled my extra chair around to my side of the desk, which forced me to scoot over. He spread an oversized calendar across my desk. The sudden commotion stirred up the air in my office, and I got a whiff of something that smelled like the beach somehow—warm and fresh, like sand and sun and just a hint of suntan lotion. For someone who looked like he'd come straight from bed, Bennett certainly smelled nice.

"It's this show in Mexico."

"We have a show in Mexico?"

"It's a boondoggle," he said, a sheepish smile crossing his face. He had a smattering of freckles dancing across his nose, and light green eyes. This close to him, I could see the beginning of crow's feet around the corners of them, and when he smiled, they crinkled up. There was something comforting about Bennett's less-than-polished persona. "You know how this industry is."

This industry was online advertising, and many of the sales reps were making a killing putting together advertising packages for businesses in what was essential a completely new medium. My company was one of the first to sell splashy advertisements with movement and animation. We called them interstitials, and the sales reps at Adtrack were even cockier than those I'd known at All Night Media. They had a right to be. They were constantly sought after by other companies and were considered some of the savviest players in the developing field of online advertising. Big, over-the-top events were the norm. There was no reason why it should surprise me to see a show on Bennett's calendar in Cabo San Lucas.

"So you don't want to go to Cabo, Ben?"

"Oh, it's not that. I can't. My parents need me for some big event that week, and they won't change their plans."

My eyebrows shot up. Bennett was clearly older than me. I hadn't thought of him as someone's kid, but of course everyone had parents. He just seemed like such a grownup when I'd first met him. Maybe this was something I needed to work on—realizing that I'm actually a grownup, too. "Okay, so... what are you asking?"

"Wanna go to Cabo? I know you're not part of the event team normally..."

"Seriously?" Even if I was working, Cabo San Lucas seemed pretty glamorous, considering I'd been exactly nowhere out of the country in my entire life.

"I've been." He shrugged. "You could take your boyfriend."

I grinned at him. The idea of me and CJ in Cabo was even better. "That'd be great."

Was it really a possibility? The show was only about a month out, at the end of October. It'd be the perfect time to escape the city for a warmer destination.

Bennett was watching me, something dancing in his eyes. "You can let down your guard now and then, Natalie. Have some fun."

I squinted at him. Was I really so uptight? "I do have fun."

"Oh, I know. I'm sure you do." He cocked his head to the side and smiled. "You just seem serious so much of the time. For someone so young."

"Am I that much younger than you are?"

"I think you probably are. It's not polite to ask."

"I'm twenty-five."

Bennett whistled, low and long, shaking his head slowly.

"A lot younger, huh?"

He shrugged. "I guess not. Five years. Give or take."

"Okay, well, you asked. Now I get to ask something."

"Fire away." He leaned back in the chair, pulling the oxford shirt tight across his chest as his hands went up behind his head. Cords of muscle stood out on his neck, and for the second time in just a few minutes, I found myself thinking of Bennett differently than I had before.

"What's your story? Are you married?"

"That's two questions."

I waited.

He sat forward again, a sad smile replacing the open grin. "I was married, but we got married too young. She didn't really want to be married, as it turned out, so I'm not married anymore."

"I'm sorry, Bennett. It's none of my business. I shouldn't have asked."

"No, it's fine." He shook his head lightly as if we'd just been talking about the weather. "We had no business getting married anyway. Should've known better."

I wasn't sure what to say, so I resumed looking over our conference plans.

"To answer your other question," Bennett continued, "I live on the Upper West Side, and I have since I was a kid. My parents live a couple blocks north of me."

"City kid, huh?"

"Always have been. Can't imagine living anywhere else."

I watched his face as he talked, surprisingly comfortable in his presence even though the conversation was much more personal than any we'd had so far. Bennett had an easy way about him, something that made me want to keep him talking. "So you went to school in the city, too?"

"Nope. That was the one deviance from my citified ways. I went to school out in New Jersey."

I couldn't stifle the laugh that escaped my lips as a sharp bark. "Hardly far away, then!"

"Especially since every kid I knew in school went right along with me to Princeton. We came home so many weekends I'm not sure if I spent more time here or there."

"You must get along well with your family then. And have lots of friends nearby." I imagined his life, having everyone he knew so close around him. I couldn't imagine having dinner with my dad or my sister on regular weekdays. Having them three thousand miles away meant we only saw each other on holidays. If I could afford airfare. What would it be like to call New York your hometown?

"I guess I'm lucky that way. I just wish my parents would exclude me from their fundraising plans at this point."

"I can't imagine being so at home in a city like this," I admitted. "It still feels so foreign to me, so much unlike any place a person could really call home."

"You don't feel at home here?" His eyes filled with concern as his chin tilted down.

"I do, I guess. I mean, I have friends. I've been finding my way along. It's just not home yet."

"A California girl, through and through, huh?"

I laughed at that. I'd never quite been at home in California either. "Not exactly."

"Let me show you around a bit, then," he offered. "Have you been to a show yet? Done a real Broadway night out?"

"No." I laughed and shook my head, trying to imagine the girls and I out at a show. "My friends kind of try to avoid midtown in general."

I thought of Lulu's horror when I'd once suggested we go to a bar in Times Square. They didn't do tourist. Never, not at all. Although I did remember Candace mentioning the Statue of Liberty at one point, so maybe we all went native now and then.

"That's understandable," he agreed, "but if you do it right, it can be a lot of fun."

"Yeah? I'll have to think about that. I haven't seen anything."

Bennett looked at me with a half-cocked grin for a minute. "Let me take you."

I leaned back in my chair, surprised. "No, I couldn't." I wasn't sure what he had in mind, exactly. He knew I had a boyfriend. He'd met him, here in the office, so he couldn't be suggesting a date.

"It would just be a friendly night out, Natalie. Me showing you around my home, that's all."

Of course that was really all it was. "That's so nice. I don't think it's really in my budget though, to tell you the truth."

"I have some connections—"

My phone rang.

He pushed the chair back as he stood and replaced it on the other side of my desk.

I smiled and reached to answer the phone. As I pulled the receiver to my ear, Bennett turned as he left my office, calling, "My treat. Think about it."

"Hey, babe," CJ said at the other end of the line. "I'm so sorry. I have to cancel our lunch today."

My heart fell, and I listened to his excuses before agreeing to see him later that night. Irene's name was mentioned twice during the call. I'd started counting.

Chapter Six

SPAGHETTI WESTERN

Tamara

MY BUZZER RANG JUST a few minutes after six. It had been a rough day, and I'd actually left work early because of it. I didn't explain much to my manager, and he didn't ask, and I was glad. Everyone had bad days. At least that was what I told myself, and after an afternoon of sleep, I was feeling better. I'd gotten up, showered, and dressed before Spider arrived.

"You want to see my crib?" I called through the buzzer intercom.

"Hell, yeah!"

I buzzed him in and waited by the door, which I held open slightly. I listened to his footfalls climbing the three flights of stairs to my apartment. Anticipation bloomed in my gut, and I felt lightheaded knowing that Spider was in my building, that I was spending an evening with him. Besides the energy that he always inspired in me, I felt other things, too. I didn't want him to ask too many questions about my life at this point. He could be here to act as a spy. My family had been less than pleased about my decision to move away.

A long whistle came from the top of the steps, and Spider appeared, his dark hair pushed back from his forehead and spiked up in a purposefully gelled mess. It struck me as odd to see his hair actually "done." I was so used to seeing him in his hat.

"Got my exercise for the day, I guess." He laughed. The bright blue eyes caught mine, and my heart leaped as it always had when he grinned at me like I was the person in the world he most wanted to see.

"Hey, Spider." My voice was soft, almost a whisper. It was a combination of my exhaustion and a sense of awe as I watched Spider move toward me. I stepped back and waved him into the small studio apartment with a smile to cover that he made me every bit as giddy and nervous now as he always had. At this point, I was convinced that it was some kind of chemical compatibility. No guy since had made me feel as completely bowled over as Spider always had. I was drawn to him, despite everything, and leaving him had been one of the hardest things I'd ever done.

"So this is what you ran away for, huh?" He looked around the five hundred square feet I now called home, poking his nose into bookshelves and peeking into cabinets beneath the small sink in the kitchenette.

"I didn't run away."

"You know what I mean." He gave me a knowing look, one side of his mouth pulling up into a smile. He watched me a beat too long and then stood up straight, his mouth shutting into a firm line. "Hey. You okay?"

Spider knew me way too well, even after two years apart. "I'm fine."

"You taking your pills?"

"Stop trying to nurse me. I'm fine." This. This was why I

left home.

He crossed the room in two strides and pulled my left hand between us, holding my wrist and staring at my extended fingertips. I willed them to stay still while he watched, but the tremor I'd been fighting all day flexed and released them.

Spider pulled me gently by the wrist to my couch, sitting down and pulling me next to him. "The tremor's back?"

"I have good days and bad days." I couldn't meet his eye.

"Today's a bad day?"

"I'm fine. I was tired. I came home for a rest. It's just the tremor now."

"Seen the doctor lately?"

"Last week. Everything is fine."

Spider's fingers gently lifted my chin so that I was forced to look into those eyes, forced to see the concern there. "I'm worried about you."

I didn't respond. This was not a new topic of conversation for us. "Let's just go to dinner. I'm dying to hear what's got you here in the city dressed like a golfer instead of a cowboy."

He dropped my chin and looked stricken. "You thought I looked like a golfer today?"

"Were you wearing a shiny polo shirt?"

He pursed his lips and cocked his head, forcing a giggle from me despite my dark mood. "Shit. I'm gonna have to rethink my getup."

"For what it's worth, you look good tonight. More... you."

And he did. Spider had on a pair of dark jeans with a soft blue plaid Western-style shirt. His standard boots and belt buckle were in place, although the boots looked like they'd been recently shined and the buckle was a shade smaller than the ones he wore back home. The only thing missing was the hat.

"And you always look good," he said, his voice lowering.

He reached out slowly toward my chest and then pulled his hand back, looking uncertain.

Was he going to grope me? I stiffened. It wasn't like it was uncharted territory for him, but I thought he'd at least take me to dinner first.

Then he added, "Can I, uh... It's just... you missed a button here."

I looked down at my cardigan, which was fastened over a camisole, and saw that I'd misaligned the buttons, leaving the sweater bunched up in one spot. My mood deflated further. The tremor made it hard to do little things, and I'd had trouble with those tonight. One more thing to prove to Spider that he needed to gallop me home on his big white horse.

He moved in to fix my buttons, and I let him, watching his big fingers deftly refasten the tiny mother of pearl buttons with ease. "There you go."

"Let's go." I stood up and picked up my keys, eager to change the subject. I didn't have it in me to thank my ex-boyfriend for making sure I was dressed properly. "You promised me dinner, and I'm imagining a good story about your new golf-attired persona."

Spider knew me well enough not to argue, and although I could tell he was wary of me now, more worried about my health than he might have been before, he dutifully stood and held open the door for me to go out.

———

It turned out Spider had a plan. But then, Spider had always had one. Some got us in a lot of trouble in the past.

We sat across the table from each other in a way-too-romantic Italian sidewalk cafe in the East Village. The tables were draped with a checkered tablecloth straight out of a movie, and it unsettled me how completely at home Spider looked, sitting there perusing the wine list. My Indiana boy, at home with cabs flying by and horns blaring, a snobby waiter treating him like a hick because of his clothes. It all rolled right off him like he did this every day.

Spider ordered two glasses of wine and returned his attention to me. "How long have things been bad, Tam?"

There it was again, the nursemaid act. I dropped the bread onto my plate and gave him my fiercest look. "I'm fine, Spider. If you're going to make this entire dinner about my health, then I'm leaving now." I was smoldering with anger and something else, some visceral reaction to seeing him again. Whatever it was, it combined with my anger to push me close to some kind of tipping point. I'd felt off balance all day, and this was not helping.

"Relax, little buckaroo," Spider said, unruffled as usual. "We can talk about other things. Like, how about Hal?"

The fire in me burned just a tiny bit lower, but this topic was not less inflammatory. "Maybe later." My water glass shook as I lowered it back to the table.

"How's work, Tam?" Spider leaned back in his chair and watched me, his eyes seeing everything.

I dropped my hands in my lap and glowered at them for betraying me. "It's fine. It's good, actually." I looked across at Spider, and that little spark sizzled a bit. It wasn't fair for him to come here to check up on me. I really was fine, and he was here, making me feel like I wasn't, like I needed to be looked after again. "It's really good, Spider. I'm the top producer in my office this month, and I think I'm on track to be the top producer this year. I'm great at my job, and I actually love it. And there's no one here looking over my shoulder telling me what I can and cannot do!"

The waiter appeared behind Spider's chair and leaned in, his thin mustache making him look like a cartoon. "Not to contradict you, madam, but you cannot shout on our patio, please. It frightens the other customers."

I looked around, suddenly self-conscious. Several other guests were pretending not to watch us. "Sorry."

The smile on Spider's gorgeous face made me want to kick him. My face burned with embarrassment.

"You are ready to order, then?" The waiter seemed permanently bent over at the waist, and I felt we needed to order quickly just to get him to go lean over someone else's table.

We ordered. Spider's lazy half-grin pulled me in two directions at once. I hated him, but I wanted him to take me home and make me remember why it'd been so damned hard to leave him. Not that I ever forgot.

"I'm glad you're happy here." Spider sipped his wine. "It's a great town." Only he could refer to New York City as a town and have it come off sincere.

"So what are you doing in my 'town'?"

"I'm working for Poppy," he said, that slow drawl driving me nuts. Poppy was Spider's grandfather, one of the biggest cattle ranchers in Southern Indiana. "He's producing hogs and game meat now, and there's a demand for that kinda thing out here where all these fancy folks get bored fast with chicken."

"You're selling meat?"

"Like it's going outta style."

I stared at him. Spider was not a salesman, or at least I couldn't see him that way. When I closed my eyes and conjured up a picture of Gaige Spydell, he sat atop a brown-and-white paint, that long body controlling everything down to the very earth he rode on as if it was his birthright. He was a cowboy, through and through, and that was the only way I could see him. Then I thought back to the way he'd looked today in my office. Maybe to someone who didn't know, he was doing a passable job of playing city slicker.

Through the rest of the meal, I watched Spider as he talked and ate. He wasn't uncomfortable, and he handled himself here with the same ease he would on the ranch. There was no way this was his first time in the city. After he'd paid the bill and we were walking back toward my apartment, I asked the question that had been forming in my mind all evening. "Exactly how long have you been in town, Spider?"

His head snapped around to look at me, and he raised an eyebrow, the slow grin taking a moment to catch up to his surprise. "Caught me there." He laughed. "Just about six months now, I guess."

I stopped walking. "Six months?"

I was angry. Or was I hurt? How could he have waited six months to call me? Why did that make me mad? I left him. I told him to leave me alone. Wasn't he doing exactly what I'd asked?

"I don't even know how to process that." I started moving forward again, my head spinning. No wonder he was right at home here. No wonder he knew just where to take me for dinner.

He took my arm, and I wrenched it away. "I was gonna call earlier, Tam, but I wanted to give you some space."

"So why are you here now?" I turned to face him, my emotions a swirling maelstrom of confusion in my mind, my heart.

"Because I couldn't stay away any longer." His eyes fixed on mine, and the grin was gone. All that was there on his face was the hurt and pain I remembered from the day I'd told him I was leaving, the day I'd ended everything. I stopped myself from reaching up to touch his cheek. My hand was shaking too badly to do that anyway.

I just watched him as my conflicting desires waged war within me. *Tell him off. Tell him you still love him. Make him go. Ask him to stay forever.* "I have no idea what to say."

"Neither do I. But I miss you, Tamara. And I'm worried about you."

We turned and walked more slowly, side by side with this awkward reality keeping pace, tagging along between us.

"You mad at me?" Spider asked.

"No." I wasn't. I didn't think I was.

"You want me to come up? We can talk some more."

Somehow we were already in front of my building. "No." That certainly wouldn't help things. "I'm tired."

"We didn't talk about Hal."

"I'll call him tomorrow." I had words for Hal. He knew Spider was in the city, I was sure of it. He and Spider were best friends after all. I talked to Hal at least once a week. He'd been keeping secrets. Probably more than one.

"Will you call me tomorrow?" Spider's eyes twinkled, and the bravado was back.

I wanted to put him in his place for once, the cocky bastard. But the truth was that maybe I was a little bit relieved to have him nearby. But I sure as hell wouldn't tell him that.

"We'll see. Thanks for dinner."

"Any time." He pulled me close, leaned down to kiss the top of my head, and then released me. That familiar scent of leather and rain surrounded me, and it occurred to me how easy it would be to invite up, relive old times.

"Good night, Spider." I walked away, letting myself into my building without a glance back. A part of me wasn't sure he'd really been here at all. If I was getting sick again, maybe my screwed up mind had just invented this really complex hallucination, and I'd spent the whole evening living it. Though I hadn't had any hallucinations since I was diagnosed years ago, as hallucinations went, Gaige Spydell wasn't a bad one.

Chapter Seven

UPPER WEST WAFFLES

Natalie

AS I RODE the subway north that evening, the jostling ride of the express train soothed me a little. While I was happy to be headed up to see CJ, and I couldn't wait to tell him that we had a chance to go to Cabo together, there was a growing uneasiness in the pit of my stomach. We'd worked so hard to be together. I'd forced *him* to work so hard. Now it seemed like he had forgotten that, and I was beginning to wonder if I had been a conquest, if maybe half the point of his wanting me was the fact that for so long he couldn't have me. Now he did. Maybe it was time for the next conquest. Irene?

Tears stung, and I closed my eyes hard. As quickly as that evil thought had come, I knew it wasn't true. I thought of CJ, finding me in Union Square in the freezing cold, kissing me and telling me he'd wait. I thought of his sad eyes in the elevator last year when I'd walked away again. I thought about the way he'd looked when I'd finally gotten the guts to tell him how I felt, stopping him from getting in the car that would have taken him away from me forever. He'd been genuine, I really believed he had. He'd been honest and open with me, and he'd waited for me to figure out that what we had was real, was special, and was worth fighting for. So why did I feel like he was suddenly giving up the fight?

When the doors opened at 72nd Street, I got out, riding the surge of people onto the platform and up the stairs to the bustle of Broadway. CJ's apartment was just a couple blocks away. As I walked, I forced myself to stop thinking. Sometimes my brain was my worst enemy. Instead of letting it turn in poisonous circles, I turned outward, to look at everything around me as I moved down the sidewalk toward CJ's place.

The evening was alive with to his door energy, which seemed to almost always be the case in my new hometown. The breeze carried a chill and a faint scent of roasting nuts, sweet and thick, that made me eager for scarves, coats, and holidays. People hurried this way and that, some laughing, some with phones pressed urgently to their ears, talking seriously. The energy of the city carried me along, and when I reached CJ's building, I was almost disappointed. I loved feeling myself becoming a part of this place. On the elevator ride up to CJ's, I reminded myself that I'd come here on my own, that I'd be fine on my own even if things with CJ didn't work out. I was meant to be here, in New York City. By the time I got to CJ's door, my heart felt lighter, and I felt more like the girl who'd risked everything to move to an unfamiliar city—a brave, independent girl.

"Hey, you." The door swung open, and CJ stood there, wearing cotton PJ pants and nothing else. My heart raced at the sight of him, his broad strong chest tanned and shining in the lamplight, the faintest curls of blond hair leading in a line down his perfect stomach.

"Hey," I managed, stepping closer so he could shut the

door. He smelled like CJ always did, like leather and mint. Something in me settled. Being near CJ felt like coming home.

He took my bag and dropped it at the end of the couch, putting his arms around me and pulling me close. "I'm glad you're here."

"You okay?" I asked. Something seemed off.

"Just a long week." He smiled.

"It's only Tuesday," I reminded him. I hugged him closer and enjoyed the warmth of his arms, the solidity of his chest against mine, and the way my body melted into his.

"God, you feel good, Natalie." CJ was the only person in the city who didn't call me "Pepper."

We ordered sushi in, both of us lounging on his long couch in front of the television until darkness damped the energy that hummed around us, even through the walls and windows of the apartment building. As night fell, we were pushed closer together on the couch, and eventually CJ's head was in my lap. I ran my fingers through his short blond hair, loving the way it felt rough and soft all at once. We hadn't talked about his meeting with Irene, and I didn't want to bring it up. At this point, it was a sensitive enough subject I thought I should let him take the lead.

"What's going on at the new job?" he asked, his voice sleepy and drawn out.

I grinned. I was still excited about almost everything at work, such a huge change from my previous job. "Actually, I might get to go to Cabo next month. You can come, too. There's a trade show down there, and Bennett asked me to take it. You interested?"

"In going to Mexico with you?" CJ smiled up at me, his dimples making an appearance on either side of the full lips. "Absolutely."

"The schedule hasn't been approved yet, but the CEO,

John, is pretty laid back about things. I doubt he'll have any issues about it. You might just need to pay for your own plane ticket."

"Sure, I can do that. Just let me know when you know. Hopefully things will be settled enough by then to get away..."

"What's going on at your work?" I finally dared to ask, almost not wanting to know. I had an inkling how crazy things were at All Night since I'd left, and the mention of work also had the potential to bring Irene back to the conversation, something I didn't want to do but couldn't avoid.

"It's about the same." He ran a palm up and down my arm. His eyes were half-lidded and darkened. "Do you really want to hear all about David and Lanie Bill and Irene right now?"

"Not at all," I said, distracted by the way his warm hand felt against my skin. I'd be happy to never hear about Irene again.

"Good." He swiveled around, sitting up and then standing, offering me a hand as he rose. There was no mistaking the way he was looking at me, a tiny smile pulling the edge of his mouth up as he led me to the bedroom.

My skin tingled in anticipation as I followed him and climbed onto his bed. CJ was next to me in a second, one hand on the side of my face and the other in my hair while his mouth met mine. He kissed me softly at first, increasing the pressure slowly until his mouth was hot and demanding. I opened my mouth to him as his hands traced my body, and my mind let go, leaving me to the sensations coursing through me.

CJ broke off the kiss for a second, his body pressed against mine as my hands traced the firm planes of his back. He whispered into my ear, the hoarse scratch of his voice pulling sparks of sensation deep within my core. "I love you, Natalie."

It wasn't the first time I'd heard him say those words, but every time he said them, a tiny spark of surprise caught me off guard. This time, I let the spark ignite into a fire inside me, and for the next hour, I let CJ try to put it out.

———

CJ and I spent our evenings together for the rest of the week, and I tried to enjoy the fact that things seemed good between us—back to normal. I didn't ask questions about the potential job, and he didn't bring it up, so there was some tension that followed us wherever we went, but I did my best to smile through it. This topic had become a difficult one for us, probably because of my reactions to Irene in general.

It was Saturday morning before CJ finally broached the topic. "I need to talk to you about my job options," he told me as we sat at his counter, eating waffles.

"I'd love to hear about that. I wasn't sure I should ask."

"I know. You've been awesome, as usual. I'm sorry if I've been weird about it." CJ put his fork down. "I'm going to take the job with Irene's firm. It's an opportunity that I just can't pass up. The money involved, and the responsibility..."

"Of course," I said, trying to cover my disappointment. Some part of me had known that he would take the job; I just hadn't wanted to admit it to myself. "That's good, CJ. That's great! Congratulations!"

He didn't look thrilled. "I know this will be tough. I know you don't really like Irene."

"I don't even really know her, but she's not sticking around long, right?" I wasn't going to deny that Irene's presence made me uncomfortable.

"Not for long. She'll be here at first though." He looked thoughtful. "I wondered if maybe the three of us could go out. Maybe you'd like her if you got to know her a bit."

I raised an eyebrow. Getting to know Irene sounded about as entertaining as sticking a fork in my eye, but I would do it for CJ. Who knew? Maybe he was right. "We could do that," I said, drawing the words out and hoping maybe some enthusiasm would climb into them.

"Don't sound too excited, Nat." He grinned at me, and just like that, the tension evaporated. The light stubble on his jaw caught the morning sun from the window, and his dimples deepened as I smiled back. CJ was amazing, and more importantly, I trusted him. If he said there was nothing going on with Irene, then there was nothing.

"These are incredible, by the way," I said, finishing my last bite of CJ's signature waffles.

"I can show you how to make them," he offered.

"But then you wouldn't make them for me. I like it that you cook."

"I'd still cook, but then you'd be able to, too." CJ grinned, and his dark eyes flashed.

I shook my head. "No, I'm going to stay clueless in this department. You look way too hot in the kitchen. I like sitting here keeping you company while you whip up your CJ specialties."

"I should write a cookbook."

"You totally should." I carried my dishes to the sink and put them in the dishwasher. "I'll just be cleanup crew." I rinsed the waffle-making items and leaned over, arranging the stuff in CJ's tiny dishwasher. His eyes were on me, and I turned, looking over my shoulder as I bent down. "Are you staring at my ass?"

"Absolutely." He was still grinning, but something deeper had crept into his tone.

With the tension between us gone and a whole weekend ahead, I felt optimistic and almost giddy. All the concern I'd harbored over the week dissipated, and I found myself feeling lighter than I had in weeks. I was happy just to be with CJ, to get to be the girl in his life.

I walked around the counter and moved close to him, picking up his empty plate. "Are you finished with this, sir?"

"I am," he said, his voice low and solemn as a wicked smile played across his full lips.

"Let me just get it out of your way then," I said, letting my breath tickle his ear as my breast fell across his shoulder while I lifted the plate. I put it in the dishwasher, letting him watch me move, and then washed my hands before returning to where he sat waiting. His eyes were dark, and his hands reached for me eagerly, pulling me against him as his mouth found mine.

———

We occupied ourselves until it was almost time for lunch, and a sense of guilt pulled us from CJ's bed.

"We can't just stay inside all day," I said, pacing to look out the window. "It's one of those perfect fall days. We need to go out and do something. Something New Yorky."

"Pretty sure that isn't a word."

"It is today."

"Okay, what New Yorky thing do you want to do? I'm hungry." CJ stood and stretched, looking less than motivated.

"We just had waffles."

"That was hours ago. Let's go sit on a patio somewhere and let someone bring us margaritas."

"Margaritas?" It wouldn't have been the first thing that jumped to mind for me. "That doesn't seem New Yorky."

"It will be if we go to Tortilla Flats. Trust me." CJ grinned.

I didn't care much where we went, as long as we were spending the day together, so I hopped up and waved a hand at him. I'd go wherever he wanted. "I need a quick shower."

"I'll join you in a sec. Just gonna pick up this message." Someone had called while we were occupied in the bedroom.

As I undressed in the bathroom and brushed my teeth, I could hear the answering machine message starting. It was CJ's mom. I hadn't met her yet, but we'd been talking about planning a trip to Buffalo. Maybe I shouldn't have listened, but he didn't ask me not to.

"CJ, it's Mom. We got your message about the job, honey. We're happy for you. We're just... concerned. You know how I feel about that woman... I'm just... I don't know what to say, Ceej. Your dad and I are uncomfortable with the way Irene seems to keep pushing into your life. Can you give me a call please?"

I turned the water on and drowned out whatever the end of the message was. So I wasn't the only one in CJ's life who didn't like Irene. I tried not to let that message confirm any concerns I had as I stepped into the flow of warm water and tried to regain the optimism I had about the weekend, about CJ and me. The water ran from my body in rivulets and I visualized it pushing every mention and thought of Irene from my mind. I was going to focus on margaritas. Margaritas and CJ.

Chapter Eight

THE BATHROOM ON THE RIGHT

Tamara

I CALLED my brother the day after I saw Spider, putting my feet up on my coffee table and leaning back into the couch as soon as I got home from work.

"Sis." Hal's voice was flat and emotionless.

A pang of guilt hit me hard in the stomach. I should have called earlier.

My rock solid facade crumbled. "Hallie, how are you?"

That question was met with silence. Then Hal sniffed. "I'm okay. Not great. Things have been... bad. They've sucked, actually."

"Clarissa?"

"Among other things."

"Never liked her." I was lying. I liked her just fine, but if she was the reason my brother sounded like he was seconds from leaping in front of a bus, then I hated that bitch.

"She's a good person. It's not her fault."

I considered the things I might say. All of them sounded idiotic and trite, so I changed the subject. "Your boy Spider is here. I suppose you knew that."

"Isn't Spider really more *your* boy than mine?"

"Not since a long time ago." I pushed down the ire that was sidling up my throat. "Hal, why didn't you tell me he was in the city?"

"I meant to. I just... things have been busy here."

"Have you been sick?"

"Have you?"

"I asked you first." I stood up and paced around. Talking to my brother about our disease always put me on edge.

"Yeah, but Spider called me yesterday, so I know you're not doing good."

That rat bastard. "I'm fine," I said. "Just pushing too hard. I'm slowing down."

"Well, same here."

"You taking your pills?" I asked, eyeing the prescription bottles lined up in the cabinet I'd left open earlier.

"You sound like Mom."

"Are you?" Hal and I had been close in all ways. We even shared the same ridiculously rare genetic disease. It wasn't unusual for me to ask about it.

"Yes, nurse Tam."

"Good."

"Did you hear my whole message?"

"About Clarissa's news?" I was still in shock.

"Right."

"Congratulations, Hal. You'll be an amazing dad."

"Not sure I'll even get the chance."

"Is it *over* over between you? Like totally done?" My mind spun as I sat down. Clarissa was good for Hal. I wondered what he'd done to make her leave. Hal had always been a little too forceful.

"I don't know."

"Hal, what did you do?"

"Nothing. It's between us. When are you coming home?"

I sat up straighter on the couch. Hal had never pushed me to come home. He'd been the one member of my family to support my desire to get away, to be something other than the sick little sister to four overprotective brothers. "I'm not. Why are you asking me that?"

"Just kidding." But I could tell he wasn't.

I stared out the small window over my bed at the deepening blue of the sky hanging above the building across the street. "Spider said he was here to bring me back home, but then he told me he'd been living here for months."

"Yeah."

"Yeah what? Which part?"

"I knew all of that."

"Well, if he's living here, he's not exactly about to pick up and drag me back to Indiana, is he?" Confusion and anger were combining within my mind. I didn't know what I felt exactly but hoped Hal wouldn't mind if I took it out on him for a minute or two.

"What are you mad about? That he's not dragging you screaming back to Indiana? Or that he didn't look you up when he first arrived in New York?"

"What's he doing here, Hal?" The hand holding the phone shook more than usual as my heart pumped at an accelerated rate.

"Why don't you ask him?"

"I'm asking you."

"I don't know. I haven't talked to him much about that. He asks about you, but he doesn't exactly bare his soul to me. Since he left, I've only talked to him a couple times."

"If anyone else moves out here, could you let me know before they appear in my office please?"

"Deal."

I stood. A wave of homesickness hit me and I tried to walk it off by pacing in the small open area of my apartment. "You gonna be okay?"

"I don't know."

"Figure it out, Hal. Don't make me come home and take care of things."

"You can't fix this, sissy. I don't know if anyone can."

"You gonna get the baby tested?" I asked him.

"The odds of Clarissa being a carrier are so small…"

"Better to know right away." I hated the thought of Hal passing our disease on to a tiny little baby. But we'd been tiny babies, too, and we were okay. Mostly.

"If she'll let me. It'll be one more thing she can blame me for."

I shook my head, squeezing my eyes shut. "I don't like this, Hal. I don't want you to be alone. Clarissa is good for you, and she needs you right now as much as you need her. Call her."

"Sure. It's that easy."

"Start there. Start somewhere."

"I love you, Tam, but it's not your business."

"Like hell."

"Bye, sis." Hal hung up.

A painful darkness spread through me as his voice disappeared from my living room, and I sat down heavily on the couch.

———

I forced myself to slow down for the rest of the week and was feeling better by Saturday—physically, if not emotionally. Spider didn't call again, and I didn't call him. I told myself I could just go on as I had been, living a new life in a new place with none of the baggage I'd carried in Indiana. The problem was that those heavy bags seemed to have begun to spill out of the cramped closet where I'd piled them. I was good at ignoring things, though, and I just draped an imaginary blanket over that pile of crap and went on about my business.

I was supposed to have plans with the girls this weekend, but no one had set anything up. As late Saturday morning crept into afternoon, I began to feel anxious. I needed some girl time and some distraction. I called Natalie at home, but she didn't answer. She was probably with CJ. The walls of my apartment were beginning to close in, and I was feeling desperate, so I called her cell.

A loud beat filled the staticky background of the call as she picked up. "Hola," she said.

"Pepper."

"Hey, Tam!" She was practically screaming. I could hear music, but couldn't make out the song, and lots of people.

"Where are you?"

"Tortilla Flats. Come down here!"

"Yeah?" I knew that place. It was down on Washington Street just north of the Village. "Will CJ mind?"

"Tam?" CJ's voice was suddenly on the other end. "Get your butt down here. We need some help with music trivia."

"That is my area of expertise." I was only kind of kidding.

"See you when you get here."

I heard some jostling on the other end and then Natalie's voice again. "You coming?"

"I'll be there in a few." I felt relieved, if not excited. I had somewhere to go, something to do.

I called Lulu as I rode in the cab heading South, and she made plans to meet us. Candace and Gregoire were moving, but Lulu said she'd call them, too.

Tortilla Flats was a scene when I got there. Perfect. I needed a distraction from the things that were plaguing me—

my brother, Gaige Spydell, and the fact that another appointment with my too-frank doctor and a pharmaceutical adjustment were almost certainly in my future.

Natalie and CJ were at a cozy table in the corner, and I pulled up a chair. As tables near us left, we dragged them over. By the time Lulu, Maggie, Candace, Gregoire, and Natalie's neighbor, Tom, had joined us, we had a large part of the patio to ourselves.

Paper lanterns hung overhead, several pitchers of margaritas sat on the table, and a man with a microphone was wandering between the tables, running a music trivia contest, just as CJ had said.

"Cheers, *señorita*!" Tom held up his glass and leaned into my shoulder.

I smiled at him, holding up my margarita. I took a sip and put it back down. I really wanted to drink it. And I really couldn't.

"That's no way to treat a perfectly good shot of tequila." Tom nodded at my glass.

My fingers traced the plastic cactus holding up the globe of my drink. "I know, but tequila and I have never been close." I winked.

"Something else?"

I shook my head. "Nah. I came out for the company. And the food."

Tom raised an eyebrow. "People don't come to New York City for Mexican food, Tam."

"I know that. But I like cheese and chips, so I'm pretty easy to please." I pulled a chip from the basket.

"Where's the flavor of the week? No Hair? No Bed?"

I grinned. That had been an adventure. But I wasn't currently pursuing any hot Irish men with incredible hair, beds, or apartments. "No flavor this week. What about you?"

"So sadly single, but I think that guy over there might change my luck."

I followed Tom's gaze to the opposite side of the patio where a thin guy with a shock of platinum blond hair sat, staring at our table. He raised his glass when he noticed me staring.

"Was that for me or for you?" I wasn't sure if I'd accidentally flirted with Tom's guy.

"Your gaydar needs adjustment. That's all for me." Tom raised his own glass in return. A few minutes later, he'd excused himself and joined blond boy's group across the way.

"First correct answer wins shots for their party," the DJ was saying as he wandered by. "Finish this lyric: Built like she was, she had the nerve to ask me if I planned to her any harm."

My hand shot up in the air and I shrieked, catching the man's attention. Before I knew it, the microphone was in my hand and the rest of the lyrics flew out of my mouth. "So look here, I put her on the back of my bike and we went riding down by Old Man Johnson's farm!" My volume was a bit excessive, and the entire patio was focused on me by the time I finished. I curtsied and handed the microphone back, feeling my cheeks warm from the attention.

"That's correct! Shots all around!" The man fished some tickets out of his apron pocket and winked as he handed them to me, the wrinkles around his dark eyes making him look like someone's favorite uncle. "Here ya go, darlin." He had a vague accent from somewhere in the Midwest, and for a second, I wanted to hug him. Instead I thanked him, took the tickets, and forced jocularity as I turned back to my table and hooted, tossing the shot tickets into the center of our group.

"It's raining drinks!" I grinned and sat back down, hoping

my mind would quit spinning and play along with my face if I smiled hard enough.

"Nice work, Tam," CJ said with clear appreciation in his voice.

"Prince," I said. "I can't believe no one else got that."

"You hardly gave us time," Pepper said.

A waitress came out and took our drink tickets. CJ ordered the shots. When they appeared a few minutes later, hands raised and glasses met in the center of our table. "To Tam!" CJ shouted.

Everyone did their shots, and I quickly emptied mine into Tom's abandoned water glass. I raised my eyes again to find Lulu's eyes on me, a question on her lips. I shook my head and watched one eyebrow climb skyward. Lulu was not known for her subtlety, and I had no doubt she was about to make a big deal of the fact that I was not drinking. Instead, she shrugged and turned back to CJ and Pepper, who were snuggling at the end of the table.

But Lulu hadn't been the only one who noticed. Maggie was across the table from me, watching me with a concerned expression. "What was that?"

"Just not feeling it," I said.

"Something going on?" Maggie was easy to talk to and genuinely cared about all of her friends. She was probably the least judgmental of us all, which must have been why she could tolerate Catalina, her icy roommate.

I shrugged. "Not really."

"But kind of." She got up and moved to Tom's seat next to me as the trivia contest went on loudly around us. Candace and Gregoire were telling everyone how their move had gotten delayed because of a parade clogging 5th Avenue. They'd put the whole effort off until the following day. Candace was more agitated than usual.

I looked into Maggie's deep brown eyes and considered

telling her everything, but then I noticed that her eyes were red and puffy. Not very bright and Maggie-like at all.

"Hey, what's going on with you?" Something was wrong, and since Maggie was our fixer, no one ever asked her if she was okay.

Her eyes immediately flooded, and I almost wished I hadn't asked. I didn't want Maggie to be sad, and I wanted to help, but I honestly didn't know if I could handle anyone else's drama in addition to my own. I put an arm over her shoulders as she sniffled.

"I'm okay," she said finally. "Just stuff with 'Nesto."

Ernesto was Maggie's boyfriend, who lived back in Texas, Maggie's home state. They'd been dating long distance for more than a year, and all I'd ever heard was that they were blissfully happy. But Maggie, sitting here on the patio of the most festive Mexican joint in the city, with the sun blazing behind her as it set over the Hudson, did not look blissful. Or happy. Or even sort of content. She looked miserable.

"Maggie," I said, my voice lower than I wanted it to be. "What's going on?"

"I think it's ending." She sniffed and crumpled into a pile on the tabletop, sobbing quietly.

I gazed around, perplexed and a little terrified. I was not the most empathetic of the group. Pepper or Lulu would have been much better equipped to handle this, but Pepper was practically sitting in CJ's lap, and happier than I'd ever seen her, and Lulu was pouring herself another margarita and screaming out woefully inaccurate song lyrics in an effort to win more shots.

"Bathroom on the Right! Bathroom on the Right!" Lulu was standing, waving her arms at the man with the micro-phone. He couldn't *not* come over to her.

"What's that, miss? Can you repeat your answer for the crowd?"

I cringed. The guy with the mic was trying not to laugh. It was a Credence song. Everyone knew it. Everyone but my beautiful Brazilian friend, Lulu.

"There's a bathroom on the right..." she sang, a gleeful smile overtaking her face as her eyes glinted with certainty.

The mic guy cracked up then regained control of himself. "Though that was a beautiful rendition, and a very amusing guess, I'm afraid it's not right."

"Bad Moon on the Rise!" someone yelled from another table.

"Ding, ding, ding! It's actually Bad Moon Rising, but we'll take it!" the mic man shouted, making his way to the guy with the correct answer.

Lulu, for her part, looked more miserable than Maggie when she realized she was wrong.

"I want to donate my shots to her!" the guy who got the lyrics correct called out, pointing at sad Lulu.

Lulu's face went from dejected to triumphant in a split second, and she blew a kiss at the guy.

In the meantime, Maggie continued to sob quietly, unnoticed by the rest of our group. This one was going to be on me. That was about the way my week was going anyway.

"Mags," I said, bending down close to her ear. "Do you want to go somewhere else and talk?"

She nodded, and I threw a twenty on the table and then guided her out the patio gate. I smiled and waved to our friends as we walked by them, Maggie wiping her face and smiling at them as they threw questions our way.

Candace gave me a curious look and mouthed, "Call me?" I nodded and watched her lean over to reassure Lulu about Credence.

Maggie and I made our way to a quiet bar on the corner where we could talk away from Lulu's painfully bad interpretations of song lyrics.

Chapter Nine

THERAPY AND FOOTBALL

Natalie

I WAS nervous as I rode the subway down to Rector Street on Monday morning. Now that I'd had a few days to think about it, I realized I really had no idea what to expect from therapy. The sum total of what I knew about therapy could be summed up by Dr. Phil's appearances on Oprah, and I really didn't have a high opinion of the good doctor based on that, but I had high hopes for real, actual therapists who were not on television. I spent the ride down to Dr. Chase's office trying to decide how best to present myself. I wanted her to think I was cool, put-together, and generally awesome. But was that really the point of therapy?

When I arrived at the building on Maiden Lane, it was less posh than what I'd had in my head. I buzzed up to the suite and let myself in, climbing the stairs to the second floor. The building was more like an apartment building than a fancy doctor's office, but I'd been in New York long enough now to know that sometimes outward appearances were deceiving.

At the top of the stairs were two doors, one of which was standing slightly open, a dark-haired woman waiting just inside with a smile. "Natalie?"

I nodded and smiled. "Doctor Chase?"

"Call me Ronnie, please."

My spirits lifted. She was pretty and trim, and she'd just asked me to call her by her nickname. So far, things were going well.

I followed her into her office where she waved me to a low leather couch. I put my bag down next to me and sat down. "Should I, uh, recline?" I asked. Every television show I'd seen that involved therapy had the patient lying down on a couch. Or maybe those were just the cartoons.

"I want you to be comfortable, Natalie. If that means standing next to the window while we talk, or sitting on the floor, or reclining, then that's fine with me."

"Okay. I think I'm good just sitting here."

Dr. Chase had me fill out a quick form and then gave me a brief introduction. She was a few years older than I was and had worked as a social worker while finishing her graduate degree. "I thought I was going to do child psychology, but I was always far more interested in the concerns that the mothers had, and I realized that I wanted to focus on women specifically."

She sat with her feet tucked up under her, a notepad next to her and a cup of coffee steaming on the table in front of her. The office was furnished like a well-appointed living room, and I had a fleeting thought that it would be really nice to be her, to come here everyday and just hang out and chat with people.

"Why don't we talk about your expectations, Natalie. What brought you here today?"

An impulse? A wild hare? Some strange belief that I needed to master my life? "I'm hoping to get some help with decision making. I've been in the city for a year now, and I feel like I should be more assertive. I should be more in control of my own life."

"Who's in control of your life now?"

"I'm not even sure. I make a lot of choices based on what I think I'm supposed to do—what my father would want, what my boyfriend would want. Sometimes I'm not sure what exactly I want."

She nodded and made a quick note before replacing the small notepad on the table. "That's good. Let's start there. Tell me about coming to New York."

For an hour, I talked with Dr. Chase—Ronnie. She was easy to confide in, and I told her a lot about my friendship and relationship with CJ, about my mom's death and my family, and about my recent graduation to living on my own for the first time.

"You're on a great path, Natalie, and it sounds like you do a pretty good job thinking about the events in your life, understanding how they've come about. We'll set a goal to help you focus more on making choices and getting you in charge of those events so that you are steering the boat rather than being carried by the current. Sound good?"

It sounded perfect.

"Homework then." Dr. Chase gave me several sheets of paper and asked me to keep them with me and use them to record choices as I went through my daily life. "Even if it's just deciding between eggs and oatmeal. I want you to record it and write down the thought process that goes with it. I think that, over time, we'll see a pattern emerge."

I nodded, not sure I'd be willing to make notes in front of anyone else since I wasn't going to explain that I was seeking therapy.

"Let's meet again in a week," Ronnie said.

We made an appointment, and I left, emerging into the financial district feeling optimistic and hopeful. The towers of the World Trade Center rose before me as I turned south. A quick dash through the mall beneath the towers would be fun before I headed back up to work. Oh, a choice. I stopped, leaning against a building to write about the choice I'd just made to take myself shopping instead of going back to work. As I wrote about it, I changed my mind. Though it would have been fun to visit the Gap and Banana, maybe getting a few new things, I couldn't really afford new clothes at this point and I needed to get to work.

I folded the paper up and turned around, wondering if the paper was intended to make me second-guess every impulsive decision I made or if it really was supposed to just be a record. Either way, I began to remember that I'd never liked homework.

———

My office was a welcome environment when I arrived that morning. It wasn't as plush as Dr. Chase's living room-like space, but it was comfortable and it was mine. I settled in behind the keyboard and fired up the computer, waiting to see what email might await me after the weekend. Bennett's tousled head appeared in the doorway while I waited for the machine to spring to life.

"Late night?" he asked.

"Come on in, Bennett." I waved him to a chair and shook my head. "No, I had an appointment this morning."

"Everything okay?" Concern crinkled the corners of his eyes.

"Not a big deal. Everything's good."

"I just wanted to check in with you. My parents gave me their tickets to see *Rent* tomorrow night. Interested?"

I'd heard of *Rent*. I was tempted. "I don't know." I thought of the "homework" in my purse. A decision sat in front of me, and I wasn't sure what to do. "Can I take a few minutes to decide?"

"Sure, but you need all the info." Bennett smiled, and I realized how charming he was. His hair stuck up as usual, but his clothes were impeccable. The guy had a sense of style and rarely wore the standard Internet uniform every other man I'd worked with seemed to favor. He donned bright fashionable ties and great shoes, and his entire persona always put me at ease. "We'll take my folks' car and driver," he started. "And their standard Tuesday reservation at Balthazar."

"They eat at the same place every Tuesday?" That seemed both impressive and boring.

"They're creatures of habit, but they're traveling this week. The tickets are for a box at the theater—great view from one side of the stage. If I'm perfectly honest, I've never thought the seats were much better than first balcony seats, but people seem to think that having the box is some kind of exclusive thing."

"I kind of think so," I said, imagining Richard Gere and Julia Roberts in *Pretty Woman*.

"Well, there you go." Bennett's eyes brightened and I felt the warmth of his gaze from across the desk. "And if you need it stated plainly," he added, "just friends, Natalie. I know you're involved with someone and I would never want to interfere with that."

I nodded. It didn't need to be said, but it was nice to hear it.

"You're totally not my type anyway."

I tried not to be offended. "Oh, okay." My voice was flat. I needed to learn to conceal my feelings.

"Yeah," he went on. "It turns out my type is more uptight, manipulative bitch than cool Cali girl."

I couldn't help but smile. "Oh yeah?"

He smiled back. "Unfortunately."

"I'll let you know in a bit? Let me just check on a couple things." As if I had all kinds of important Tuesday evening engagements.

"No rush." Bennett rose and turned.

"Thanks, Ben."

"You're welcome." He walked out of my office, leaving me with my decision.

I pulled the folded paper from my purse and began writing:

Decision - Go to the theater and dinner with Bennett?

Immediate emotion - Guilt.

Influences, other factors - CJ.

Specifics - Is this cheating? Why do I feel like I shouldn't mention it to him?

Any other considerations - Never been to Balthazar or a NYC Broadway show.

Impulsive choice - Go!

Final choice - Go.

I rose and went to Bennett's office to accept his invitation, pushing aside the guilt I felt. I would see CJ later and tell him what I was up to. There was nothing going on besides friendship here anyway.

That evening, I struggled with whether to tell CJ about my theater plans. I'd mentioned Bennett before, and CJ was not the jealous type at all, so I was fairly certain he'd be fine with it. Then again, I hadn't been planning to go on something that sounded an awful lot like a date with the guy.

CJ and I sat side by side on his couch watching Monday night football. I flipped to Ally McBeal during every commercial, something CJ put up with even though it drove him crazy. We ate takeout sushi as the Jets gave a pounding to the Jaguars, CJ cheering with every fumble and incomplete pass the Jaguars put up. I mostly put up with football to spend time with him, but I had little actual interest in the game. The tight pants worn by the players had lost their appeal a while ago. Luckily, CJ wasn't one of those guys who insisted on shouting at the television or shushing me when a play was in motion.

"So I need to tell you something."

CJ's head snapped to the side, concern furrowing his eyebrows.

"Why are you looking at me like that?"

"No good conversation begins with 'I need to tell you something.'"

Not a great beginning. "This is not a big deal, I promise."

"You're kind of freaking me out." His dark eyes had not left my face, and I was beginning to worry that going out with Bennett was a bigger deal than I thought.

"I made plans for tomorrow night, that's all."

CJ's shoulders visibly relaxed, and he smiled. "Oh. The girls?"

I shook my head. "No, actually. A friend from work. I've told you about him before. Bennett?"

CJ looked confused. "That's a dude, right?" One of his eyes squinted at me.

"Yeah, just a friend. His folks have tickets to see *Rent* that they're not going to use. I've never been to a show, so he invited me to go with him."

"Oh." CJ was staring at me, his expression indecipherable. "Okay." He shrugged.

"Does it bother you? I'll tell him no. It's just a friend thing. I swear."

"I know. I trust you. It's fine."

"You kind of look like maybe it isn't."

"I can't pretend to be excited about it. I didn't know you hadn't seen a show." He shrugged again. "I just wish you were going with me instead, that's all."

That. That was what I loved about CJ. He was rarely anything besides painfully honest. I always knew where I stood.

"I'm sorry." I contemplated calling Bennett to cancel. Or I could just tell him at work tomorrow. But that didn't feel right either. We really were just friends, and I did want to see *Rent*. "I'll cancel if it bothers you," I said. "But it really is just a friend thing."

CJ shook his head, and a reluctant smile lifted the corners of his mouth. "No, I trust you. Go have fun. Just let that Bennett guy know that I'll pound him if he touches you."

It was a joke, but my mind called up an image of CJ and Bennett. I wasn't sure who would win in that match, actually. Bennett was about the same size as CJ, if a bit older.

"He won't."

"Is he taking you to dinner first?" CJ's eyes were on the game now, but his attention was still on me.

I hesitated. That sure did make it sound more like a date. "Yeah. To Balthazar."

CJ turned back to me and sighed. "I wish it was you and me instead of you and him."

"I'll cancel."

"No. Go have fun. Have extra fun for me. I'll expect a full report. I'm not going to be having any fun tomorrow night, that's for sure." CJ handed me the remote as a commercial filled the screen.

I flipped to Ally McBeal even though I'd lost track of the plot. "What are you doing tomorrow that's no fun?"

"Irene and I are setting up the office space she found. Basically moving desks, setting up computers..."

I swallowed hard. An image of CJ and Irene pushing furniture around an empty office space filled my mind. In my evil imagination, he was shirtless, and they were laughing, a bucket of fried chicken on one of the empty desks with a bottle of red wine. I let the stupid vision go on far too long. I knew this because it devolved quickly into barefoot dancing and feeding each other fried chicken. But that wasn't really romantic. I erased the fried chicken from the vision, trying to think of something sexier that they could feed each other before I stopped myself. Even my imagination was indecisive. And I hated the entire vision anyway. I was sure it would be nothing like that, but sometimes I was my own worst enemy.

"Still with me?" CJ was staring at me like he was trying to figure something out.

"Sorry, yeah. I had an image of you guys eating fried chicken and dancing instead of setting up an office."

"What?" CJ laughed.

"I know. I'm a moron." I laughed too, but something dark and pointy lodged in my gut. "I guess I'm a little jealous."

"You're the one going on a dinner date, and you're jealous?" CJ shook his head, but his voice was soft. "We're together, Natalie. We both know that, and that's what matters." He took my hand, the game forgotten as it blared on before us. "How about if I set up drinks with Irene later on this week? Then you'll see that there's no threat there. She's just a mentor and a friend."

I nodded, despite not relishing the idea of sitting across from Irene with her dark sultry eyes and excessive cleavage. "Okay."

Chapter Ten

THURSDAY IS THE NEW FRIDAY

Tamara

THERE AREN'T a lot of things that shock me in life, but hearing Maggie tell me that she had decided to move back to Texas did the trick. For some reason, I thought of all the other people around me as permanent fixtures in the city landscape. They moved and changed, but to me, they were fixed. I was the newcomer. It never occurred to me that we were really all the same that way. So few people I'd met were actually from the city.

"His mother died, and now his dad is sick," Maggie explained. "And 'Nesto is under so much stress."

We sat in the corner of a quiet bar near 14th Street, and I listened while Maggie poured her heart out.

"I don't really think he wants to break up either. I just think the stress of the distance... the fact that I'm really not there to help him with all of this... It's just becoming too much."

"And you're really willing to give up your life here and move back home for a guy?" I was shocked. We were career women. We were tough and independent. These girls who had come to mean so much to me in such a short period of time had changed my view of girls in general, and of myself. They were the ones who helped me understand that it wasn't selfish to want a life for yourself. It wasn't wrong to want to go in a direction different from your family. Maggie was a successful brand manager for one of the biggest packaged food companies in the world. Her future was secure, and her career path went straight up. Here she was, about to walk away from that. For a guy.

"Not a guy." Maggie smiled through her tears. "For 'Nesto." She sipped her wine and then stared at the glass before turning back to me, her voice soft. "I've been with him since we were kids. His parents were like my step-parents. He's family to me, but I'm also in love with him. I've never doubted that he was the one, but I've also always known that one day we'd have to make a choice. When I first came out here, the plan was for him to follow me. Then his mom got sick and now his dad, and there's no way that our original plan is going to work. He's trying to let me go because he knows I'm happy here. He sees the success I've had, and he doesn't want to be the reason I give anything up."

I nodded. Yes and yes. "But you're going to give it up."

She shook her head. "Not really."

I raised an eyebrow.

"Well, yes. I'm giving up the city and the job. And being close to you guys. That's what is making me so sad. I'm giving up the possibility of what my life might have been here, if I'd stayed."

"You haven't left yet."

"But it's decided. I'm going home. I just need to help Catalina find a new roommate."

"I can't believe it." I couldn't figure out how I felt about Maggie leaving. Part of me felt like she was giving up, giving in. Another part of me admired her for knowing so completely what was right for her. "I'm going to miss you."

She smiled, and a bittersweet comfort fell between us. She was happy with her decision, and I had to be, too.

"But I'm throwing a kickass farewell party for you before you go."

"I'll take it!" She picked up her drink and took a long sip. "Now tell me what's going on with you."

I shook my head. "Nothing."

"You dumped a shot into a glass of water. That's alcohol abuse."

"I'm pretty sure your definition differs from the official one."

"Be that as it may..."

"Just didn't want it, and didn't want to take shit for not doing it."

"Well, here's your shit. It's concerned shit, though. What's up?"

"I'm just cutting back." Which was true.

"Any particular reason?"

I shook my head. "I just want to keep my blood a little bit more undiluted."

She was squinting at me, and I could see that she knew there was more to it. "Something else going on?"

"No. I just... I can't drink a lot. I did for a while when I first moved here, but it's really not good for me. Some people just can't handle alcohol as well, that's all."

She nodded. "Okay, but you'd tell me if it was something serious?"

How could I tell her that my whole life constituted "something serious"?

I nodded back.

"So this party," she said. "When will that be?"

I grinned, happy for the distraction. We spent the rest of the evening avoiding serious topics, planning the farewell to end all farewells.

———

I saw my doctor monthly as it was, but with the tremor increasing in severity and my constant friend exhaustion insistent on riding shotgun on a daily basis, I scheduled another appointment. Dr. Charles was kind enough to work me in on Tuesday morning after a visit Monday to make a small deposit of bodily fluids.

"Okay, Tamara," Dr. Charles said once I was seated in her office. "Your urine shows copper levels higher than I'd like, and your blood count is pretty low. Since the tremors are worsening, I'm going to recommend cessation of the penicillamine."

"If I stop taking it, won't my copper levels get worse?"

She nodded. "I wasn't quite done. I was going to suggest an alternative therapy. One that might not have the same adverse effects."

"Trientine."

"I see you've done your homework."

I nodded, hating the fact that my disease and regular visits with my doctor took up almost all of my free moments. I knew more about the way the liver processed copper than any sane person should.

"We'll see how you respond. I'd like to see you at the end of this week and then again early next week to see how it's going. Are you taking your B?"

I nodded again. "Yes. Taking the vitamins, buying ridiculously expensive bottled water—which I have to lug home four blocks and up three flights of stairs, by the way—and avoiding alcohol. Mostly."

"Mostly?" She raised an eyebrow.

"I do have a life. And friends."

"Well, unless you have a friend who's your blood type and wants to donate part of their liver, I'd go for 'totally' instead of 'mostly.'"

I sighed and stared up at the ceiling. I felt like I handled my disease pretty well. But when it interfered with things I wanted to do, it pissed me off. I looked back at the doctor. "But the Trientine will help with the tremors?"

"It should. We're going to watch closely for anemia, and I want you to call if you start feeling nauseated. There's a small chance the neurological symptoms could worsen a bit before they get better. Call me if they do."

"Okay."

The doctor scribbled a prescription and handed it to me. "Fill it right away, okay? And Tamara... no drinking."

I nodded.

"How's your brother doing?"

"Fine, I think." I should ask Hal about his medication. He'd always tolerated treatment better than I did, though. He hadn't developed the neurological symptoms that went along with Wilson's disease. At least not that he'd told me about.

"I'm glad to hear it." The doctor stood, walked to the door, and turned back around. "I want to hear about any changes for the worse, but I think we'll see things get better in the next couple days."

"Thanks." I rose to follow her out as I silently cursed the stupid gene mutation that made my liver retain copper and made my life impossible at times.

I filled the prescription and took it with me to work, where'd I'd been forced to set up an easy week to accommodate my exhaustion. I sat behind my desk for a bit, shuffling through contracts and messages.

My mind wandered. When I'd first been diagnosed as a teenager, no one had known what was wrong with me. I'd started losing my ability to concentrate in school and turned into the clumsiest kid around. I crashed through doorways, tumbled over stairs, and generally caused a ridiculous scene for weeks before my mother suspected it might be more than klutziness. My handwriting was the tipoff, she said. I'd had perfectly round swoopy letters as a kid, dotting my I's with ridiculous hearts. By the time my Wilson's was diagnosed, I could barely write my own name legibly, and the tremors had begun.

No one suspected anything with Hal because he had no symptoms at all, but when they finally identified Wilson's, after thinking I had everything from Multiple Sclerosis to ADHD, they tested all my brothers for the disease as well. Hal's copper count was off the charts, and it was only a matter of time before he would have ended up in the hospital with liver failure. If nothing else, my stupid symptoms potentially saved my brother's life.

I picked up the phone, intending to call Hal and check in, but found myself dialing Lulu's number instead. What I needed was some light and distraction, not tales of divorce and depression. I'd call my brother later.

"Lu," I said when she answered. "We have a party to plan. Call your man-nurse friend."

"That's Andrew's friend, not mine. I don't have man-nurse friends."

"Not the point."

"Wait, you want to go out with him?" She sounded excited suddenly. Lulu was the master of the sudden change of attitude. "That's great!"

"No, I do not want to go out with him. I want to use him for his bar."

"I'll ask Andrew," she said slowly, "but I'm not sure I understand what I'm supposed to ask."

"Ask him if we can throw a party at man-nurse's bar this weekend."

"Okay!" Her voice higher. "What kind of party?"

"Maggie's going away party."

"Oh." Now she sounded sad. I loved that Lulu was completely transparent and that her emotions were so pure and strong that I could practically see her pouting face, from just one word uttered on the phone. "I don't want Maggie to leave."

Maggie had told everyone after we'd talked. No one was happy.

"Me either. But the least we can do is send her off right."

"You're right. I'll find out about the bar. What night?"

"Friday?"

"Bars are busy on Fridays. They might not want to let us use the place if it means losing other business." Some people were street smart. Lulu was bar smart.

"Good point." I thought for a minute. "Thursday?"

"Thursday might be bad. Thursday is the new Friday."

"It is?" What the hell? "Well, it won't hurt to ask." I was getting frustrated.

"Okay. I'll ask. I'll call you back when I know."

"Thanks, Lu."

I couldn't keep up. Since when was Thursday the new Friday? I spun around in my chair and stared out the windows at the buildings around me, contemplating how fast things could change.

I had just taken the first dose of my new medication when the phone rang in my apartment.

"Hey, sweetness."

Spider.

"Hey yourself." I cursed myself. That sounded like I was flirting. I couldn't help it. Damn damn.

"What've you been up to?" He sounded like he was lounging on a couch somewhere, a long spear of hay tucked in one side of his mouth.

"Nothing interesting," I told him, settling back onto my own couch. Why, I asked myself, did I suddenly want to extend this conversation forever? We'd barely said two words, but already a deep sense of comfort was descending through my body, pushing away the tension that the week had brought. "You'll be pleased to know that I got a medication adjustment today."

"Thanks for telling me that. You know I worry about you."

"I know you used to."

"I think you know I still do."

This was dangerous territory. Part of me wanted to hear that Spider had never gotten over me, that he'd take me back in two seconds if that was what I wanted. But I'd left him, and everything else, behind. For good reasons. Spider would always be part of my past, and the fact that he was laser-focused on my condition meant that he'd never be able to see me any other way. I'd always be that vulnerable little country girl he had to protect. I wanted to be so much more than that. Someday, I'd need to be with someone who'd never seen me that way in the first place.

"How's the meat biz?"

"Poppy's a happy man." I could hear the slow grin spread across those incredible lips. "Think I'll get to see you again anytime soon?"

"I don't know." I wanted to see Spider, I definitely did, but I didn't know if I could trust myself around him. We still shared crazy chemistry. It would be too easy to fall into old habits. I didn't want to encourage him—or myself—but I found myself saying, "There's a party next week. I don't know the details quite yet, but maybe you could come out and meet some of my friends." They'd help keep me in check.

"I'd like that."

"I'll call you when I've got details, okay?"

"Sounds good. You call me if you need anything. Take care, Tam."

When the line was quiet, I replaced the phone gently, trying not to kick up any of the strange feelings that were settling around me. I missed Spider. I wanted him. I needed to let him go. Again.

Chapter Eleven

WHO THE HELL IS TIM?

Natalie

BENNETT and I spent the whole day Tuesday passing each other in the corridors at work, sharing strange little smiles. I was looking forward to our not-date, but I was also feeling nervous about the entire thing. He'd said it was just an evening between friends, and I definitely didn't think of him as anything more than that, but there was an aura of excitement and fun surrounding our plans. A town car and a driver, and the whole dinner and a show thing, had me feeling like I was about to spend an evening playing pretend. This wasn't my usual life. I was going to be pretending to be a grownup, a very fancy New York City grownup.

I was staring at a sales campaign I was supposed to approved on my computer screen, but my eyes weren't focused on work. They were seeing past snippets of my life. That idea—pretending to be something I wasn't—had plagued me for as long as I could remember. If I really looked at it, I was a grownup. I wasn't making believe at anything. I was a marketing executive, playing an important role for a public company. I was a twenty-five-year-old woman, living on my own in one of the biggest cities in the world. But it all felt like an act in so many ways. I didn't feel any different inside from the little girl who'd sat at her mother's feet, arranging felt dolls and imagining she was a princess. Only the circumstances around me had changed.

"Natalie?" John stood in my doorway, eyebrows furrowed in concern.

"Yes, hi, John!" I sat up straighter. Since coming to AdTrack, I hadn't had much time with our CEO. He made me a little bit nervous.

"Do you have a few minutes?" He stepped into my office.

I had flashbacks to when David at my old company had told me he was hiring a VP above me. That had resulted in disaster. As John settled into the chair across from me, I hoped bad news wasn't coming.

"I know you've taken on a lot since coming here to AdTrack and that you've got a few responsibilities you didn't have back at All Night."

I nodded, my stomach starting to churn.

"I'm guessing maybe you're a little overwhelmed—I know we're a smaller company. I expect everyone here to wear several hats. You know that our ad salespeople make affiliate deals, too; our events team pitches in for investor meetings. Even Julie up front parses industry news for me."

I nodded again. Where was this going?

"Part of your job is proofing the campaigns that go out and making sure everything is tight. No typos, no awkward wording."

"Right." We designed a lot of ads in house for clients, and I was the last eyes on them most of the time.

He sat forward, taking a deep breath, removed a couple of

rolled up sheets of paper from his breast pocket, and smoothed them on my desktop. "So this one here. For the executive charter airline OneHop?"

I'd seen that campaign. Recently. My gaze dropped to the page.

"So here it says, 'We Get You There on Tim.'" John raised his gaze to me. "Who the hell is Tim?" He smiled and shook his head.

A deep heat rose up my neck, causing sweat to bead on my upper lip as embarrassment surged in me. "Oh my gosh." My voice was a low whisper.

"And this one for the bookstore invites people to 'Exploit a good book today.'" He stared at me. "Natalie, you can't use spell check on these."

I nodded. "Are these live?"

"Not anymore. We have to fix them for free and refund the money already expended on the campaigns." He smiled at me, a sad fatherly smile that did nothing to help the fact that I now felt both like I was pretending to be a grownup and was completely unqualified to be one. "Don't freak out. We all make mistakes. But mistakes cost money, and they piss off the ad reps because they ruin our credibility. How can the guys sell campaigns if one of their selling points—our in-house production—is complete crap?"

"Right."

"I need you to be more diligent."

"Okay." I felt like a child being scolded.

"I know you have a lot of other work with the PR firm and our event roster, but this is really important, too."

"Of course."

"Why not allot a specific portion of time a couple days a week for going through these? Have some really focused time —no phone calls, no emails, no interruptions. Just so you can focus."

I thought of the last group of ads I'd proofed. I'd been on the phone with Candace at the time. I cringed. Did any of those invite people to ride on Tim? "That's a good idea."

"Okay. Thanks. You do good work, Natalie. We all have a thing or two to learn. That's what life's about." John stood and gave me one last long look, his brown eyes friendly under the mop of messy blond hair. He looked more surfer than CEO, but that's part of what the Internet Industry was about—people got where they were based on capability and ingenuity rather than via some ladder chiseled from tradition.

"I'm sorry, John."

"Not a big deal." He spun and was gone, leaving me withering at my desk wondering if I was in any way qualified to be a grownup.

I'd been blasé about my job. I'd assumed I could do it with my eyes closed because of the time I'd spent at All Night. In reality, I'd been in this industry for just over a year, and I was only twenty-five. Work needed my attention, and I needed to figure out a way to give it more. A wet rag of shame balled up inside me, and I swallowed hard.

"Hey, you." Bennett appeared in my doorway wearing a huge grin. "Excited?"

The theater. Dinner. I nodded.

"Yeah, you look thrilled." His smile dropped. "What's wrong?"

I shook my head. "I'm okay. Sorry. Just work stuff. I'm excited. What's the plan?"

"I'll come pick you up, okay?" His voice softened. "Dinner's at six. I know it's early, but the show starts at eight. Pick you up at five-thirty?"

I looked at the clock on my monitor. It was already after three. I'd picked out a dress to wear but needed to shower. "Sounds good. Thanks, Ben."

He nodded, looking uncertain, but then slid away down the hallway.

I had one hour to get through the rest of my work. I focused on the words on my screen, self-doubt kicking his jolly little legs back and forth as he perched on my shoulder to help.

———

I was ready when the car came, waiting with my head poked out the fire escape so Bennett wouldn't feel like he had to come up. The long dark car rolled to a stop, and Bennett stepped out, his hair tamed and his tall body dressed in an impeccable suit. Even from two stories above, he looked amazing, and an unfamiliar interest bubbled in me. Could I be attracted to Bennett? I didn't think so, since I didn't doubt my love for CJ even for a second, but he did look good. I chalked the strange feeling up to perspective—I was just used to seeing Bennett in the office.

"Ben!" I called.

He glanced up, squinting into the late afternoon light.

I waved, and he smiled when he saw me. "I'll be right down!"

When I met him on the curb, he gave me a low whistle. "You clean up nice, Pepper."

"Thanks." I blushed as he held the door open for me and I slid in. After we were seated, I added, "not so bad yourself."

"You ready for a traditional New York City night out?"

I'd had plenty of New York nights out, but I doubted many of them had been very traditional. "I am."

The restaurant was somehow both huge and intimate. We were seated in a dark corner that felt very private, and I enjoyed the opportunity to gaze around. Even on a Tuesday evening, the place was humming with an energy that I'd only ever felt in the city. So many different people with so many different lives were running these intersecting courses all around me. It was heady, and the buzz was one of the things I loved about my new home. I just wished I didn't feel so outside of it all.

"Champagne." Bennett handed me a glass, and we toasted.

The table allowed us to sit side-by-side, facing outward, and it was much easier to talk than it would have been if we were forced to lean across the table across from one another. It also afforded great people watching, since we were looking out across the space.

"What about them?" Bennett said, angling his glass toward a couple just a few tables away.

I sipped my champagne and used my tiny binoculars. The couple was probably in their forties. She was trying pretty hard, I thought—hair meticulously done up, too much eye makeup—but her hands were unmanicured, and I got a distinct sense that she was someone's mother from the worry lines around her eyes, and the gentle slump of her shoulders. The man was smooth and refined, wearing an impeccable suit with a trendy contrast tie and shirt. He held her hand, and his mouth had a hungry shape to it as he watched her speak, his gaze never leaving her face.

"They're in love," I said. "I don't think they're planning to stay long." Dessert was already in front of them, but neither one was paying any attention to it.

"I don't think it's love," Bennett said. "He's got a tan line on his finger, and she looks like she's seeing bacon after dieting for fifteen years. They're having an affair."

I turned to him, shocked. "You can tell that across a restaurant?"

He smiled at me. "I guess I've seen enough to recognize it."

I remembered then that Bennett had been married once,

and it sounded like his wife had cheated. "Wow." I scanned the room to find something to distract him from any negative memories, but our food arrived before I'd managed to do so.

Dinner was incredible, and the prix fixe pre-theater menu had us out the door just in time to get to the show. I was a bit woozy from the champagne and the wine, but a slow warmth spread through me as I became more comfortable. By the time I sat in the box at Bennett's side, I felt like I was glowing with contentment.

The theater was ornate, the heavy curtain and all the seats covered in red velvet. Gold accents were everywhere, and the long boxes that hugged the walls gave us an excellent view of the audience arriving below. The ceiling was a multi-colored carved structure that drew my attention for long minutes as I stared at the ornate woodwork.

"I feel like we're in a palace," I breathed, leaning close enough to Bennett to get a whiff of whatever clean-smelling cologne he wore.

He smiled at me, taking my hand where it rested on my knee and squeezing gently. "Thanks for letting me bring you out, Pepper. It's fun to see the city through your eyes. I've been here so long I'm jaded." He leaned in and kissed my cheek, and I smiled back at him.

We watched the audience arrive below us, voyeurs in our fancy box in the air. I watched the people with fascination, dressed in everything from jeans and sneakers to long flowing gowns to... a girl in a black dress and pearls with a French twist on the back of her head and cat eye makeup. Catalina. I ground my teeth. Of course Catalina would show up here. It was exactly my luck.

I watched her take the arm of the suit-clad guy with her as they moved toward seats in the fourth row just below us. I clenched my teeth, working to keep my dislike for Catalina from coloring the otherwise lighthearted and exciting night

I'd been having so far. Catalina had pursued CJ when I'd been too uncertain to do so, and they'd shared a kiss that still made jealousy burn a prickly fire in my gut.

I watched her perfectly coiffed head as she leaned in close to her date and decided to forget that she was here. I wasn't going to let Maggie's irritating roommate ruin another second of my life.

I pushed my gaze beyond her, pointing people out to Bennett and laughing as he continued our game of figuring out what their backstories might be.

It felt odd to sit here, so close to Bennett, talking in intimate whispers as the theater darkened, but it also felt wonderful. Bennett was a friend, and everything about the evening had been incredible so far. I was floating on a cloud of happiness. Only in a little place at the back of my mind did I wonder what CJ and Irene were up to or have a thought about what CJ would say if he saw me sitting so close to another man. Had I not been about to see my first show, in the company of someone who smelled so good, I might have been a little bit jealous or feeling guilty. But there was nothing between Bennett and me, and as the orchestra jumped to life, electric guitars calling a promise into the heavy silence of the darkness around me, I felt only contentment with where I was at this moment.

The show was overwhelming and completely absorbed my attention until the lights came up for intermission. It was like being in a dream, and when I came back to myself, I was perched on the edge of my seat, leaning forward, and still squeezing Bennett's hand in my own. I turned to him, unable to keep the grin from my face, and dropped his hand. "I'll just let you have that back. Sorry."

"I didn't mind." Bennett was watching me intently, a warm smile on his lips and his eyes shining. "You look like you're enjoying yourself. That makes me really happy."

"I love it," I said, still floating on the last notes of the act that had just ended. "It's not exactly uplifting—"

"AIDS isn't really a joyful topic…"

"But it's so amazing. The singing, the music, the coordination of all the people and the lights… I've never seen anything like it."

"So it isn't just that you haven't been to Broadway…" Realization lifted his chin as he finished the thought. "You've never seen a show. Period."

"Period." I smiled. "I'm a virgin."

Damn it. I didn't need to flirt with the guy. It was bad enough I'd been holding his hand for an hour.

"Shall we go get a drink and stretch our legs?"

"Sure." I followed Bennett to the lobby and excused myself while he waited for the bar. The line for the restroom was ridiculous, and by the time I got back to Bennett, the theater lights were flashing, signaling us back to our seats.

He held out my wine and winked. "You're gonna have to slam it."

"Seriously?"

"You can't take it to the seats."

"A girl's gotta do what a girl's gotta do." I took the plastic glass from him and leaned my head back. If I'd learned anything from time spent with Candace, it was how to down a shot. This was just a little bigger shot.

When I lifted my head again, the glass drained, Bennett was grinning with wide eyes.

"I was kidding."

I cringed. "Oh. Sorry. That wasn't very polite."

"No, but it was *awesome*." Bennett took my arm as I dropped the cup into the trash.

We climbed the stairs together. The lobby was almost empty, and we were some of the last people still not in our seats.

"Tonight has given me a whole new appreciation for you, Pepper."

I smiled at him. "And me for you."

I didn't even have time to think before Bennett paused on the step next to me and leaned in, his lips meeting mine softly. I'd like to say that I flinched, pulled away, or at least asked him to stop, but the moment was heady, the company was warm and wonderful, and a full glass of wine was combining with all of it to alter my view of the world, if only for one night.

Bennett's mouth was soft, and his kiss was gentle and sweet. It was just a brush, a slight warm pressure that made my skin tingle, and something inside me jumped to life at the suggestion of a possibility I hadn't considered. And then it was done.

I stared at him for a second, his green eyes cloudy as he watched my face. His eyes crinkled and his mouth opened, but a movement at the foot of the stairs caught my attention and I turned fully, cutting him off before he'd even spoken.

Catalina stood at the bottom of the stairs, looking up at me with an amused smile on her face.

An icy cold fear sheathed my body, stripping away any happiness I'd found that night. Had she seen Bennett kiss me? Or was her expression only an outward sign of her dislike for me?

I turned away, and Bennett followed me. Neither of us said anything else as we slid back into our box, the theater dark around us.

I couldn't get the image of Catalina to go away. What would she do if she'd seen the kiss? She didn't have reason to see CJ regularly at this point, but I wouldn't put it past her to go out of her way to track him down and report on what she'd witnessed.

The remainder of *Rent* was enjoyable, but as the music

wound down and the audience stood to applaud, a weight settled upon me and the realization of what I'd done—and of what Catalina might do—began to swirl in my mind.

Bennett walked me to my door when the town car delivered us home, and I thanked him, keeping space between us. "I had a wonderful time."

"I did too, Pepper." He had a hand on my elbow.

I was relieved that he didn't lean in as I fished my keys from my purse. "I'll see you tomorrow, Bennett."

"Good night."

The door behind me closed with a crash of finality, and I stood for a moment in the small confined lobby of my building as guilt began to bubble within me. That kiss. That wasn't just friendly. What kiss was? What had I done?

I didn't climb the stairs to my apartment. Even though it was after eleven on a weeknight, I turned and knocked on the door to my left, each rap of my knuckles sounding like the dull beat of my traitorous heart.

————

The door swung inward after just a few minutes, and my neighbor Tom stood before me, wearing some kind of silky kimono thing.

"What are you wearing?" I asked, unable to keep the smile from my face as I took him in, standing there wrapped in silk, his chest hair springing up in the low v-neck.

"You came down here to bang on my door at this hour to make fun of my robe?" Tom made his back straight, pretending to be offended.

My eyes widened as I had a thought. "Oh. Are you alone?"

He grinned. "I love that you think I might not be, but I am. Come in?"

I stepped past him into an apartment that was the exact

shape and size as my own. Tom lived directly beneath me. We'd met last year thanks to Tamara's proclivity for oversized footwear and Tom's sensitive ears.

"You're so fancy." One hand smoothing the flouncy skirt of my pink dress. "Drink?" he asked, even though he didn't look excited about the prospect.

I shook my head. "No thanks. Can we talk for just a sec? I did something."

Tom's eyes danced. "Something or some*one*?"

"Nearly."

"Oooh." Tom sat on the leather couch that hugged one wall, motioning me to join him. "What have you been up to this evening in your fabulous frock, Peppercorn?"

"I saw *Rent*."

Tom's mouth made a frown, but he didn't look terribly sad. "Ah yes. The swan song of my people."

I raised an eyebrow at him. "Anyway."

"Yes, go on."

"Uh, Tom... Your, um, your robe..."

Tom looked down and then grinned. His robe was gaping open, and it was clear he wore nothing underneath. He pulled it shut and tucked the ends underneath him. "Sorry."

"Didn't see much."

"Don't be hurtful. There's plenty to see down there."

"You know what I meant." Tom was always fun for banter, but I'd come for more than that. "So tonight," I began. "I went out with a guy from work, just as friends."

"Noble intentions. Destined for failure."

"Right. So he kissed me. Or we kissed. I don't think I kissed him. But..."

"But he's not CJ."

I nodded, guilt making my heart feel leaden. "There's more."

Tom leaned forward. Sometimes I thought he enjoyed my drama a bit too much.

"Someone saw."

"When you go kissing people in public, that's the risk," he scolded.

"It was Catalina."

"The bitch?" He spit out the word.

I nodded.

Tom contemplated this information, shaking his head. "And where is the golden god tonight?"

"That's a whole other issue. He's with Irene."

"The cougar?"

I kind of wished all my friends would stop calling her that, but I couldn't deny that I shared their image of her. "Yeah, the cougar."

"And they're doing what, exactly?"

"He's going to work for her. They're setting up the office."

"That's a flimsy tale if I ever heard one."

"What?" It hadn't occurred to me that CJ might be lying.

"Setting up the office? Like installing phone lines? Moving furniture? Why wouldn't they pay someone to do that? She's in finance, right?"

I nodded. I was an idiot. "I don't know."

"Well, it's possible," he said quickly. "God, you look like I killed your hamster. I'm sorry, Pepper. I guess it's possible. CJ doesn't seem like the lying or cheating type."

"He's not." There must be a good reason why he and Irene needed to move desks themselves. "But evidently I am."

Tom leaned forward and took my hands from my lap, stopping me from wringing them. "Sweetie. It was a little slip. You didn't do anything wrong."

"I kissed someone who isn't my boyfriend. That's not doing something right."

"True, but sometimes you need to know what's out there to know what you've got."

I watched his face. He seemed to believe what he was saying, his eyes wide and honest. "Doesn't make it right."

"No, but it does make you human. You slipped. It isn't a big deal. Trust me. I'm lord of the slip, but I tend to slip into someone else's bed anytime I find myself in a relationship. That's why I avoid those suckers."

Tom was joking, but I was pretty sure a part of him was being honest. I'd seen plenty of men coming and going from this apartment, although Tom managed to be somewhat discreet. "So what do I do?"

"Normally I'd say do nothing. Move forward. And I'd say that whatever you do, you should *not* tell CJ."

"Don't I owe him the truth?" How could I live with myself if I didn't tell him?

"Think it through. If you tell him, will he be upset?"

"Of course."

"Will it change anything?"

"Probably." The thought of watching CJ's face fall as I told him I'd kissed someone almost broke my heart.

"Like I said, that's what I'd normally tell you to do."

"But Catalina saw."

"Or she didn't... you don't know." Tom leaned back into the red-fringed pillows on the couch. "The question is, if she saw you, will she tell CJ?"

"I've gotta think she would, just to hurt me."

"Is she really as bad as we think?"

I gave him a dark look.

"Okay, so you tell him."

"And then he breaks up with me."

"Maybe not. And if he's banging the cougar, it won't matter."

I cringed. "Too harsh."

Tom gave me a small smile. "Sorry."

"I don't know what to do." My voice was a piteous whine. I hated myself more in that moment than I had in a long time.

"Here's what I would do. Wait until the next time you see him. If he knows, you'll know right away. And then you tell him before he can tell you that he spoke with bitchy pretend-Hepburn girl."

Catalina seemed to believe she was in a constant historical reenactment that demanded she play the part of Audrey Hepburn at all times—except I'd always thought that Audrey Hepburn was probably a nice person. Catalina was not.

I didn't have a better plan, so I nodded. "Okay. Thanks, Tom."

"Go to bed, Pepper. It's late."

I stood and hugged my friend before heading back upstairs. I'd screwed up, but Tom was probably right. I'd have to wait to see if Catalina planned to tell CJ anything. And I still didn't know if she'd actually seen anything. She might have appeared at the foot of the stairs after I'd kissed Bennett. But there was enough to be concerned about in the idea of CJ's girlfriend standing in intimate silence in a near-dark theater with another guy, I supposed. It all came down to one question—how much did Catalina really want to hurt me?

———

In Dr. Chase's office the next day I found it difficult to make eye contact. Dr. Chase was poised and refined, with a shining wedding band on her finger. I was sure she didn't run around kissing men who were not her husband.

"Why do you think you kissed him, Natalie?" It was a simple question, asked innocently over a steaming cup of tea as Dr. Chase sat on the couch next to me with her feet tucked up beneath her.

"I have no idea. Because he was there? Because I'm an asshole?"

She shook her head. "I don't think you're an asshole. I think you made a decision, and because you didn't give it any thought first—or did the homework we agreed upon—you don't know why. This is the point of that exercise."

"I couldn't exactly whip out the paper and make notes while I stood there with him looking at me..."

"No, Natalie. You're right—you couldn't have done that. But the point of the exercise is for it to become second-nature. If you do it regularly, you'll be able to analyze a decision in your head."

I nodded. I could have done that. "I got swept up in the moment, I guess."

"And that's what you said you wanted to change."

"It is."

She nodded. I envied her. Dr. Chase was calm and focused. She exuded an air of confidence and direction. I was certain she didn't go running around dark theaters kissing men she shouldn't. And I was pretty sure she didn't cry herself to sleep worrying that she'd ruined everything she'd worked so hard for in one fell swoop of stupidity.

Chapter Twelve

MAN-NURSE

Tamara

LULU WAS able to get the man-nurse to potentially commit to letting us use the bar for Maggie's send off party, but he wanted to show me the space and make sure we were okay with the way things would operate during the party. As it turned out, Thursday night was a big night for them, as Lulu had suspected, but he was willing to accommodate us.

I took a cab to the bar on Mercer and stepped onto the curb out front, distracted by the bright green facade. There was no sign, but the huge picture window that faced the street made the place look interesting if not inviting.

The tall hunky dark-haired guy standing in front of it added some interest, too. He watched me take the place in and then walked toward me with a hand outstretched. "Tamara?"

I shook his hand. "Gabriel?"

"Nah, everyone calls me Gabe."

Actually everyone called him man-nurse, but I wasn't going to tell him that. "Nice to meet you. Thanks for taking the time."

"For a friend of Dr. Barton? Not a problem."

Dr. Barton. The formality of it made me laugh. "Sorry, I forget that he's a doctor. He kind of goes by 'Lulu's boyfriend' in my circle of friends."

"I've heard about your circle," Gabe said with a smile.

"Oh, really?" I shifted my weight, enjoying a moment in the sunlight, chatting with this handsome stranger. He was all shoulders and legs, tall and broad, a faded light-blue T-shirt with some kind of skateboard design pulled tightly across his chest. He wore a plaid shirt open over it, slim denim jeans, and Converse sneakers. "What exactly have you heard?"

"That you're all ridiculously fun, that you party like nobody's business, and..." He looked around, and a hand rose to rub his shoulder as a blush crept into his cheeks. "That you're all smokin' hot."

It was my turn to blush, but I played it off by pulling out my arrogant card. "And?" I spun in a small circle.

"Oh, and humble, too." He laughed.

I stopped and raised an eyebrow at him. Time to change the subject. "So the outside is nice... Can we go in?"

He pulled keys from his pocket. "Sure. Follow me."

Gabe unlocked the door, and we stepped into a dark open space with a long stainless steel bar gleaming against one wall. In the dim filtered light coming from the window facing the street, the place looked pretty nondescript, but when he flipped a couple switches behind the bar, I began to see the appeal.

Framed mirrors hung on many of the walls, along with life-sized Warhol-style portraits of old-school Hollywood celebrities. Marilyn Monroe looked down from behind the bar, and Clark Gable faced her on the other wall. The low banquettes and dangling chandeliers gave the place an old school vibe, too.

"I like it." I kept my voice low. Something about the open space demanded reverence.

"I'm glad." Gabe was watching me turn in a slow circle, taking it in. "There's another room back here with a bar."

He led me through a wide doorway and down a step. Tables lined the walls, but the center was open, under an arched ceiling. The bar in the back also stood beneath wooden arches, and there was a Moroccan feeling to the upholstery and decor here. Still old school chic, just less continental.

"Cool," I said. "So how would you work it for the party?"

"How many are we talking about, do you think?"

"Not more than thirty. Maggie has a lot of friends, but I think we're keeping it pretty low key."

He nodded, peering around. His dark brows furrowed over the amber eyes. "You guys want the back room?"

I looked around. "Where does the dancing happen?"

He lifted an eyebrow and grinned at me. "Sometimes people dance back here, but most of the craziness happens downstairs in the club."

"There's more?" The place was a labyrinth.

"Yeah, a DJ and a dance floor downstairs. Another bar. I thought you wanted to keep things low key, though, so I'd put you up here where you can actually talk."

"Could we have this room and still be allowed to go down and dance?" I tried to imagine keeping the girls from dancing and pictured a knock-down drag-out fight ensuing. Natalie had once body-checked a bouncer who'd tried to stop them from dancing at a bar uptown.

"Definitely." Gabe grinned, revealing nice white teeth. One of his front teeth had a small chip in the corner. There was a story there, and I found myself wanting to hear it.

I pulled my eyes away, realizing I'd been staring. "This is great. Do you need a deposit or anything?"

He shook his head as we walked back to the front. "No, of course not."

"Oh, one more thing," I spun on my heel and turned, but Gabe wasn't watching and he crashed right into me. His hands gripped my upper arms and pulled me back to keep me from toppling over. "Woah!"

"Oh, man, sorry," he said quickly. "Are you okay? I'm so sorry." His warm hands stayed on my arms, and his eyes filled with concern.

"I'm fine. Just surprised me, that's all." I stepped back, and his hands fell back to his sides. I considered moving close to him again. What was that smell? Something like the ocean, something briny and warm, but clean at the same time.

"What were you saying?" he asked.

"A drink. Do you think we could come up with a special drink for the night? For Maggie?"

"Sure. Like what?"

"She's from Texas," I said, thinking aloud. "And she's Mexican. She knows a lot about tequila."

"Not stereotypical at all," he said, his voice gently scolding.

"Yeah, but it's true. If the stereotype fits..."

His face was serious, and he dropped his chin a bit. "I'm a nurse. I might be a little sensitive about stereotypes."

Oops. Hit a nerve. "Sorry."

He smiled again. "Okay, so something a little different then? How about mezcal?"

"Mez sure." I laughed. I had no idea what mezcal was.

He smiled, revealing his dimples, his eyes dancing. "I'll take care of it. It'll be fantastic."

We walked back up to the front, solidifying times and

other details. After he locked the door, we said goodbye and I turned to flag a cab out on Canal Street.

"Hey, Tamara?" Gabe was beside me again, his long legs keeping pace with my always-quick cab-grabbing walk.

I stopped. "Yeah?"

"Would you want to go out sometime? Grab a bite?"

I agreed before my mind even really processed the question. If I needed a distraction from a certain sexy cowboy, here was a good one. We didn't set a date, but I settled into the cab, content that I'd be seeing him next week for the party. We could figure it out then.

———

On the cab ride back to my office, I called Lulu.

"I met him."

"Who? What are you talking about?"

"The man nurse."

Lulu squealed. "And?"

"And he's nice. We booked the bar for next Thursday. There's a club downstairs, and he's making a special drink in Maggie's honor."

"But what about the man-nurse?"

"I told you. He's nice."

"Tell me the good stuff. Is he nice looking?" She drew out the last word.

"He is. In a grown-up skater boy kinda way."

"So he is immature?" Lulu sounded eager to find a category to drop Gabe into. I suspected he might not be that easily quantified.

"I don't think so. He's... interesting."

"Good. It's about time you found someone interesting."

"He asked me out."

"Even better! When?"

"We'll figure it out." I paused. "Hey, Lu? I know this might drive a serious wedge between Pepper and me, but do you think we should ask Catalina to help out with this party? She and Maggie are close."

Lulu clucked. "She and Pepper are not exactly friendly."

"Thanks for the news flash. I still think we need to call her."

"I'll do it if you want."

"I want." I didn't mind Catalina, but I needed to get back to focusing on work. Things had been lagging.

"What do I tell her?"

"Time and date, to be on her best behavior with Pepper, and to invite some of Maggie's friends that we don't know. But no losers or jerks. Except herself of course."

Lulu giggled. "Okay."

"Leave that last part out." Sometimes Lulu was very literal.

"I will. Talk to you later."

I spent the rest of the day wishing three things: I wished I didn't feel constantly queasy on my new medication, I wished I could stop thinking about Spider, and I wished that Gabe hadn't turned out to be so cute. All I needed was one more hot man in my life who I couldn't possibly have.

As I closed my eyes and leaned back in my chair for a quick rest, I realized I couldn't do a single thing about any of those things. I swallowed hard and decided to focus on the stuff I could control. Like work.

Chapter Thirteen

COCKTAILS WITH A COUGAR

Natalie

WEDNESDAY FOUND me sitting at my desk, stirring my coffee and nursing it, along with a healthy portion of guilt, slowly. No matter what Tom said, I wasn't sure that keeping the truth about my slip from CJ was a good idea. And I had no idea what to do about Catalina. Part of me wondered if I should just call her. That would be the mature thing to do, certainly, but I wasn't a good keeper of my own secrets, and there was a fair chance that even if she didn't see anything, she'd know everything by the time I was done babbling.

I knew cheating was not a small crime. I'd had similar experience in this area before, but I'd been on the other side of it. My college boyfriend had been boyfriend to another girl. I'd found out about it when the two of us had a gothic lit class together, and Aaron, our mutual boyfriend, had gotten confused about who was writing the essay on Poe and who was writing about Horace Walpole. He was no lit major, and his constant references to *The Tell Tale Heart* and *The Pit and the Pendulum* at first seemed like a charming effort to understand my world a little better until I realized that he seemed to think I was writing about Poe. Needless to say, hilarity did not ensue. Aaron, unlike Tom, seemed to think that telling the whole truth was the best policy, and I relived his dual relationships in painful detail while he admitted everything before I finally managed to end things.

Though hearing the truth had been painful, living as a fool —believing that he loved me, that he was faithful—that was probably worse.

I'd been staring at my computer screen, wondering what to do for the better part of an hour, when Bennett appeared.

"Hey." He stood just beyond the threshold, looking uncomfortable and uncertain. "Can I come in?"

I forced a smile. I didn't want Bennett to be awkward around me at work. As he tentatively stepped into my office, settling in a chair, I realized that one tiny kiss had the potential not just to ruin things with CJ, but to seriously alter my world at work, too. "How are you?" I asked, struggling for a topic that felt like our usual banter and coming up with only pleasantries.

"Good." He nodded, his hair back to its usual messy state. "Hey—"

"About—"

We both began at once.

"Go ahead," he said, running his hands through the mess of hair.

"You."

"I just don't want things to be weird," he said. "You know, because of... everything. Last night." He shrugged.

"They aren't. I mean, they totally are..." This wasn't going especially well. "But they don't need to be. I don't want them to be either."

"I really like you, Pepper—"

"It didn't mean anything—"

Talking at once again.

He looked stricken before recovering himself. "Oh. I mean, of course not." He lifted one shoulder, shrugging it off.

"No, what were you going to say?" What *had* he been about to say?

"Just that I hoped it wouldn't mess things up with you and CJ. Are you going to tell him?"

I opened my mouth and then closed it. That was the question, wasn't it? "I don't know."

"Dude perspective?"

I shrugged. Maybe straight dude perspective would somehow be more helpful than the gay dude perspective I got from Tom last night. "Okay."

"Don't tell him." Bennett dropped his voice to a near whisper.

There it was again. "I don't know..."

Bennett's green eyes were shining, liquid. "I'm sorry I've complicated things for you."

"It isn't your fault. I had such a nice time with you. I just got caught up."

"Me too."

We sat in silence for a minute, the heaviness of the quiet seeming oppressive and solid.

"Can I ask a favor?" Bennett asked, bending forward slightly.

"Of course."

"If you tell him, will you let me know?"

I nodded. Why? Why would he care?

Bennett continued, "In case he comes in here, or I meet him out sometime. I need to know if he knows. To prepare myself for the punches."

"I don't think he'd hit you." I imagined CJ punching Bennett. It wasn't an easy image to conjure.

"You never know."

I smiled at him, sad to have shadowed such a fun night out with such a stupid error. "Thanks for everything, Ben. I had a great time."

"Me too." Bennett stood, looking like a dejected kid. Then he pulled his shoulders back and regained himself. "See ya."

Later that day, CJ called, and I was almost relieved that he didn't seem to have much time to talk.

"Drinks later?" he asked. There was nothing in his voice to make me believe he might have spoken to Catalina.

"Okay," I said, still feeling terrible.

"With Irene?" He said these words slowly, anticipating that I'd need time to absorb them.

"Really?" It was inevitable. Why not now, when I was at the bottom of my pit of self-loathing? The thought of sitting across from her, the idea that she and CJ might be involved in any relationship beyond the professional, turned my stomach. Despite my own slip, the thought of being cheated on again —this time by someone I really and truly loved, someone who could actually be the guy I wanted to end up with—it was almost too much to process when my mind was already stuck plowing through the repercussions of my own unfaithful behavior.

CJ sighed.

"Okay. Yes. When, where?" I tried to sound like a girl up for anything, enthusiastic and bold.

"Meet me at my place and we'll go together. Upper West, a bar called Sacha's. Can you be here at six? Maybe we'll go grab dinner after?"

"That sounds good."

We hung up. It did sound good. Seeing CJ, sitting at his

side, having a quiet dinner. It all sounded good... until I contemplated the cougar sitting across from us with her heavily made up eyes and impressive cleavage. I hoped she'd wear a turtleneck.

———

Irene was waiting at Sacha's when CJ and I arrived. We'd walked from his apartment in the cooling evening air, and I'd attempted to pretend that it was just a regular night out. I held CJ's hand and tried to live in the moment, as CJ was always able to do. It wasn't easy, though. The girls had just called to tell me that Catalina was helping to plan Maggie's send off party, and now I was on my way to have a cocktail with a woman who I was sure I pretty much detested. And somewhere inside me, a constant well of guilt bubbled away, burping and belching a filthy malaise that threatened to choke me from the inside out.

Irene sat at a tall round table with two chairs facing her, and she waved CJ into one that seemed to have been placed strategically closer to her than the other. A casual observer would assume that she and CJ were together, and that I was alone, sitting across from them. I ground my teeth and smiled.

"Hello, Cassidy," Irene purred, standing to open her arms and give CJ a hug. My jaw began to ache from the pressure of forcing my teeth together. "And you must be Natalie." She reached a hand out to me, and I shook it, but at the last moment she gave me her fingers only, so I ended up gripping her limp fingers instead of her palm. A move engineered to make me feel like a moron. It worked.

Smile still plastered painfully across my face, I slid onto my chair.

"So you're in some kind of advertising, Natalie?" Irene asked once the cocktail waitress had taken our order.

"My company does online advertising, but I'm actually in marketing."

She nodded, her eyes watching me with a fierce interest.

Since she didn't respond, I continued, "I'm actually the director. I manage branding... handle the corporate communications, PR... I deal with the agencies, approve creative for clients..."

CJ squeezed my leg. I was babbling, unsure what the hell to say but desperate to sound important to this woman. I closed my jaw, grateful when the drinks arrived.

"Well, that sounds nice." She nodded.

Nice? Really? I took a long draw of my citron and tonic. Lulu always said that vodka could solve most problems. I planned to find out if she was right.

"Natalie was pursued by a headhunter," CJ told her. "She was phenomenal at All Night Media and had her pick from of a bunch of opportunities."

That wasn't exactly true, but I felt like I needed Irene to think highly of me, so I left it alone.

Irene smiled politely. "I suppose you're not too happy that I'm keeping your boyfriend occupied and exhausted all hours of the day and night, but Cassidy knew I'd ride him hard. He told you we have a history?"

CJ looked uncomfortable, and I thought I might throw up from the innuendo.

"We go pretty far back," she was saying. She scooted her chair closer to CJ and looked at him adoringly.

"So the new firm is going well?" I ventured, not sure what to ask but desperate to keep myself in the conversation.

"It's not really a new firm." Irene dipped her chin as if she was speaking to a child. Her bright red lipstick was feathering around the sides, and I took small satisfaction in the wrinkles that appeared in her forehead when she made her eyebrows come together to scowl at me.

"It's a new branch of the same firm Irene runs up in Buffalo," CJ said, shooting me a smile that told me he knew every thought running through my head at that moment. "And I think we're getting pretty close. Irene's brought in some great brokers, and a few of the guys are coming in from Buffalo."

"And Cassidy will oversee the whole endeavor." She beamed at him.

I watched them discuss some details of the opening, which was going to be the following week. She leaned in close to him, and her deep v-neck was certainly revealing, but there was something off about the way she flirted. There was something in her eyes when he spoke, when she spoke about him. Something that looked like pride. I could only guess it was because she felt like CJ was her prodigy.

CJ, for his part, didn't seem to be acting any differently around me than he usually did—maybe a little bit more nervous as he tried to make sure that I didn't leap across the table to eviscerate his boss and mentor. He definitely didn't know about the kiss with Bennett. Maybe Catalina would stay in her little Tiffany box and leave us alone.

The vodka was beginning to work in my system, and I felt warmer and looser. The looseness traveled to my mouth, unfortunately, and as soon as my next words were out, I regretted them. "So I guess you taught CJ everything he knows, huh?" It wasn't the words. It was the snarky tone I let seep into them, and even CJ stared at me with a disapproving eyebrow raised.

"I wouldn't say that," Irene said, obviously picking up on the sexual connotation with which I'd infused the statement. "Though he probably gets a bit of his decisive nature from me."

Even CJ looked at her askance when she said this.

She quickly explained, "I mean, we've spent a lot of time together. Many of his... formative experiences. I mean, not in a parental way, of course."

What the hell was she talking about?

CJ was staring at her, potentially as confused as I was feeling about the weird detour into parental topics.

"CJ's parents are great people. Very nice. Very... qualified." This extra explanation didn't make things more comfortable. Neither did the fact that Irene stood abruptly after uttering these words, pushing her stool back and excusing herself to the bathroom. "Excuse me. I'll be right back."

She teetered away on sky-high zebra heels, and I stared at CJ. "What the hell was that about?"

"I don't know. She's been a little strange lately. Maybe I should've warned you." He looked glum.

"I wouldn't know the difference. I think she's strange in general. What do you mean, though?"

"I can't put my finger on it. She likes to ask me about my folks, about growing up. It's always been a topic with her— she says she likes to understand where people come from, but I haven't ever heard her question the other guys. She means well. She's a good person, Natalie." CJ scooted his chair closer to mine, and the ticking irritation in me settled a bit. He slid his hand onto my knee beneath the table and leaned over to whisper in my ear, "We don't have to stay long. We'll go get a quiet dinner, okay?"

A happy warmth spread through me. I could tolerate this a bit longer as long as I was sure that CJ was here with me, and not with Irene.

When she reappeared, Irene approached the table looking less than pleased. She paused before sitting, noting the rearranging of furniture that had happened in her absence. Irene gave me a tight lipped half-smile, an acknowledgement of my proximity-to-CJ victory, I guessed.

"So Irene," I said. "How long do you plan to stay in the city?"

Her eyes flitted to CJ and then back to me. "As long as I need to." She took a sip of her red wine. "There are so many things that need to be settled before I can go."

"We're in good shape though, right?" CJ seemed unsure. I hated seeing him uncertain of his abilities, but he'd told me several times that he might be in over his head in his new role. That was something we shared. I didn't seem to be cut out for my new job, either.

"We're in great shape." She beamed at him. "You're doing just fine."

We stayed another half hour, and things didn't get much more comfortable. I had another drink, so I cared just a tiny bit less about how not comfortable they were. When we stood to leave, Irene looked suddenly sad, and it struck me that she might be lonely. Once I'd had the thought, I realized that I didn't really care.

"We've got dinner plans," CJ told her, "but thank you so much for the drinks. I'm glad you guys finally got to meet."

She smiled, her eyes still cold. "Me too. So nice to meet you, Natalie."

"Have a good night." I couldn't help but gloat a bit. She clearly wanted to spend time with CJ, and I was winning in that department. Her motivation for wanting to be with him, however, was suddenly unclear to me. I didn't think she actually wanted him in a sexual way. So what exactly was her intention?

Chapter Fourteen

FATEFUL FAREWELLS

Tamara

I KEPT my head down and focused on work for the week leading up to the party. Lulu spoke to Catalina, and I emailed all of Maggie's other friends, making sure everyone knew where to be and at what time. Otherwise, I was a nauseated real-estate machine. I closed three deals between meeting Gabe and seeing him again the following week, and when Thursday rolled around, I was ready for a break and some girl time.

We met early at Natalie's apartment on the West side.

I took in the spread of appetizers covering the surface of her kitchen table. "You made food?"

"No, I ordered food." Lulu came to the door to give me a hug.

"It's for me," Maggie said, smiling. "I complained that we never eat enough, and then we go drinking. It's not healthy."

"But it is fun," I chirped, picking up a piece of bruschetta.

I was glad there was food. Maggie was right. Health was something I needed to focus on, unfortunately.

"Drink?" Candace hugged me and went to the sink.

Lulu leaned in. "She's got a new metaphor."

It had been Manhattans not long ago. She'd preached something about getting through the stiff alcohol to find the reward at the bottom—the cherry. They were way too much for me. But with my liver, anything would be too much.

"Can I make my own drink?" I asked.

Candace narrowed her eyes. "You don't even know what I'm making. It's a Moscow Mule. Vodka, ginger beer and lime."

"And the metaphor? Let's have it."

"Vodka's easy," she began. "Smooth and innocuous, right? But the ginger beer has a hot bite."

I nodded. "Okay."

"It's a metaphor for sex." She waggled her eyebrows.

"No it isn't." I didn't see it at all.

"Then you're doing it wrong. It should be smooth and unassuming sometimes, and hot and spicy at other times."

"I'm not doing it at all," I told her. "But I like hot and spicy."

"Why aren't you having any sex?" she asked, taking a step forward as if I was about to divulge a secret.

"I'm fasting," I quipped. I didn't want to have this conversation with her. "Move."

Candace finished making her own drink, and I stepped to the sink, pouring myself a ginger beer with ice. No alcohol, but interesting enough to fool my taste buds. Luckily, Candace wandered to the middle of the apartment where Pepper and Maggie were sitting on the futon, heads close together as they talked. I didn't need her asking why I was avoiding alcohol. I didn't want to tell any of my friends. New York City—these girls—this was the first time in my life I'd been just Tamara. They knew me as fun and strong and wild, and I was keeping it that way.

Tom came up, and we turned up the music and talked and danced until Candace turned it back down and interrupted everyone's conversations.

"Tamara is not having any sex. This is a solvable problem, and I say we fix it tonight."

"Need a rabbit?" Lulu asked. She'd given Pepper a fancy vibrator as a housewarming gift.

"Maybe," I said. "Guys, this isn't a topic for discussion. I'm on a man break." Images of Spider flitted through my mind. I'd emailed him details about the party, unsure whether it was the right thing to do. Gabe would be there, after all, and I wanted to get to know him and see if he could help me focus on someone other than Spider. Maybe I wasn't really on a man break after all.

"Well, I'm not," Candace said.

"Are you going to tell us how hot Gregoire is again?" Pepper asked, looking wary.

"No. I'm going to tell you how creative he is. This story involves Crisco and plastic wrap."

"Seriously?" Lulu looked interested, leaning in with her eyes wide.

Candace nodded, swiveling her shoulders and standing taller, proud to be the center of attention.

"Save it," I said. My mood was darkening, and Candace's habit of bringing the conversation constantly into the sexual realm wasn't helping. "We're celebrating Maggie. So unless your story involves her, we'll hear it later."

"I want to hear it." Lulu pulled Candace into a corner. Tom followed them over.

Maggie beamed at me. "I'm gonna miss you guys all so much. Thank you for planning my party."

"Catalina helped," I told her, though in reality Catalina's

contribution had involved emailing a couple people. Lulu and I had done the rest.

"I'm worried about her," Maggie said.

Pepper cringed visibly but leaned in. "Why?"

"She didn't take the news that I was leaving very well, and she's been almost angry about it. She's not happy about having to find a roommate."

"She seems angry about pretty much everything," Pepper said, not quite under her breath.

"Does she have a couple months to do it?" I asked.

Maggie nodded. "I'll keep paying rent until she finds someone. I'm staying with 'Nesto back home, so I don't need to pay rent there."

"But you don't have a job there," Pepper pointed out.

"I have some savings."

"Don't let her bleed you dry. If you keep paying rent, she has no incentive to find a roommate." Pepper was quick to think the worst of Catalina.

Maggie shrugged. "I'm not worried about that. We've been friends forever. She wouldn't take advantage."

Pepper snorted but then looked sorry. "Has she been acting weird at all?"

We all turned to look at her. "What does that mean?" I had to ask loudly to be heard over the shrieking coming from the corner where Candace was still telling her Crisco story.

"Just..." Pepper's face fell. "I went to see a show with a guy from work. And it was just... I got caught up in the moment. The theater was all *Pretty Woman*, and it was dark and velvety and romantic... and I kissed him. When I stopped it, I saw Catalina standing there. I think she saw us."

"Oh, shit." I had no idea what to say, but I gave Pepper a hug. Catalina was definitely dangerous where CJ was concerned.

"I know." She sounded completely miserable. "I don't even

like the guy, I mean... not like that. And I love CJ. But if he finds out..."

Maggie shook her head. "Catalina wouldn't tell him. She's not like you think, Pepper. You guys just got off on the wrong foot. Do you want me to talk to her? Make sure she won't tell anyone what she saw?"

Pepper didn't look any less miserable, but she agreed to let Maggie talk to Catalina. I, for one, believed Catalina would do whatever she wanted, regardless of anything Maggie said, but I was a skeptic.

"Hey, ladies." I stood. "We've got a party to go to. Bottoms up."

Everyone downed what was left of their drinks, and we headed downstairs to catch a cab. When we got down to Soho, there was a line spilling out onto the sidewalk in front of Gabe's club.

"What's this place called?" Maggie asked, her face lit with excitement.

"No name."

"That's a stupid name."

"No, it literally has no name."

"That's equally stupid," Maggie said.

"It's a really cool place," I assured her.

Catalina was standing in line, an annoyed expression on her face as she watched us all arrive together. She quickly flitted to Maggie's side as I approached the bouncer.

"Hi, there. We're here for Maggie's party?" I hadn't expected things to be quite so crazy. People in line were shooting us angry looks and making irritated grumpy sounds as we stood in a group at the front of the crowded sidewalk.

"Tamara, right?" the bouncer asked. He was huge, as bouncers tended to be, but he was unusual in that he was wearing a skirt of some kind.

"Sir, is that a dress?" Candace pointed at his exposed legs, looking up at him with wide eyes. Obviously, she had already had enough drinks to be forward.

A flit of annoyance passed across his dark face before he found a smile. "It's a lava-lava. I'm Samoan," he said with more patience than I thought Candace deserved. When he stood, I understood how he could get away with wearing what was, essentially, a skirt. The man was huge. He towered over me at what must have easily been six and a half feet, and he weighed three hundred pounds at a minimum.

"I bet she's the first person to give you shit about it," I said.

He grinned. "Most people don't have the balls. You guys can go on in."

I thanked him and smacked Candace on the arm as she walked past me. "Behave."

"Never." She cackled as she swayed into the club.

Gregoire and Andrew were already inside, and Pepper had CJ on the phone within minutes, urging him to hurry down and meet us. "No!" she wailed. Her face fell as she stuffed the long phone back into her purse. When she saw me watching, she leaned in to talk above the thumping beat. "CJ has to work. He's not coming."

"Oh, Pepper, I'm sorry."

Catalina sidled up to us, lifted an eyebrow, and snorted as she pushed between us to get to the bar.

"Bitch," Pepper whispered under her breath.

I was about to try to console Pepper, but at that moment, Gabe appeared with a wide smile. "Hey, Tamara! I'm happy to see you. How's everything working out? Is this okay?"

"We just got here," I said. "The giant in the skirt out front let us to the front of the line."

"Don't let Josefa hear you call it a skirt."

"A little late for that, I'm afraid. Candace already took care of that."

Gabe glanced to the door, but Josefa still sat on his stool, calmly checking IDs and providing a somewhat menacing gate to the incredible interior of the club. "He's a good guy. Great bouncer."

I nodded. I didn't doubt it.

"Get you a drink?" Gabe walked me to the bar where my friends were busily ordering, chatting and scanning the room.

"Club soda?" I suggested.

Gabe didn't question my order. Rather than bothering the bartender, he let himself behind the bar and poured it for me, grabbing something for himself in the process. He put a martini glass on the bar and then poured an orange drink into it from a shaker, topping it with a lemon curl. "You don't have to drink it, but you at least have to taste the Maggie Mezcal Martini.

He looked so proud of himself that I couldn't deny him. I took a quick sip and smiled at him. "It's fantastic."

"On the house," he told me.

I shook my head. "It's really good, but I'm not much of a drinker these days."

He didn't question my statement, and I wondered if maybe I'd found the right way to discuss my alcohol celibacy. Most people in my life wouldn't accept the declaration that easily.

Gabe and I chatted for a few minutes, and then I turned to introduce him to the girls, who evidently didn't need to go downstairs to the club to dance. They were tearing it up in the narrow space between tables as the Santana song *Smooth* wound its way around the growing crowd. He was friendly and welcoming, and I found myself liking him even more as he shook hands and made small talk with my friends. Tonight, he wore dark jeans and a button-down blue shirt with a faint sheen and an understated pattern. He looked cool and easy-going—and handsome. I watched him with something bordering on attraction, although I told myself it was just fascination. This was a guy totally comfortable in his environment, among strangers but at home. I envied him in a way. I felt like I had something to prove, but Gabe seemed to be interested in proving things only to himself.

After meeting each of my friends, Gabe turned back to me. "Do you have a few minutes to sit?"

I nodded, enthralled with my own perceptions of him.

We took seats on a bench along a wall, just a few feet from where my friends seemed to be enjoying themselves tremendously. Andrew and Gregoire were buying drinks for the girls and talking with their heads close—dude talk, no doubt—and the girls were laughing and smiling. Maggie looked like she was having a great time, and I felt like I'd succeeded in giving her an official send-off.

I sat facing the door, and Gabe faced me, leaning forward with his elbows resting on his long denim-clad legs. "What do you think of the place now that there are people in it?"

"It's amazing." I meant it. "Seriously. You've got all kinds of people in here, and it's such a happy environment. I really like it, Gabe."

He grinned.

"You have a partner, right?"

He nodded. "Yeah, Sefa."

I cocked my head, not sure who he was talking about.

"The guy in the skirt out front."

"Oh!" Of course. "So he's here when you're at the hospital?"

"Yep.".

"So what's the plan? I mean, long term? Are you going to pick one or the other, club or hospital?"

For the first time, Gabe's smile dropped and he looked uncertain. "I have no idea. Nursing pays really well, and that's where my education is, right? But I love being here. I love being around people who are happy, who are having a good time. It makes me feel like I'm doing something good."

"Nursing doesn't make you feel that way?" I laughed at the idea of a nurse who didn't think he was doing something good.

"No, it does. It's just... it's serious, you know? The stakes are higher. People aren't always well, and some die." His amber eyes shone.

He looked so sad I wanted to reach out and hug him, but just as the idea occurred to me, a tall lean figure appeared in the doorway and paused, looking around the space.

A chill went through me as Spider strode into the center of the space, his sharp eyes finding me immediately. I stood without even thinking about it and then looked down at Gabe. "I'm so sorry," I said. "A friend of mine just arrived." I walked away from Gabe, and it didn't even occur to me how naturally I'd done it. How easy it was to fall back into old patterns and take my place at Spider's side.

"Hey, darlin'," Spider drawled as I got close. He took me in his arms, giving me a warm hug before releasing me.

"Hey." I didn't know what else to say. A smile covered my face that I wished I could dial down a few watts, but I was happy to see him.

"That banner says 'farewell.' Is this your goodbye party? You comin' home, Tam?" He grinned at me, his eyes dancing.

"You wish. I'm not going anywhere. This party is for my friend Maggie."

"Well, I guess you'd better introduce me, then."

Inviting Spider had been a whim, and now I had to introduce him to the girls, which would result in endless questions and pointed barbs full of innuendo. It was too late to rethink the whole thing, so I took his arm and guided him toward the noisy bubble of girls who were my best friends.

Pepper, Maggie, and Candace stopped talking and turned

to stare openly as I approached. I was glad to see that CJ had finally arrived and was supporting a swaying Pepper. I guessed that Pepper's disappointment on the phone must have been convincing enough to get CJ to decide that work wasn't that important after all. Lulu and Catalina were engulfed in some conversational bubble that had them talking simultaneously two inches from each other's face.

"Girls, CJ," I said, standing in front of my friends. "This is Gaige. He's from Indiana. We grew up together."

How else could I introduce Gaige Spydell? I could have said, "He was my first everything." I could have told them that my heart still beat faster when he was near and that he could send my blood surging just by tracing his fingers up the side of my neck. But I didn't.

"Y'all can call me Spider. Tam does." Spider gave each of the girls a hug and a kiss on the cheek. Charming. Way too charming.

I let the girls gush over him, peppering him with questions as I stood at his side. Once he'd said hello, he returned to me, still talking to my friends but with one hand protectively on my low back. His hand was warm, and it made the nerves up and down my back spring to life, as if they were suddenly more sensitive than any other spot on my body. Why did he still have this effect on me? Why couldn't I let go of Spider?

As Spider's fingers sent my mind reeling, I tried to get a grip on myself. Not only were my emotions suddenly tuned to a very high frequency, but my whole body felt like it was buzzing—and I hadn't had more than a few drops of alcohol all night. The party went on around me, and the volume of the crowd seemed to increase at the same time as my vision narrowed. Although Spider's touch warmed me just moments before, a cold freeze crept over my skin as I stood at his side. Panic began to bloom in my chest. What was happening to me? A sense of doom overtook me, and I moved in closer to Spider's side, looking for some connection to the world around me. Even as I stepped toward Spider, I felt as if I was actually moving away from myself, watching from just a few feet away. Spider was the first person to notice when I slipped to the floor, my entire body trembling as I dipped beneath the surface of reality and lost consciousness, my breath catching in my lungs in painful gasps as life left me behind.

BIG MEN CAN WEAR SKIRTS

Natalie

"I'M REALLY SORRY, babe. Irene really needs me here for a while. I'll make it. It's just going to be later than I thought."

CJ sounded sincere, but the vodka in my system was bringing my emotions closer to the surface than normal. Combined with the roiling guilt and self-doubt I'd been feeling, it was no great surprise that I snapped at CJ when he offered his excuses.

"CJ, Irene always needs you lately. What about me?" I hadn't seen him in days. Not since we'd had drinks with Irene and then dinner afterward. While the sharp edges of my guilt had softened, seeing Catalina tonight had me on edge.

"There is nothing going on," CJ said, his voice still placating, soothing.

"I know that." I felt like I was shouting over the music. "I just want to spend time with you. And Maggie's leaving the city."

"I know. I'll be there, I promise. Give me an hour?"

I drank for an hour. When CJ finally arrived, I was less put together than I'd been in weeks. Work had been insufferable lately, with John watching every move I made as if he was waiting for me to screw up again. He'd also said something in passing about hearing that I'd be vacationing in Cabo on the company, and it didn't sound good. Bennett was walking on eggshells around me, and I couldn't blame him. Plus Catalina was here, watching me with accusing eyes. Maggie had promised to talk to her, to make sure she wouldn't out my indiscretion to CJ, but it didn't settle the unease I felt at seeing her up close and personal, all Hepburned out as usual.

"Hey, babe." CJ put his arms around me and pulled me in for a kiss. "I was outside in line for twenty minutes. I called you a bunch of times. One word from you and I'm sure that giant out front would've let me in."

"Sorry," I said. My phone was buried in my purse, and it was crazy loud in the bar.

"This place is awesome. Is Maggie having a good time?"

We both turned to see Maggie dancing, her arms around Lulu and Candace and her head thrown back. "I think so," I said.

We went to the bar together, and CJ handed me another of the special drinks that the man-nurse club-owning hottie Tamara had been chatting up all night made. I turned to introduce CJ to the man-nurse, only to find that Tamara had moved on to yet another good-looking man. This one was tall and polished with purposefully spiked dark hair and chiseled cheekbones. He wore a western-style shirt and boots, and he was definitely pulling it off.

As the drinks hit my system, I realized I needed a minute away. I excused myself to go to the ladies room, where Candace found me.

"Who the hell is the tall drink of water with Tam?" she asked.

"No idea," I said, my voice echoing inside the stall. "He's pretty hot though."

"Understatement," Candace said. "Hey, you might not want to take too long in there. Catalina moved in as soon as you walked away from CJ."

"Shit! Are you sure?"

"Sorry, Pep."

I pulled myself together and raced out of the bathroom to find Catalina standing alone near the bar, CJ nowhere in sight. Had she told him what she'd seen? Was he so angry that he left the party? Dread filled me, but it mixed with anger as Catalina spotted me and gave me a smirk.

"If you're looking for CJ, he went outside to take a call," she said, her voice full of something I couldn't identify.

I ignored her and walked to the door, leaning out and smiling at Josefa. I could hear CJ just a few feet down, barking into the black flip phone he held to his ear. He sounded angry and impatient, and he looked upset. I cringed and headed back inside. I felt somewhat unhinged. The drinks weren't helping. It was at least ten minutes before CJ finally stepped back up to my side, looking aggravated.

"You okay?" I ventured.

CJ turned to look at me, a look I couldn't quite read in his eyes. Before he could answer, Tamara walked toward us with the cowboy. She introduced him as a childhood friend. I greeted them, struggling to behave normally, and the guy kissed me on the cheek. I kept an eye on CJ the whole time. His face was inscrutable, and my heart was slowly shriveling up into a painful lump.

Tamara stepped closer to Gaige, and I wondered fleetingly what the relationship really was. They certainly seemed like more than friends to me, and she looked like she was practically swooning in his presence. I was torn between terror over whatever Catalina might have been whispering in CJ's ear and the desire to behave naturally so as not to give anything away—in case Catalina had just been saying hello—when I realized that Tamara wasn't just swooning. She was literally sinking to the floor, her skin a pallid yellow.

Gaige caught her in his arms, flashing a look of terror around at us as he lowered her to the floor and her entire body shook and spasmed.

"Call 911," he said, his voice level but loud enough to command attention.

Gabe, the bar owner, dashed behind the bar and made the call while everyone else backed away from the center of the room where Gaige had lain Tamara down, her head on his lap.

Andrew dropped to Tamara's side, his hand on her neck as he took her pulse. He rolled her to her side, speaking in serious tones with Gaige as he lowered her head to the hard ground.

I gripped CJ's arm, wishing I hadn't had quite so much to drink. I had no idea what to do. After a moment, all the girls knelt at Tamara's side, shielding her a bit from the gawking crowd, which had begun advancing. They'd overcome their surprise and were now leaning toward curiosity, I guessed. I didn't want Tamara to be a spectacle to them—she would hate that.

Gaige was new to me, but it was clear that Tamara was not new to him. He was keeping her close, whispering softly in her ear, devastated worry on his handsome face.

When the EMTs arrived, the music had stopped and Tamara was the center of attention. Her body had stilled, but she still didn't appear to be conscious. A cold fear gripped me. What the hell was wrong? Andrew barked orders to the emergency workers, and I was grateful to have an emergency department doctor among my circle of friends.

We stood on the sidewalk, tears running down our cheeks, as our friend was loaded into the ambulance on Mercer Street.

"Where will you take her?" Maggie asked Andrew as he and Gaige climbed into the ambulance behind the stretcher.

"St. Vincent's," Andrew said. "Meet us there."

We watched the flashing lights disappear down the block and then stood still on the sidewalk for a long minute, looking into each other's frightened faces for some hint of explanation.

"Let's go," CJ said, pulling me toward a cab that had just pulled up along the curb.

The others followed suit, and soon we were racing in stops and starts to find out what had happened to Tamara, praying she would be all right.

———

Lulu was in the cab with us, and she spoke enough to make up for the fact that CJ and I didn't seem to be speaking to each other.

"Andrew was incredible. I'm so glad he was there. What do you think happened? Do you think it was alcohol poisoning?"

"She wasn't drinking." I'd noticed that the last few times I'd seen Tamara she hadn't been drinking. I'd considered questioning her but had been a little wrapped up in my own head and hadn't managed to ask her why. Now that I thought about it, I'd never seen her drink much.

"Of course she was." Lulu sniffed. "Oh my gosh, do you think she took something?"

CJ shook his head, and I glared at Lu.

"What if she was experimenting with something else, and she didn't tell us?"

"She wouldn't do that." I was sure that wasn't it.

"I hope not." Lulu was quiet after that.

The ride to St. Vincent's seemed to take forever, and CJ's silence formed a suffocating cloud that settled over me. I glanced at him a couple times as we rode, but he was staring out the window at the city flying by.

Once we'd arrived, Lulu took charge. She was a familiar face to most of the staff, and she questioned the admitting nurse inside the emergency room and came back out to give us a report. "No one can go in yet. They're running some tests and still working. She will almost definitely be staying, though, so once she has a room we can go see her."

"Is she conscious, Lu?" Maggie's voice was small, scared.

Lulu nodded. "The nurse said yes. Andrew will come tell us something as soon as he can. I told the nurse we'd be in the waiting area out front."

We left the emergency room and made our way to the chairs clustered in the hospital's main entrance area. Just as we were sitting, CJ stood again. "I'm going to get some air," he said.

I watched him walk out the door of the hospital and dread turned my stomach. I couldn't tell for sure if he was angry with me, or if this was just a reaction to this horrible situation. It didn't seem like a coincidence that his mood had shifted so totally just after speaking with Catalina, but then the whole thing with Tamara had been pretty traumatic.

I leaned over and put my head on Lulu's shoulder. She put her arm around my shoulders, and we sat like that, taking comfort from one another. The others sat around us, Gregoire and Candace whispering across from me, Catalina and Maggie silent and staring at the television overhead. Gabe had come and was sitting on Maggie's other side, twisting his hands as they rested on his knees. I wondered if he somehow felt responsible, since Tamara had collapsed at his bar.

The night, which before had felt so festive and exciting, had turned cold and foreboding. The darkness pressed against the windows reminded me of a predator, and I felt like no matter what we did, there was something fierce and hairy waiting to attack.

When CJ finally came back inside, his face was every bit as grim as it had been when he'd gone out. His eyes didn't meet mine as he took his seat next to me again. It was like sitting beside a monolith. I was certain he knew. I wanted to leap across the aisle and rip Catalina apart, but I couldn't meet her eyes either. In that moment, maybe more than ever before, I hated myself.

———

After about an hour, Andrew came down to tell us that Tamara was awake, that she was going to be okay, but they hadn't yet admitted her, and we couldn't see her. He disappeared again, and we waited some more. At some point, I fell asleep, my head on Lulu's shoulder and my heart yearning to lean in the other direction and feel CJ's warm arms around me. He had slid down in his chair and was resting his head against the back of it, his eyes closed and his long legs stretched out before him. He was right next to me, but it seemed like he was light years away. I drifted into a tortured sleep, fueled by too much alcohol and a deep sense of foreboding.

When Andrew came back, everyone was sprawled across the waiting room, curled up on chairs or laying across the long benches. He woke Lulu, so I was jostled awake when she stood to throw her arms around him.

"How is she? Can we see her?"

Andrew smiled. "She's okay. Spider's with her for now, and they're both sleeping."

I stood next to Lu. "What happened?" We spoke in hushed tones. It was the midst of night, and it felt like the entire world slumbered around us.

"She's sick, guys. It was good that Gaige—I mean Spider —was here. He knows her history. She's been sick since she was a kid."

"Sick how?" Lulu asked, her face pulled long with worry.

"A genetic disease. I'll leave it to her to explain. Why don't you guys go get some decent sleep and come back in the morning? There's nothing for us to do here tonight."

I really wanted to see Tamara, reassure myself that she was all right. I needed to know that something that had broken tonight might have a chance at being fixed. A glance at CJ told me nothing about the odds of that situation righting itself.

"Thank you, baby," Lulu wrapped her arms around Andrew and kissed him. It gave me a tiny bit of joy to see Lulu so happily settled, but it also reminded me that I'd had the same chance, and I'd ruined it. Andrew and Lulu said goodbye and he disappeared into the depth of the hospital once again.

We woke our sleeping friends and shared the news. Eventually, we stumbled out to the street, flagging the few cabs that drifted by on the dark patches of night fog.

CJ and I walked to my apartment on 15th Street, since it was only a few blocks north. It took me two blocks to find my voice. "I saw you talking to Catalina," I began.

He turned and stared at me, his eyes narrow.

"I just wondered what she had to say," I tried. "I know you guys have a history..."

"You're jealous?" His voice was thin and tired. "First you're jealous of Irene, and now of Catalina?"

I shook my head. "No." How could I fix this when I wasn't sure what was broken? "I just... I'm tired. I'm not making sense."

"Not much makes sense tonight. Let's just get some sleep and we can talk tomorrow."

When we got to my apartment, we found ourselves facing opposite directions in my queen-sized bed, and I wondered how everything had gotten so completely screwed up.

Chapter Sixteen

ORGANS AND ORDERLIES

Tamara

I WOKE IN AN UNFAMILIAR BED, every muscle in my body screaming in pain. Evidently I'd been hit by ten thousand elves with sledgehammers, each one intent on breaking a bone. I groaned involuntarily as I tried to sit up and look around.

"Hey, darlin', don't rush it." Spider appeared at the side of my bed.

As he helped me to a sitting position, I saw the chair where he'd been sleeping. There was a thin blanket pulled over it. Spider's clothes were wrinkled, and his hair was sticking up much less artfully than it had the night before. My mind raced back to the party, but I'd lost a huge chunk of time. I stared around me, feeling lost, my throat dry and scratchy. I was in the hospital. Again. And Spider was here at my side. Again.

Memories of my youth came scrambling back at me, a

dark tide of familiar horror threatening to erase everything I'd discovered in myself since then. For so long I'd been in and out of the hospital, and it was just like this—the cold sterile room, the beautiful boy at my side, his eyes full of fear.

I squeezed my eyes shut to stop the tears. "Water?"

Spider stepped away to get water, and I wiped at my eyes, the IV in my arm hampering my movements and making me angrier still.

"Here you go." He put the straw to my mouth, and cool liquid soothed some of the fire within me. "I'll go see if I can get the doc to talk to you, okay? Hang tight."

I sat in the room alone for a few minutes, trying to piece together the end of the night. Spider had come into the club. I'd introduced him to my friends. And then somehow I'd gotten here. There was no doubt my friends knew more about what happened between then and now than I did. And that they knew much more about me now than I'd ever intended to tell them. I dreaded seeing their faces next. I'd watched it on everyone who ever knew me as a sick teenager, and I never wanted to see it again. Pity. I hated their pity. It did me no good, and it limited me, stopped me from becoming anything beyond the little sick lump of a girl who needed their sadness and despair.

If I'd had the strength, I would have ripped out the IV and run away from the hospital. But I knew without trying that my legs would fail me. Something had gone wrong, and now everyone had seen behind the curtain I'd hung to protect myself. Everything was ruined.

Spider came back in, Andrew on his heels, Dr. Charles behind him.

Andrew put a hand on my shoulder and leaned down to kiss my cheek. "Had us worried there, Tam."

I had no doubt Andrew had taken care of me, so I thanked him, my voice thin and weak.

"It's good to see you alert, Tamara." Dr. Charles stepped up close to the bed. "I'm glad you were with friends when this happened."

"What happened?" I croaked.

"You had a seizure. I think the medication swap might've had something to do with it, but it's just a more serious version of the symptoms you've had before."

I nodded. This was not the first time I'd had a seizure. "So the new medicine isn't working."

Dr. Charles shook her head. "I don't think we can assume that. I've run some tests, and your levels are actually improving. Seizures at nighttime are not unheard of on Trientine. Did you eat last night, Tamara?"

I tried to remember if I'd eaten before going to Pepper's house. I shook my head. "I don't think so."

"And were you drinking?"

"No. No alcohol. I had a club soda."

"I think your blood sugars dropped, and that set off the seizure. You really need to eat properly. Your body needs stability and balance as much as you're capable of providing it, okay?"

I nodded. This was my fault. I was an idiot.

"So here's the less good news. Though your copper serum looks good, your liver function has actually decreased. I don't think it's critical yet, but I'm going to recommend we add you to the transplant list."

My heart fell. Liver transplant? I'd always known this was possible, but I thought I was managing well enough that I would never need it.

Spider put a hand on my shoulder and squeezed. "Can I donate?"

That was Spider. Willing to do anything, even give up a vital organ. I owed him so much, and I should have been grateful and thanked him. But I was angry about all of it, and so I stayed silent, fighting the tears that threatened to reveal more than my collapse already had. I was terrified.

Dr. Charles smiled at Spider. "We'd have to do some tests for compatibility," she told him, "but we also need to look for a donor with a similar body size. Tamara is only five three. How tall are you, Gaige?"

"Six three."

"You would probably not be the best match, but we'll definitely test you."

I looked up at Spider. His face fell, and he looked for a moment exactly like he had as a kid—the freckles splayed across the bridge of his nose, his eyes sweet and vulnerable.

Then his bravado came back up. "Well, she's got three brothers to try, but they're tall bastards, too. How'd you end up such a pipsqueak?" he asked me.

I shook my head. I didn't know how I'd ended up with a lot of things.

———

Later that day, I had a steady parade of friends through my room at the hospital. Spider joked about putting up a velvet rope outside and charging a cover. He refused to leave. I watched him joke and cajole the nurses and anyone else, coddling me and catering to my every need. He probably would've peed for me if I'd let him, but the bathroom was the only place I actually had a few minutes to be alone, to process.

I sat on the edge of the toilet, my head in my hands. The world was swimming, and I felt like shit. The knowledge that everyone who knew me would see me differently now was much worse than the physical weakness and pain. I'd had to call my boss, and he'd assigned a different agent to handle my current clients. There went my goal of being producer of the year. Beyond that, my frailty was now something everyone at work knew about. The world of New York City real estate was cutthroat and competitive. It was no place for weaklings. There was blood in the water, and I'd be lucky to survive the year at my firm now.

My friends were being brave now, but they would tiptoe around me after this, and I dreaded seeing them in the real world. They'd ask how I was every time they saw me, aware that there really was a reason to ask. Their overprotectiveness would drive me nuts. Maybe Maggie wasn't the only one leaving the city soon. Maybe it was time for me to find a new life, too.

Despite my annoyance and irritation, I also recognized that I was vulnerable, and I was sick. Reestablishing care in a new city was no small feat. Especially if a transplant was in my future.

Tears of frustration rolled down my face, and I let myself sob into my hands, stifling the noise so Spider wouldn't hear.

"You okay in there, Tam?" He was at the door.

"I'm good. Right out." I ran the water in the sink and washed my face. Makeup had smudged around my eyes, and my hair was a ratted mess. When I shuffled back out, Pepper had arrived, looking nearly as bad as I did. "Hey, girl," I said.

"Hey yourself," she said, putting a hand out and helping me into bed. "I thought Lulu was the attention hog in the group. You totally outdid her with that one last night. The ambulance ride was a nice touch."

"Thanks?"

Pepper looked embarrassed and ducked her head, her long blond hair swinging into her face. "Sorry. I'm not good in hospitals."

Natalie's mom had died just a couple years ago after battling cancer. I guessed she'd had a few experiences with hospitals. "It's fine. I'm happy to see you."

Spider hovered for a few minutes and then excused himself so we could talk.

"That is one very nice looking cowboy," Pepper said. "And I don't know anything about it, but I'd guess that he cares a lot about you."

"We've known each other forever."

"In the biblical sense?"

"That too." I tried to keep my mind from replaying some of my favorite memories of those days. Spider and I had a favorite spot in Daddy's barn where we would lay down a blanket and make out... and sometimes do much more. "He's a good guy."

"I think there's a little more to it," Pepper guessed.

"There is, but I'm not going backward. Spider is my brother's best friend. And my past."

"He seems pretty present," she said.

"Thanks for coming." I laid a hand on her arm, changing the subject. "How was your night before I pulled my stunt?"

"It was going downhill, actually." She ground her teeth, her jaw clenching as she squeezed her eyes shut. When she opened them again, they shone with unshed tears.

"Oh no. What's up?" I leaned forward. At least we weren't discussing my health, but I hated to see Pepper sad.

"I think Catalina told CJ she saw me kiss Bennett at the theater. I think he was about to say something about it when you passed out."

"So I totally saved you?"

"I guess so. Or just delayed the inevitable. He slept over but literally said like three words to me. He left this morning before I woke up."

"That doesn't seem good." I didn't know what to say. "Maybe he's just stressed out. Didn't you say work was really crazy for him with the cougar lady?"

She nodded but looked doubtful. "I think he knows about

the kiss. And since I don't know for sure, now I feel like maybe I should just tell him about the stupid kiss, and like maybe I should just come clean about absolutely everything and tell him about what happened with Damon too. What?"

I wanted to stop her from talking, but my lack of energy and creativity stopped me from managing it. CJ had walked through the door as she was about halfway through her sentence. His face was stony and his eyes were cold and distant as he walked to the side of my bed.

"Girls," he said, finding a smile and leaning down to kiss my cheek. "How are you, Tamara? Better?"

Natalie looked like she was about to throw up, her face turning gray as blood drained from her features.

I nodded. "Yeah, much better."

Spider came in, and the guys did the standard dude greeting handshake-one-arm-hug thing. "You doin' okay, man?" CJ asked.

"As long as Tam's okay, I'm good," Spider said.

CJ and Spider pulled up chairs and chatted about the city, about Spider's meat sales and CJ's new venture. Pepper didn't speak a word and continued to look freaked out. I kicked her beneath my covers, but all I managed to do was make her jump about two feet off the bed and shriek, causing the guys to stare at her.

"Sorry, I..." Her eyes searched mine frantically and then darted to CJ and back. "I actually... I need to get back to work. I forgot that I..." She stood, moving to the door. "I'll see you later."

CJ's shoulders fell as the door closed, and he stared after her for a moment. "Do you know what the hell that was about?" he asked, turning to me.

"I think you guys need to talk," I said. I knew that didn't help, but it wasn't my place to tell him what was going on, and I had enough issues of my own.

———

Once my parade of visitors stopped, I drifted off to sleep, still angry about the whole situation. I'd talked to Hal at one point during the day because Spider made me call him. He threatened to come out and bring Mom and Dad, too, but I convinced him there was nothing he could do. Having Spider here made him feel better, I think.

The nurses woke me every few hours that night, taking vitals and being overly vigilant. When the final nighttime check came, I awoke to find soft gray light filtering into the room from the windows and a long, warm, heavy weight at my side breathing softly. I was wrapped in Spider's arms, and his head rested next to mine on the pillow, my back pressed up against his solid chest. I had no memory of him coming into bed, but it appeared he'd been busy while I slept. I could tell he'd taken a shower. The skin of his arm smelled clean and fresh, and the shirt sheathing his skin was not the same one he'd worn to the party. I saw a bag of clothes in the chair next to my bed and realized Spider must have gone to my apartment. The old stuffed dog I used to sleep with—the one who had long since been banished to my dresser top—was cradled in my arms.

The dark-haired nurse who took my vitals that final time said nothing about the man sharing my bed. She clearly knew there was nothing going on, and I hated to admit that I probably looked happier in that moment than I had in days.

I breathed in Spider's familiar scent and pictured a vast indigo sky and heard the sound of cicadas singing at dusk. I could practically smell the Indiana air, the scent of crops being cut down as summer wound through its final days. I didn't want this man in the city. I didn't want him wrinkling the fabric of my new life, and I didn't want him complicating everything that was already so complex. But maybe it was already too late. My life wasn't new anymore. The past had come back with a vengeance, and having Spider come along with it was the only thing keeping me from losing my mind. I might send him away when morning came, but for now, in the diffuse-filtered light of my new reality, I took comfort in Spider's strong arms and ever-steady heart.

Chapter Seventeen

STRATEGY DRINKS

Natalie

I NEEDED to talk to CJ, yet I couldn't bring myself to do it. If he hadn't know about anything before, if Catalina hadn't spilled the beans at the club, he surely knew now, and there was no denying it when I was the source.

I'd left the hospital and gone home, pacing the floor of my tiny apartment until Tom had come upstairs to see what was going on.

"Is this some kind of new workout, Pepper? Because I'll totally go out to the park with you. But you're wearing a groove in my ceiling."

I told him about what had happened at the hospital.

He put a hand over his mouth. "Oh shit."

"I know."

"How's Tam?"

"I think she's okay. But I mean, not really. Because I guess she's really sick." I didn't know what to make of Tamara's situation. Part of me wondered if she'd go home now, but I selfishly hoped not. We were already losing Maggie.

"Yeah." Tom was one of Tamara's biggest fans. They exchanged fashion advice regularly, and he'd been one of the first people kneeling over her when she'd collapsed. The worry was etched into the lines around his mouth. "So what will you do about this CJ debacle?"

I shook my head. My relationship with CJ had been a long time coming, and now that it was solid, I'd ripped it to pieces. "I don't have a clue."

"Call him. Better yet, go over there."

I nodded. "I should."

We sat on my futon staring at one another, each lost in thought, when my phone rang. I stood and walked to the window where the phone sat on the sill. "Hello?"

"Natalie? It's John. Were you in today? Did I miss you somehow?" His voice was high pitched, aggravated.

I didn't think I could feel worse than I had before the phone rang, but it turned out that I was capable of even lower emotional depths. I'd completely forgotten that it was a workday. I was so wrapped up in the drama surrounding Tamara and now CJ. "Oh God," I managed.

"You missed the agency review. That *you* scheduled. That *you* insisted I be present for."

I heard myself gulp. "I'm so sorry. A friend got really sick last night..."

"Natalie, I know you're young. But this is a real job. With real responsibilities. If you had an emergency, then I deserved a phone call to let me know I'd be handling things on my own. Or you should have set up someone else to handle things in your absence. Planning backup for yourself is part of being a professional."

I was being lectured. By my boss. On a Friday night. And I completely deserved it. I sat down hard on the floor, silent tears pressing their way out. I didn't even care. I was giving up.

"I'm so sorry," I repeated. "I just..."

"I don't like this, Natalie, but I can't give any more warnings. You're on very thin ice at this point."

"Okay." I was pretty sure that meant I was inches from losing my job.

"I rescheduled with the agencies for next week. Monday. I expect you to be here and to be prepared. We don't have room to screw this up again. And by we, I mean you."

"Got it."

"Have a good weekend."

That was very doubtful. I hung up and slumped over, curling into the fetal position on the floor as Tom stared at me.

"Oh, honey, nothing can be that bad."

"It is," I wailed. "I'm a complete fuckup. I've ruined everything. Literally everything."

Tom shook his head. "You can't just lay here wallowing in a pile of sad girl on the floor." He stood, looked around, walked to my closet, and rifled through it. "Here, put these on." He held out a pair of velvet pants that I'd borrowed from Lulu. They were burgundy and tight, and they were my very favorite. I didn't know I could ever feel about pants the way I felt about these.

"No..." I moaned.

"I'm taking you out. You have ten minutes to get ready. We're going to see Tam, and then we're going to have some strategy drinks."

"Strategy drinks?" I asked from inside the cocoon of my arms.

"Drinking. To come up with a strategy."

"Of course."

The door crashed shut as he exited, and I hauled myself

to my feet before I had time to start crying again. I'd focus on Tamara for now. My life might be a shambles, but her problems were real. As I thought about it, I realized that Tamara being sick only added to my own sorrow. I cried while I got ready to go out. Applying mascara was quite a feat.

———

I presented myself at Tom's door ten minutes later to find him in the shiniest of his shiny shirts. When Tom wore a shiny shirt, it meant two things: shots and dancing. Often on a bar.

"No," I moaned. "It's not a shiny shirt night."

"It's Friday night, Pepper. There is no better shiny shirt night. Unless it's Saturday. But only after ten. Or Tuesday if we're talking about Madame Sizzles on the Lower East."

"Madame Sizzles?"

"Your people don't go there."

"I guess not."

"Shiny shirts are *de riguer*."

"Of course they are."

"All right." He pushed me out of his door and marched out behind me. "Flowers and chocolate first, shots after."

We arrived at the hospital to find Andrew, Gabe, and Spider all crowded around Tamara's bed.

"I guess you're taken care of in the hottie department," Tom quipped.

Spider and Gabe blushed, and Andrew shot Tom a look that said he'd heard it all before.

"Hey, you," I said, stepping up between Tamara's admirers. "It seems you're being looked after pretty well."

"Too much testosterone in here," she said, grinning. "Give us a minute, guys. Tom, you can stay."

"Of course I can." Tom took a chair next to Tamara's bed.

The guys left, and I sat down next to Tom. "How long are they keeping you?"

"Dr. Charles says I can go home tomorrow."

Fear spiked in me. "Home, home?"

"No, she agreed that I could go to my apartment if someone stays to keep an eye on me. I can't work for two fucking weeks." Tamara frowned.

"Do you want me to stay?" I offered, knowing that there was no way I'd be able to feed that excuse to John. I had the agency review on Monday, and it sounded like I this close to being fired, a thought I really hadn't digested fully.

"No," she said, something odd crossing her face and making her look guilty for a moment. "Spider is going to stay with me."

Tom raised an eyebrow comically high. "He is, is he?"

Tamara glared at him. "He's taken care of me before. He knew about all this... from when we were young."

"You've been sick for a long time?" I asked. Why had she kept this from us?

"That's why I moved here." She didn't explain further. I didn't press, but I was curious about the disease, about Tamara's decision to leave her support network and live in New York alone.

"We brought you chocolate." I grinned and held up the European chocolate truffles Tom had scored at the specialty shop on Seventh.

Tamara smiled but shook her head. "That's so sweet, but you guys should eat it."

Tom looked offended. "A girl does not say no to chocolate. What kind of woman are you?"

"The kind that has to watch her copper intake. Can't eat chocolate."

"Dreaded disease!" Tom said, mocking horror and raising

a wrist to his forehead like a southern belle with a case of the vapors.

"That is pretty shitty," I agreed.

"Blows." She nodded and shifted in her bed. "What are you guys doing tonight? Tom's in a shiny shirt, so I know you're going out dancing."

I shook my head. "No dancing."

Tom ignored me. "I'm doing a strategy session with Pepper since she ruined her life and is about to lose her job. Strategy drinking is one of my gifts."

Tamara frowned. "I wish I could help, Pepper."

"I know," I said.

"I've totally got this, Tam," Tom assured her.

We stood and kissed her goodbye. "Talk to you tomorrow," I said.

"You better. I'll need an update."

Spider came back in, and I gave Tamara a pointed look. "So will I."

The guy she called Spider was ridiculously cute, and he seemed to be head over heels in love with her. Today he was dressed in a long-sleeved T-shirt and jeans that hugged lean, muscled legs. The boots were gone, but there was still something about him that called to mind tractors and horses and hot, sweaty work that probably required him to remove his shirt.

"See ya," he called as we went into the hallway.

"Let's go, Peppercorn," Tom said. "We have problems to solve, and only copious amounts of vodka are going to do it."

I followed him to the elevator, doubtful but willing to try pretty much anything to undo all the damage I'd done.

———

Tom took me to a dive bar that I'd never been to and doubted I would ever find again, somewhere south of Houston.

I took in the smoke-stained walls and tattered barstools. "This does not look like shiny shirt territory."

"This is get-drunk-cheap territory. And this place has special meaning to me."

I wondered how a dark musty bar with a photo of James Garner hanging on the only wall not covered with television screens could have prominence in Tom's life.

Our first shots arrived as we perched at the end of the bar closest to the door. "This was where I first came out."

"Oh." I hadn't thought about Tom ever not being out. He was comfortable in his skin, completely at home with who he was. Or at least he sure seemed it.

"Yes, oh. I was at NYU. Broke and drunk, and on a date. With a girl. A really nice girl who I most definitely didn't want to kiss, let alone fuck."

"Poor girl."

"We're still friends. Don't worry." Tom ordered another shot. "But this bar right here..." He gripped the edge of the bar as if to show me how sturdy it was. "This is a place where decisions get made. Where souls are bared and true desires are uncovered."

"Deep." I threw my second shot back and felt it burn down my throat, landing in the pool of deep regret and self-pity swirling inside me.

"So let's solve this," Tom said. It was hard to take his problem-solving face seriously when his shirt was reflecting the spotlights above the bar, making him look like a kid with a flashlight under his chin.

Still. Solutions. Yes, those were what I needed.

"So we have no idea what exactly CJ knows."

"Right."

"And you're sure this relationship is worth saving?" Tom cocked his head to the side.

"What? Yes!"

"Don't get hostile. Needed to make sure."

I sipped the beer that sat next to my empty shot glasses. We'd need to figure something out soon or else I wouldn't remember whatever we came up with.

"Well, given those two things, I'd go for the 'honesty is the best policy' thing."

"Ugh." Dread filled me. I wasn't afraid CJ would be angry with me. I was more terrified of experiencing something akin to the shame I felt when my parents had said things like, "I'm not mad. I'm disappointed." I knew CJ would be disappointed in me. I knew he'd be hurt and upset, and even imagining his face as I told him I'd essentially been unfaithful ripped my battered heart to pieces.

"Start with honesty about how you feel about him. Tell him how you feel about everything you two have been through and about how upset and sorry you are. And then tell him what happened."

"Okay..." That didn't seem like a terrible plan.

Tom sipped his beer, his eyes never leaving mine. "Once you get started, he'll be certain you're going to tell him you cheated on him. Like really cheated. And when he finds out it was just a silly little kiss, he'll be so relieved he'll forget to be angry."

I was skeptical, but it was a better plan than the one I had, which involved avoiding the issue completely until one day, at seventy or eighty years old, CJ would finally catch me somewhere, sitting in a park with my walker at my side, and I'd have to come clean. "What about the Damon thing? I wouldn't have told him, but that was the last thing I said when he came into the hospital room, so I'm pretty sure he heard it."

"That was before you were with CJ. And Damon is ridiculously hot, so you should get a free pass." Tom giggled. He was getting tipsy.

"That isn't helpful." Damon was ridiculously hot. He'd been a sales rep at my previous company, and I'd kissed him one night before CJ and I were together. I hadn't been cheating but doubted CJ would be thrilled to know that he'd shared lips with Damon, who was a confirmed man-slut. One who was gorgeous, of course.

"You now have a strategy," Tom declared. "Down the rest of that and lets go someplace where my shirt can be properly appreciated."

We finished our drinks and stepped outside. The rest of the evening was spent under flashing lights and disco balls, a blur of drinks and men and multiple shiny shirts. By the time I'd left the club Tom had dragged me to, my ears were ringing and my stomach was churning. I was feeling better, though.

At least until I got home long after midnight to find CJ sitting on my futon, waiting for me with a dark look on his face.

Chapter Eighteen

HOME, BITTERSWEET HOME

Tamara

WHEN I WOKE SUNDAY MORNING, Spider was asleep in the chair by the window, and I was alone in my hospital bed. I'd gone right to sleep when Tom and Pepper had left, and at some point in the night, I'd woken to find Spider next to me again. Everything that had happened in the last few days had been so surreal that I wondered if I'd dreamed him there, holding me. Maybe that was what my subconscious really wanted—to be back in Spider's arms, in his bed. His dark lashes were thick against the tanned skin of his cheeks, his long legs extended and his hands clasped on his chest. He'd been here for three days now, and even if I hated the circumstances, I had to appreciate his constancy.

"Hey," he whispered, his eyes fluttering to life to find me watching him.

"Hey," I whispered back, lying on my side.

"Let's break you outta here, girl." He grinned and then yawned, stretching long limbs out and flexing the muscles in his torso against the thin soft T-shirt he wore. After the stretch, Spider stood and stepped over, leaning down to kiss my cheek and smooth my hair back. "I'll go see what we need to do to make it happen this morning."

"Thanks.".

When he was gone, I sat up and dropped my feet over the edge of the bed. I was getting dressed. In real clothes. I was getting the hell out of here. Even if Spider thought this nurse-maid thing was going to continue, I was going to set him straight. I was a big girl, and I was feeling better since the doctor had increased the dosage of my new medication. It was time to see what I could salvage of my independence, get myself on damage control. I needed to get back to work, and two weeks off was an unreasonable expectation.

I stood and immediately sat back down. Waking up turned out to be more exhausting than I would have expected, and my body still ached. Fine. Slow then. I stood again, with much lower expectations, and carefully picked up the bag of clothes Spider had brought for me. He had packed everything I needed—meaning the man had been through my underwear drawer—and I took my things to the bathroom. It took longer than I would have liked to get dressed, and by the time I was trying to get my hair into a ponytail, I was spent. I gave up, carrying the hairbrush back to the bed. I would rest and then try again in a few minutes.

"...'Rarin to go home today..." Spider's voice preceded him into my room.

The same small dark-haired nurse I'd seen in the early morning light followed him. She gave me a smile and asked how I was feeling.

While the nurse took my vital signs and filled out my

discharge papers, Spider moved close to me, taking the brush from my hand. "Can I help you?" he asked.

I nodded.

With careful hands, Spider ran the brush through my tangled long hair, holding the locks above any knots so it didn't pull while he brushed them out. Then he smoothed everything away from my face and into a ponytail, handing me the brush back with a smile that made my heart falter. Spider had a little sister, and he'd done a lot of work raising her while his mom worked in the next town over from ours as a school principal. He had experience making ponytails.

"Thanks."

"No sweat."

We waited patiently for Dr. Charles to come discharge me, but time seemed to drag on endlessly. Finally, after sitting through two hours of the Today Show and something that followed which was cleverly titled Later Today, she arrived to sign me out.

"Rest," she said as I stood. "Lots of water, take your B, and don't miss a dose of the syprine."

"I got her, Doc," Spider assured her, his cowboy cockiness rising to the surface.

"I'll see you in my office in one week," she told me but nodded at him as if he would be in charge of that, too.

I shuffled from the room, practically giddy to be free. I just wished my body didn't feel so heavy and slow.

When I'd been settled onto my own couch with more painful daytime television filling the screen, I felt like I'd accomplished something huge just in making the long trek home. Despite the desperation I'd experienced at realizing the magnitude of this health setback, I also knew that I had to push forward. On my own. This was part of leaving home, of being independent.

"Thanks, Spider," I said. I meant it, but I needed him to go.

"You say that like I'm going somewhere."

"You are."

He raised an eyebrow at me and then plopped himself onto the couch next to me. "I ain't."

I cringed at the country he coaxed into his voice, making his point in the most stubborn and irritating way he knew how. "Look." I turned to face him. "I owe you one. You saved me, you really did. I don't know what I would have done the last few days without you, and I'll always be grateful. But I'm home now, and I'm good."

"You're not good." He said it softly, his eyes fixed on mine. "And you can say whatever you want, but I'm not leaving you here like this. You can barely walk across the apartment, Tam. Until you're strong, I'm staying right here."

I sighed in frustration, rubbing my hands over my eyes. "I don't know how else to say it, Gaige. I've been polite."

"You're hardly ever polite, but you make up for it by being cute." The cocky half-grin again.

He wasn't taking me seriously, and it was pissing me off. I didn't have the energy to fight him, so I drove the point home another way. "I'm asking you to leave, Spider. I've been nice because I didn't want to hurt your feelings, but you won't go, so here it is. I don't want you here. I had a life here in New York without you, and it was a good one."

His eyes were on me, evaluating, but he made no move to stand.

So I continued, "I left for a reason, Gaige. I left *you*. I ran across three whole states to put distance behind me, and you might have noticed that I never came back. I never called; I never wrote."

Spider's eyes darkened, and he sat up straighter next to me, uncertainty playing across his beautiful face.

"I don't want you here. I don't need you anymore." A little crack began at the bottom of my heart as I said these words, and as soon as they were unleashed, I regretted them.

Spider's mouth opened for a second, and his eyebrows went up as pain flashed in his eyes. It took every ounce of restraint for me to keep my hands in my lap, to stop myself from putting my palm to his face and saying the words that would take away the hurt I'd just inflicted. But I didn't. I waited for him to get up and leave so that I could go back to the life I'd so carefully constructed, away from everything that reminded me of the frail little girl I once was. And him most of all.

After a minute, his face hardened. "You better mean it, Tam. You better be sure you mean it, because if I walk out this door, I'm not coming back in. You're on your own. I love you. I always will. But I'm not going to force myself on you. Or on anyone. Tell me you mean it, and I'm gone for good."

I had known that if I pushed him hard enough, Spider's pride would win out. Guilt at having manipulated the one man I knew better than anyone seized me, but I needed him to go. I nodded.

Spider stood up. "God dammit, Tam." He pulled the discharge papers from his pocket and flung them down on the couch beside me. "You better take care of yourself, then. Follow these orders and get yourself well." He picked up his things and walked to the door, his long body filling the space once he'd pulled it open. "Goodbye, Tamara." His voice was broken and ripped, and it sounded exactly the way my heart felt when that door clanged shut again, sealing me in my lonely apartment just as I'd wished.

For the better part of an hour, I stared at the closed door from my spot on the couch, partly because I didn't have the energy it would take to get up and do anything else and partly because I was wishing with all my heart that Spider would change his mind, ignore my stupid demands, and come rushing back inside.

Chapter Nineteen

THE OPPOSITE OF GOOD

Natalie

THE DOOR CLOSED behind me with something that sounded like finality, the hollow click of the lock mirroring the fearful beat of my heart.

"Hi," I said, turning to face CJ as he sat on my futon.

He glanced at the clock hanging in the kitchen before turning his gaze to me. "Have a good night?" he asked. It was code. I was drunk, but it was clear enough that he didn't care if I'd had a good night.

I shook my head and took a seat next to him, leaving a foot between us. A foot of ice and anger. "No. All I did was think about you, about how much I needed to talk to you."

He nodded. "Me too."

There were so many words that I wanted to say, and my mind raced around itself trying to remember what strategy Tom and I had settled on. I just kept remembering hearing myself talk about Damon and kissing people and watching Tamara's face fill with horror as CJ walked in behind me. I'd already said all the wrong things, and now I had this limited opportunity to fix it. CJ was here. He had come here on his own. He wanted to fix things too. I wasn't going to get a better shot at this.

"CJ..." I paused, staring at my peeling pink nail polish and willing the magical words to come, the words that would fix everything. "I don't know what Catalina said to you..."

"Seriously?" Anger flashed in CJ's eyes. "I came here to talk about what *you* said. What I heard you saying. You're still upset that I talked for two seconds to Catalina?"

I shook my head. "No, I just... I thought she might have said something about..." Oh God, what was I saying? My mouth just kept going, stumbling along. "Never mind. I know you heard me talking to Tamara at the hospital, and I just... I need to tell you how much I care about you." That was the strategy, wasn't it? Tell him how much I cared.

CJ looked incredulous, shaking his head slightly back and forth, his eyes still simmering. "I care about you too, Natalie, but... is it true? What I heard you talking about? About Damon? Did you kiss him?"

I could fix this. If CJ thought it was all about Damon, and if Catalina hadn't said anything, then I could fix this. "A long time ago." The words rushed out, and my voice was almost a squeal. "Before we were together. When I was first at All Night. It was a stupid mistake, and nothing ever came of it. It was nothing. It was just a stupid kiss." *Stop talking, Natalie.*

CJ's face darkened, and he stared at his hands. "Wasn't Candace dating Damon before you and I got together?" He raised an eyebrow and looked back up.

I nodded. I wanted to tell him they weren't dating when it happened, but they were. I'd beat myself up for weeks about it. And now... was this really the thing that was going to drive me and CJ apart? "But it was a silly mistake, it happened late one night... It was nothing."

"It's something to me," CJ said slowly. "A kiss means something to me. And I bet it would have meant something to Candace." He stared at me, wary, the way you watch a dog you think might not be completely friendly.

"I feel terrible about this," I tried. "But I was so confused back then... We couldn't be together, and I thought about you all the time, and you were all I wanted..."

"So you kissed someone else."

"No!"

CJ stood up. "I don't think I want to hear more, and I'm pretty sure I don't want to hear about any other kisses." He walked toward the door and turned around, his eyes sad and dark. "There was another kiss, wasn't there?"

CJ waited, poised to leave my apartment—poised to leave *me*. He looked tired and angry and so, so beautiful, his golden hair catching the light from above the kitchen sink. I had to find a way to make him stay, to make him give me another chance, but I couldn't lie to him. I nodded, just a tiny confirmation of everything I'd done wrong.

He turned around without expression and put a hand on the doorknob.

I crossed the floor to stop him. "CJ." My voice was a whisper.

When he turned back around, his face was angry, but wetness welled in his eyes. "We had to fight so hard to be together," he said, his voice like a velvet hammer, soft and fierce. "And you care so little that you'd just throw it all away? I don't understand, Natalie. I don't think I'll ever understand." He shook his head. "I hate it, but maybe Irene was right about you."

Shock pricked at my brain, and my eyebrows rose. "Irene?" Why did that name keep coming up?

"She warned me you were too immature for me."

"Of course she told you that. She thinks you should be dating *her*!"

He sighed. "I guess now I understand why you've been jealous, but you should know that just because you've been out kissing people doesn't mean I have. I would never do that to you. Never."

"CJ..." Tears were streaming down my cheeks. I wished we could figure out how to move forward together, as we'd done before. The one thing I'd always been able to count on was CJ's constancy in my life, in my heart.

He pulled the door open and walked out without looking back.

I followed him onto the landing. "CJ!"

He didn't look at me as he went down the stairs. I heard the front door of the building slam, and the sound echoed through me, dissolving my heart to dust in my chest.

I dragged myself back inside, my vision tunneling in despair. Had I really just torn apart the best thing I'd ever had? I turned the knob of my front door, but it wouldn't release. It had latched behind me. I sank to the ground, my head against my front door as I sat on the cold, filthy gray linoleum, locked out of my home.

Eventually I got up and went down to Tom's, banging on the door until he woke up to let me in. "What..."

I stepped into his apartment, still sobbing. "CJ was at my place. I tried to talk to him, and I ruined everything. He left. And then I locked myself out."

"Oh, honey." Tom took me in his arms, pulling me to his shoulder as I shook. "We exchanged keys last year, right?" He stepped away and began digging through a cluttered drawer in the kitchen. "I'm never going to find it in this mess." He yawned and closed it. "How about this... You can have the couch. Let me make it up. We'll get you into your place tomorrow."

I nodded and stepped back, wiping at the wet black smudge I'd left on Tom's white T-shirt. "Sorry," I whispered. I was sorry. For so much. And there was no undoing any of it.

Tom pulled sheets and blankets from a chest and opened up a sleeper sofa. I helped him make it up, took off my shoes, and crawled in, tears still running down my face. I was glad he'd given me dark sheets so the mascara I didn't have the energy to wash off wouldn't ruin them.

"Goodnight, Peppercorn." Tom pushed the hair back from my forehead. "Things will look better tomorrow. I promise."

Something about the sweetness of Tom's action reminded me of the way my mother had tucked me in as a child, and there was more comfort there than I would have imagined. I squeezed my eyes shut, trying unsuccessfully not to think about CJ. Eventually, my exhausted mind stopped spinning and I slept.

When I woke up, Tom was gone, but a note was folded next to my head on the pillow. I unfolded it and wiped the sleep from my bleary eyes.

Out for a run. I'll bring back breakfast.

I stared around me for one oblivious moment, trying to remember how exactly I'd ended up at Tom's. Then the entirety of the previous night came crashing back down on me, its weight forcing me back down under the covers. I'd just pulled the blankets back over my head when Tom came in, whistling as he entered.

"Rise and shine, Peppercorn! We've got bagels and lox!"

I did like lox. I pushed the covers down.

"You need to go wash your face." He suppressed a grin. "There's Kiehl's on the sink. Go!" Tom basically shooed me off the bed and into the bathroom, and the sound of him folding up the couch clanged around me as I cleaned myself up.

It was pointless, really. I was a complete disaster. My face was pallid and puffy with makeup smudged from my forehead down to my cheeks, and my eyes were red. I washed as Tom had instructed, and the result was just a shinier clean version of the previous disaster. I sighed and returned to the living room after using the bathroom.

Tom was laying out a small feast on the round table next to the window. "Capers, red onion, and poppyseed bagels," he said. "Cream cheese and lox."

My stomach grumbled loudly, but I wasn't sure I had the energy required to actually eat. I felt like I was moving through dense liquid, motivation and desire gone from me in the face of everything I'd destroyed the night before.

"You'll feel better if you eat," Tom chided. "And then we'll figure out how to get you back into your place."

I nodded and smeared cream cheese on half a bagel, sitting down across from my friend. "Thanks, Tom." My voice was scratchy and pathetic.

"It'll get better, That's the best part of all this. All the bad stuff has already happened, right? It can't get any worse."

"I'm not sure that's the right way to comfort someone." I took a bite.

He shrugged. We ate in silence. Tom was right. I felt a fraction better when we were done.

"So do I have a key to your place?" Tom asked. "I feel like I do."

I nodded. We had exchanged keys, but we'd never needed them before. He opened the cluttered kitchen drawer again and began digging. I peered over his shoulder and willed my key to rise to the top of the mess.

"Maybe in here." Tom pulled open a second drawer that overflowed with takeout menus. He pulled them all out and scooped up several keys from the bottom of the drawer. "I should really label these." He held them out to me, and I picked up the one that looked most like mine.

"I'll go try it," I said.

It took three tries, but finally I got back into my apartment. Tom had things to do, and I had a self-pity party to throw. I thanked him for everything and went straight back to bed when I got inside, where I stayed all day Saturday and most of the next. The phone rang several times, but the caller ID never showed CJ's number so I didn't answer it. The sound rang unheeded, a cold and lonely trill in the vacuum of my space.

———

I dragged myself from bed Monday morning and stumbled into work where I sat zombielike at my desk for the first few hours, staring into my computer screen as my mind replayed every second of the last few minutes I'd spent with CJ.

There was no fixing it. I'd taken what we had and crumpled it up, and then I'd set it on fire and stomped on it for good measure. I'd fucked it up so completely I couldn't see a single possibility for redemption, save CJ just deciding randomly to forgive me. With Irene's needling influence at his side, I was sure that would never happen.

Bennett stopped through after my third cup of coffee, which had failed to make a dent in my mood. Now I was morose and jittery. "You look awful," he said.

"That's not very kind."

He shifted his weight and seemed hesitant to sit down.

"Just wanted to check in, see how things are…" Bennett knew there was something wrong, and he probably knew it had something to do with him.

"We broke up." I threw it out there. No use dancing around the issue.

"You told him?"

"More or less."

"Should I buy a gun?"

I shook my head. "He'd never blame you. I made the choice. I screwed it all up." I managed to say this without tears spilling down my cheeks.

Bennett's face fell anyway. "I'm so sorry, Natalie."

"It's not your fault. It'll be okay."

He nodded, and eventually excused himself from my office, looking relieved to get away.

Morning dragged into afternoon, and I tried to focus on getting through the emails I'd missed Friday. Many of them were about the agency review I'd skipped because of Tamara's collapse. I started reading them, something pinging to life in the back of my mind. Agency review… I remembered John calling to yell at me about missing it…

I bolted out of my chair, slamming my thighs into the edge of my desk when the chair didn't roll back. "Shit!"

The agency review. John had rescheduled it for today! But what time? I leaned over, sifting through the meetings in my calendar and found that it was scheduled for one o'clock. Here. It was twelve-thirty. Somehow I'd managed to stare into space for three full hours and now had about fifteen minutes to try to look prepared.

As I scrambled around my office pulling files and trying to assemble the creative plan I'd come up with the week prior, John appeared at my door. "Ready?" he asked. He wore a pressed suit and tie, his hair shone, and he had a simple leather portfolio under one arm and a cup of coffee in the other hand. He looked like a Ralph Lauren ad.

I stopped my frantic movement and looked down at what I'd pulled from the closet this morning in blind misery. I was wearing jeans. They were black, but they were definitely denim, and with the ratted flats and Chanel logo shirt I'd covered them with, it was pretty clear I was not dressed for an important meeting. The beauty of the Internet industry was that on most other days, my outfit would have been just fine, but there was an unspoken understanding that we were still professionals. We dressed when it mattered. And today it mattered.

"You're not ready." John said it plainly. "You forgot."

I wanted to argue, but denial was pointless. I opened my mouth and then thought better of it, closing it again. "I'm sorry. I'm not feeling well today." There. That was truth.

John shrugged. "I'm sorry to hear that, but I've got to tell you that I don't really give a shit. You're not throwing up or bleeding. Natalie, a professional puts on a suit and keeps going when there's important business to be done." He was silent then, and I got the sense that he was thinking deeply about something that would end up being very bad for me.

We stood facing each other in my office, and I realized that what was left of my world was teetering on the brink of disaster. "I've got the creative brief," I said, fumbling with the folders I'd gathered. "The brand strategy we talked about last week."

He nodded. "Good. Give those to me. You can't represent AdTrack looking like that. I'll talk to you after the review."

I handed him the folders and watched him turn to head to the conference room, where our agency would be expecting me to meet them and review their plans for the year. Where I was expected to show up, be a professional, and do my job, regardless of the fact that my personal life was in the shitter.

But I couldn't do that because John had just turned around and walked away. I'd watched a lot of men walk away from me in the last twenty-four hours.

The phone on my desk rang, distracting me from the fact that John had promised to come back and talk to me after the review. I doubted he would only want to discuss the way the meeting turned out.

"Natalie Pepper." I always answered this way. I thought it had a serious ring to it.

"Hey, you," Maggie said. "I'm leaving tomorrow, and I just wanted to say goodbye. I don't know if I'll get to see you again."

"Oh, no," I wailed. "Really? Tomorrow? I wish you weren't going."

"I know, but I'm actually really looking forward to the next part of my life, to being with 'Nesto all the time. He's already talking about buying a house, about having kids."

"Oh my gosh! Are you ready for all that?"

"I think so," she said, sounding happy and calm and pretty much the opposite of everything that I felt. "We've always talked about being together. It just feels like this is finally the right time."

"I'm happy for you."

"You don't sound super happy. You sound really upset, actually. Is this a bad time?"

"I think maybe this month is a bad time."

"What's wrong, Pepper? CJ? The cougar?"

"I wish."

"What?"

"It's me. I cheated on him, and he found out, and he left, and I've ruined everything." I dropped my forehead to my desk with a painful clunk.

"No," Maggie said softly. "You cheated on him? Like really

cheated?" I could hear Maggie's disapproval, and it drove the dark stake in my heart a notch deeper.

"I didn't sleep with anyone. I kissed someone. Two some-ones, kind of."

"How do you kind of kiss two people?"

I moaned in answer. "I can't talk about this now. I have to get back to work. I'm in trouble here, too."

"Oh, no. Pepper, it will get better. I promise."

I wondered at the truth of that. "I'll miss you, Mags." I would. Maggie was a rock. She was our cheerleader and our champion. But I was happy for her, too. "I hope Texas delivers everything you want."

"Thanks, honey. I'll call you as soon as I'm settled to hear how much better everything is. You'll see."

"Okay."

"Bye."

I hung up the phone, feeling like another light had just switched off. All the bright spots in my life were dimming.

It got darker still when John stepped back into my office an hour later.

"How was the review?" I tried to sound chipper and proactive and not at all like a slacker in jeans and a T-shirt.

"It was fine. But, Natalie, the thing is..." John looked up and down the hallway and then stepped inside my office, pulling the door shut behind him. "This isn't working, Natalie. I took a chance, and it didn't work out."

I tried to convince myself he was talking about the agency review.

"I have to be honest. I haven't seen a lot of effort from you in the past few weeks. You started out strong, but between the creative slip-ups and this mysterious show in Cabo San Lucas, I find myself wondering if you're really here for the right reasons. And now, today..." He ran his hand over his forehead, shaking his head. "But I don't want to just let you go. I know you tried. I think maybe you weren't prepared for the level of responsibility you were given here." He scratched his head. "Let's say you were laid off and I'll give you three weeks severance?"

I was being fired. The darkness that had swirled inside me opened up into an endless dark hole, and I tumbled over the side and fell endlessly downward, spiraling into the abyss.

Chapter Twenty

BACK ON THE HORSE

Tamara

FOR THE FIRST three days of the week after my collapse, I stayed home. I set up a command center from my couch and was on the phone most of the time with the agents who'd been assigned to take work off my plate. Mostly I let them know that there was no way in hell I was giving up commissions to them after I was the one who brought in the clients and I was the one who did all the work to set up the sales. All those schmucks needed to do now was close. And for that? Sorry, but they weren't taking my hard-earned money.

A few things became resoundingly clear after those three days: One, I could not stay in my apartment any longer. Two, my co-workers were either idiots or assholes. Most were both. Three, I felt much, much better.

So, that Thursday, I put on a power suit and took myself to work. I hailed a cab, because I didn't quite have the energy to deal with the walk and the subway, so it took a little longer to get up to Columbus Circle, but at least I got to enjoy the view on the way up. I didn't spend much time north of my own neighborhood, except at work. I knew Natalie was on the Upper West a lot at CJ's place, and Maggie and Catalina lived on the Upper East, but no one in their right mind went over there if they didn't have to. To me, the Upper East Side was the land of ex-fraternity boys and fledgling account executives. Maggie insisted that it was nice and talked about long strolls by the river and big stores that couldn't be found anywhere else in Manhattan. I didn't walk, especially now, and there wasn't much I really needed to buy.

The area around my office was clean, and the streets felt wider than in other parts of the city. Well-dressed people moved quickly along smooth sidewalks, heading to work or to power meetings in the buildings that soared into the sky. The exception was the area around the park. Fifty-ninth Street was smeared with a wide swath of tourists, wandering around looking lost with their fanny packs and children. I swore that even if I left the city one day, I'd never come back as one of them. There was nothing wrong with being a tourist, but New York had become the home of my heart—the place where I grew up, in a way. I couldn't imagine not being an "insider" here, not knowing exactly where I was going and what I was doing. I wasn't very good at being a tourist anyway.

My co-workers raised eyebrows and uttered surprised greetings as I made my way to my office. I dumped my stuff in my office and went to gather my files from those who were supposed to be handling my clients.

"Thanks," I said to Monica, a dowdy thin girl who was overly fond of chewing gum. "I've got it from here."

"I was showing them three places today," she said, a whine in her voice.

"I'll handle it." I flipped open the top folder. "You're showing them the ones on top?"

She nodded, her bottom lip sticking out.

I looked up and cocked my head at her. "Tell you what. When I die, you can have all my clients, okay?"

She huffed, and I walked back to my office. She'd planned on showing two studios to a couple with a baby on the way. She was a moron. I called them as soon as I sat down and cancelled, explaining the mistake and promising I'd have three appropriate properties to show them the next day. The morning flew, and I felt better than I had in days. It was good to be back.

I was in the groove, and when my desk phone rang after lunch, I was surprised to find Catalina on the other end. We weren't the best of friends, but then, I didn't carry a grudge against her like Natalie did.

"I thought maybe you could help me find a roommate," she said. Her voice was cold, as usual.

I wondered if Catalina ever broke a smile or laughed. She'd been prim and proper since the day I'd met her, and that was the only side of her I'd ever seen. I wondered idly if anything had come of her witnessing Pepper's kiss and reminded myself to check in on Natalie as soon as we hung up.

"We don't really do that here," I told her. "There are some places that do, though. They're called things like 'Roommate Finders.' You might try the phone book." I wasn't being sarcastic, but seriously?

"I know. I filled out a form over there. I just thought you might know of something. I'm not fond of the thought of gambling with something as important as this."

I tried to picture Catalina gambling on anything and couldn't make the image work. "I'll keep my ears open, okay?"

"Are you feeling better?" There was a different tone in her voice. Was that sincerity?

"I am. Thanks for asking. How are you doing?" I realized I'd never had more than a polite conversation with Catalina as I asked this.

She sighed. "I'm really sad about Maggie leaving, but I know she's following her heart, so I'm happy for her. It's just really quiet at home now. I hate being alone."

"Why?" I couldn't understand this. "I love being alone!"

"We're pretty different people, I think. You're this fierce independent woman. I doubt anything bothers you."

"Really?" She had no idea. "A lot of things bother me. Mostly other people. That's why I like being alone!" I was only kind of kidding.

"Well, I don't do well with silence." She left it at that, and I kind of respected her for it. And weirdly, there was a part of me that wanted to find her a roommate based on that one simple statement.

"I'll see what I can do," I told her, my brain beginning to turn as it worked on this new challenge.

"I really appreciate it."

"I'll call you back in a day or two."

"Thanks." She sounded unhappy.

I actually felt sorry for her. It had never occurred to me to be friendly with Catalina, but it seemed like she could use a friend or two. It would be a tough sell to Pepper, but maybe she didn't need to know.

I hung up and took a deep breath. It was the first time I'd stopped moving all day. I was exhausted, and it was only noon. I also felt an aching sadness that I wasn't used to. I'd hurt Spider. I'd made him go, and I knew his pride would keep him away. Although I'd left my first love once before, it felt different this time. The first time he'd been too hurt to say anything, and I'd gone before he'd had a chance to talk me out of it. This time, both of us older and maybe a bit wiser, he'd been honest with me about his feelings. And I'd turned my back on him.

Beyond the gloom inside me was another unwanted feeling. Exhaustion. Normally I'd grab coffee at this time of day, but that was on the restricted list due to my decreased liver function. Stupid liver. I guzzled some water and picked up the phone again.

———

Pepper wasn't at her desk when I called, so I left a message and tried her cell phone. Most of us had moved on to the sleek new flip phones that had come out, but Pepper was loyal to the phone she'd gotten when we'd all first discovered cell phones, and the thing was like a brick. As it rang endlessly, I pictured her struggling to pull it from her bag, a fight I'd witnessed often. She had to buy purses based on their size—not many could be small and cute and still accommodate the brick phone.

I tried her apartment just in case and was surprised when she actually answered.

"Hello?" Her voice was muffled and groggy.

"Pepper, it's Tam. What are you doing home? Are you sick?"

"Oh, hi. No. Not sick. Wait." Her voice picked up a bit of energy. "You're sick though. Are you at work? I didn't recognize the number. Aren't you supposed to be home for two weeks?"

"Eh." I made a noncommittal noise that said we were not discussing it. "What's going on?"

"I got fired." It was a quiet wail.

"Oh, shit. Why? What happened?" Pepper had been a high-powered Internet marketing director for as long as I'd know her—or that's how I'd seen her, anyway. When we'd met, she was the one taking the rest of us to the parties, making introductions. Between her and Candace, I'd always felt my friends were basically destined to run the industry.

"I got all distracted. Stuff with CJ... I just fucked up. They were right to fire me."

"So, are you interviewing? What are you going to do?" I felt a sense of desperate urgency that Pepper's voice didn't seem to carry. What was she doing?

"Tam, CJ and I broke up."

It got worse. "Oh, God, I'm so sorry. For good?"

"I don't know. I think so."

"Did Catalina have anything to do with this?" I started to feel guilty for feeling sorry for the little Hepburn wannabe.

"I actually don't think so."

Guilt relieved.

"If she saw anything, I don't think she told CJ about it." She paused. "It had more to do with the conversation he walked into at the hospital, when I was talking about Damon. He figured out that Damon wasn't the only person I'd kissed." She sounded completely miserable, her voice shaky and thin.

"But Damon was before you were together!"

"He knows that Candace was dating him. I think he's just completely lost respect for me. He thinks I'm a horrible person..." She began sniffling loudly.

"Oh, Pepper..."

"How are you? Are you better?"

I wasn't. As afternoon wore on, I was feeling less well and was actually wondering how I would get home. I didn't even have the energy to go down and hail a cab. "I think so."

"The doctor said so? I'm surprised Spider let you out of his sight long enough for you to go to work."

The sadness in me sprang to life, acknowledged and therefore somehow more prominent. "He didn't. I made him leave."

"Why?"

The room was darkening, and I felt weak, like I might pass out. "Um, Pepper? Is there any way you could come up here to my work?"

She hesitated, and I imagined she was in her pajamas, unbathed and wallowing in her misery. "I could, I guess."

I slumped back in my chair. "Okay. Please. Soon."

"Are you okay?"

"I don't think so, actually. Can you please come get me?"

"I'm on my way, Tam. Hold on."

I hung up and closed my eyes, turning my chair so no one would see me if they walked by. I didn't have the energy to close the door. Coming in had been a terrible idea.

———

I have no idea how long it took Pepper to get to my office. I was just glad she'd been there before and seemed to remember how to find me. When she came in, I was out—whether I just fell asleep or if I actually passed out, I wasn't sure, but Pepper told me later I'd been tough to wake up. She took in my state, went downstairs to hail a cab, and asked it to wait at the curb. Pepper helped me out, grabbing the files from my desk, and somehow we got to my apartment. I barely remembered the journey, but I heard about it all as Pepper reported it to the handsome nurse who was waiting at my apartment when we pulled up.

Gabe actually picked me up, carried me up the three flights to my door, and tucked me into my bed after removing my jacket and shoes. I felt like a child, Gabe and Pepper chatting in the living room as I lay in my bed, watching them through the IKEA bookcase that I used as a room divider. I was too exhausted to try to talk or to protest being treated like a sick kid. I felt like a sick kid.

"She shouldn't have gone back in," Gabe was saying. "I don't understand why that guy Gaige would let her. He was supposed to be taking care of her."

"I think they have some history that makes it more complicated," Pepper said.

"Well, whatever." Gabe actually sounded angry. "I read her discharge report, and she's supposed to have someone here with her. She'll be weak for a while."

"I can stay," Pepper said. "I'm, uh, between jobs at the moment."

"Good." Gabe was banging around in the kitchen. "I doubt she ate anything this afternoon, either, so her blood sugar probably crashed, which only makes things worse."

He was right.

I watched them move around each other, getting something ready for me to eat. Gabe wore jeans and a T-shirt again, with the same Converse sneakers. He was tall and moved with some kind of liquid grace that made me think of water. Even though I didn't feel good, I liked watching him as he worked, the lean muscles in his arms flexing while he pulled things from cabinets and the refrigerator like he'd been here before. When he carried a plate toward me, he wore a smile that actually made me feel better. And when he sat down on the edge of my bed, I got another whiff of a smell that I identified with the ocean. Gabe was all liquid and salt air, warmth and sunshine. I couldn't help but smile back at him.

"Thank you," I managed, although I felt like I was speaking from inside a fog bank.

Gabe handed me a glass of milk and a sandwich. "Drink the milk first. You'll feel better once the sugar hits your system."

I did as I was told, and a few minutes later, I did actually feel my head clearing.

"You've got to be more careful, Tamara." Gabe's amber eyes held my gaze, serious and focused. "Your liver function is way down. Your body's trying to deal with that, so you can't throw it more challenges."

"The doctor said it was decreased. She didn't say 'way down.'"

"I read the charts. Andrew read the charts. It isn't good, Tam. That's why you're on the donor list." He shook his head. "You can't just put your head down and force your way through this."

I smiled at him. How did he know that was how I dealt with every problem in my life? He was insightful and smart. I liked Gabe. A lot. But even as I basked in the confident aura of his company, the sad emptiness that Spider had filled didn't go away, and I found myself wishing Gabe were him instead. "Message received."

He stood and looked at his watch. "I've gotta get to the hospital. I'll be off after midnight, but I'm coming to check on you first thing in the morning."

I nodded, and Pepper did, too.

"I'm not going anywhere," she assured him.

"You're a good friend" Gabe planted a kiss on my cheek and hugged Pepper before leaving.

"He's adorable," she said as soon as the door clicked shut.

And he was. But he was no Gaige Sypdell.

Chapter Twenty-One

FIST? MEET GUT

Natalie

STAYING with Tamara gave me something to do, a sense of purpose that distracted me from CJ's absence from my life and my newly unemployed status. I went home to get a few things and was sad—though not surprised—to find that he still hadn't called. CJ had left, and there was some finality to it that made me shudder. I knew that if we had another shot, I was probably going to have to be the one to take it, but I had the distinct sense that my stature in CJ's mind had shrunk considerably when he'd found out that I'd not only cheated on him but kissed someone one of my best friends was dating.

There was a message from my dad, and I listened to it with a deep sense of shame. "How's my hotshot executive daughter doing? I'd love to visit you out there soon, Nat. Give me a call!"

Dad had been threatening to visit for a while. And while

I'd love for him to come see me, I had been so distracted with my own happiness that for a while I just didn't give it much thought. Now there was no way my dad could come. Not until I fixed everything. Dad needed to see me doing well, not failing. Again. In his mind, I was always failing. I'd only just begun to climb out of that pigeonhole he'd dropped me into, and I wasn't about to sink back into it now.

Back at Tamara's, I tried my best to entertain her, but she was so tired she didn't require much.

"I guess you're mostly here to make sure I don't make a break for it," she said after a nap.

"I think I could take you if you tried it."

She gave me a weak smile. "So, here's a question for you..." I could tell from her tone that I might not like where she was headed, but I'd promised to help her. "Feel like playing real estate agent?"

"What are you talking about?"

"I have clients tomorrow. I'm supposed to be showing them some properties."

"There's no way you can go. I can't believe you're even thinking about it."

"I'm not. I'm thinking about *you* going." She raised an eyebrow at me.

"I don't know the first thing about real estate, Tam."

"All you have to do is walk this nice couple through three apartments. The keys are with the doorman in each building, and you just flash my badge and take 'em up. We can be on the phone the whole time, so if they have questions about fees or co-op approval or whatever, I can talk to them."

"So they'll know I'm not you?"

"No one would ever mistake you for me." She cackled, and I knew she was feeling a little better.

I agreed to her plan, and she loaned me a suit to wear the

next day. I was uneasy about playing real estate agent, but then I had nothing better to do.

———

Tamara's plan went off without a hitch, and while the couple didn't want to pull the trigger on any of the three apartments, they were really happy with the things they saw and asked if we could find a few more for them. I agreed, and Tamara said I'd been a great assistant.

"I hear you're looking for work," she joked as we chatted on the phone after I'd finished. "Want to think about real estate?"

I considered it. "I might. I don't know…"

"Luckily, you've got a friend on the inside."

I agreed that when she was feeling better and back at work it might be fun to shadow her for a while, see what it was all about. In the meantime, I needed to talk to Allan Page, Tom's friend who was a headhunter and had found me my last job.

"Yes, call him and start interviewing for sure," Tamara said. "Just give me a couple weeks to show you how fun it is getting to see the inside of four-million dollar lofts we'd never get into otherwise!"

"Deal."

"Can we make another deal?" Her voice was smaller, and she sounded like a little kid suddenly.

"Okay."

"Can we please leave the apartment tomorrow? I have to get out and see some people!"

"Sure. Wanna have dinner with everyone if they're free?"

"Yes." She sounded relieved. I couldn't blame her.

I called around and set up dinner plans for the following night.

Andrew and Lulu got a late reservation at a place in the Bowery, and Tamara and I took a cab down to meet everyone.

"You sure you're up to this?" I asked her.

She nodded. She was glowing and her eyes shone. She looked much better. I'd taken her to her appointment with Dr. Charles that morning, and the doctor was happy with her improvement.

We were seated at a long table in the back of the rustic space, and it was fun seeing everyone together. I'd invited Candace and Gregoire, Andrew and Lulu, and Tom. Tamara settled between Tom and Candace and looked around happily. "I never thought I'd be so excited just to be out to dinner," she said.

"We're so happy you are," Lulu said.

"You look good, Tam," Andrew said, nodding his approval. "Gabe was pretty worried the other day. I'll have to report that you are following orders and taking care of yourself."

"He's a good guy," Tamara said.

Lulu raised an eyebrow.

"Don't read anything into it," Tamara scolded.

"It's because he is a nurse, isn't it?" Lulu asked.

"Don't be ridiculous," Candace said. "It's because she's already spoken for. You met the hot cowboy... What was his name? Scorpio?"

"Spider." Tamara's voice was practically a whisper, and she was staring beyond Candace toward the long bar on the opposite side of the room. At Spider. His long tall frame was instantly recognizable, and if it weren't, the boots were a pretty clear giveaway. Tamara hadn't been explicit, but she had made it clear that she and Spider had been through some kind of falling out.

"What are the odds?" I asked, feeling immediately sorry I'd let Andrew and Lulu pick the place.

They looked sorry, too, as we all turned back to one another, trying to figure out whether seeing Spider would send Tamara into any kind of health-related emergency. He'd been a very touchy subject. And the fact that he was at the bar with his hand on the knee of the dark-haired girl perched on the stool next to him didn't help.

"This place was just profiled in Time Out," Andrew said. "I guess lots of folks are checking it out."

"Now we just need CJ to show up and the night will be complete." Gregoire shook his head.

CJ's name was like a fist to the gut, which is what Gregoire actually got from Candace.

He winced. "Sorry."

"It's fine," I said. The whole table was watching me now, except Tamara, whose gaze never left Spider at the bar. "I screwed up. It's my own fault. I do need to talk to him, though. I just don't really know how."

Andrew leaned forward. "We had a few beers last night. If it makes you feel better, he's completely miserable."

"That doesn't make me feel better."

"I just thought you'd want to know. He hasn't exactly... moved on." Andrew said.

I nodded, a tiny spring of hope welling inside me.

Halfway through our meal, Spider and his date left the bar, and Tamara's line of sight. She didn't talk much for the rest of the meal, and she looked exhausted again by the time we got into a cab outside.

"Are you all right?" I asked as the city lights streaked past our windows.

She shook her head. "Not really. But I will be. It's just weird seeing him here, in my city. And seeing him having a life... without me."

That was completely understandable. I couldn't imagine seeing CJ with anyone else like that. While I didn't really know what Spider and Tamara were to each other, I knew exactly what CJ meant to me. I had to talk to him. I had to try.

———

Tamara didn't speak much once we got to her apartment. She hugged me, thanked me for a nice night out, and then went to bed. I'd been sleeping on her couch but figured that maybe a night on my own would be a good thing. I could call CJ, see if he'd be willing to talk. Or listen.

I took a deep breath once I'd settled myself on the couch and then dialed CJ's apartment.

"Hi, Natalie." He didn't sound excited to speak to me, but at least he'd answered.

"Hi." My voice was smaller than I wanted it to be. "Do you have time to talk?"

"It's pretty late."

It was. My watch said it was one o'clock, but I knew he'd be up. "Want me to try again tomorrow?"

"No. It's okay." There was no warmth in his voice, and I got the sense that this conversation might be something he just wanted to get through, be finished with.

"I owe you an apology."

"Yeah, you do." I wished I could see his face, have a better sense what he was thinking. I missed the way his dark eyes widened when he was making a point, the way his full lips always gave him away when he was trying not to laugh.

I closed my eyes. "I'm so, so sorry, CJ." Tears squeezed beneath my lids, and my chest felt like it was filling with my sorrow. "I was stupid and confused. I was jealous of Irene, of all the time you were spending with her. I know it doesn't make a difference. But the kiss—the other one—it didn't mean anything."

"And the kiss with Damon? Did it mean something?"

"No. Definitely not." I shook my head. "No, I'm just... God, I'm just stupid."

"You aren't stupid," he said slowly. "You're actually really smart. And that's part of why this is so confusing. I just don't get it."

"I know..."

CJ sighed. After a painful moment, he said, "I don't know if I can forgive you, Natalie."

Cold fear iced my blood. Was he really going to break up with me for good? My muscles went rigid, waiting for his next words.

"Cheating is... It's just something I've never understood, and it's a deal breaker for me. I'm hurt, and I'm really, really angry. I would never do that to you." His voice had gone emotionless again, and it was practically a whisper.

"I know... I..." I had no words to fix this. "I'm so sorry."

"I don't know if I can trust you again."

Tears streamed down my cheeks, and I wished I hadn't called. At least then I could go on hoping there might be a way to mend things.

"Now isn't a good time to deal with this anyway. The firm opened this week, and things are a disaster. There's something going on with my parents, something..." He sighed, and I realized he wasn't going to confide in me now. "I just have too much to handle, and I can't juggle this, too."

"Maybe..." My mouth was moving before I knew what I was going to say.

But CJ didn't let me finish anyway. "I'll call you, Natalie, okay? Give me some time. I just... I need some time."

"Oh. Okay."

"Bye." He hung up, sounding sad and defeated. The pain in his voice was like a knife to my gut. CJ had trusted me. He'd loved me, and I betrayed him for no good reason. I was a stupid girl, and I got caught up in the moment. I'd do anything to take it all back, to rewind the clock and never kiss Bennett. Or Damon. I was still that girl in high school no one was interested in, or at least she still lived inside me, and any time a man showed the littlest bit of interest, I got carried away with the novelty of it. But I knew enough to have figured out that I didn't want them. I had the best guy I'd ever met. I would get him back if it took me the rest of my life.

I curled into a ball on the couch and cried until sleep came.

———

I spent the next week with Tamara, talked with Dr. Chase on the phone, and also met with Allan Page. Dr. Chase was polite but sounded unsurprised about my change in employment status. I'd hoped she might sound a tiny bit disappointed when I told her I'd have to suspend my visits with her, but she didn't. Maybe she thought I was a lost cause. I was definitely suspecting it was true.

Allan, the headhunter, told me that he wasn't sure about finding me a job at this point. Things had changed dramatically since the last time he'd placed me, he said. Since I couldn't use John as a reference, he wasn't sure about my prospects. Real estate was looking likely. So was homelessness, since there was no way I could pay my rent once my paychecks stopped, and my last one was only a week away.

"Got any super low-rent options?" I asked Tamara as we dug through listings.

"You know that's not where I play," she said before realizing I was asking for myself. "Oh, honey... No... I didn't even think about your job and the apartment! Oh no!"

"I'm going to have to give it up. Do you think there'll be a penalty for breaking the lease?"

"Not if I have anything to say about it."

I'd sub-letted my apartment from a guy Tamara worked with, one who was practically her lap dog. I hoped his enthusiasm for her would help me move with little damage to my credit rating or non-existent cash flow.

"But, Pepper, where are you going to go?" She stared at me.

I shook my head. I'd have to go back through a roommate service and find something I could afford. "I guess I'm looking for a roommate."

Her eyebrows shot up, and a strange look crossed her face. "I do know of something, actually."

"What?"

"It's on the Upper East, but hear me out."

I rolled my eyes. I'd spent too much time with Lulu and Candace to have an open mind about the Upper East Side, but I was desperate. "Let's hear it."

"Two bedrooms, low eighties, and Second Avenue. Well-decorated and super clean, doorman building, high floor."

"Sounds expensive." But good.

"Eight hundred."

That was half what I was paying now for my studio. This could work. "Who lives there?"

Tamara squinted at me. "Don't get mad, and just promise you'll think about it."

I got the idea I wasn't going to like this.

"So I talked to Catalina the other day..."

"You've got to be kidding." I felt my spine go stiff. "She hates me. She'd knife me in my sleep. I could never live with her!"

"Maggie did," Tamara said.

"Maggie's a saint. Catalina's a serious pain in the ass. She's totally out to get me! Even if I was okay with this, she wouldn't be."

"Maybe not normally, but there's one little thing that might help."

"What?" I couldn't believe we were still even discussing this. I turned back to the listings on the screen in front of us.

"You're both completely desperate."

"Shit." I closed my eyes. Even if I could imagine it, she'd never agree to it. Living with her? I couldn't imagine a more pure form of torture.

"I'll call her."

I shook my head. "Give me one more week. I'll figure something out. Maybe I'll find a fantastic job..."

Tamara looked skeptical, but she put down her phone.

I didn't know what I was going to do, but I didn't think I could live with Catalina. If we had to live together, one of us would certainly end up dead.

Chapter Twenty-Two

HEPBURN IN SWEATS

Tamara

I FOCUSED on getting better for the next few days. Pepper helped me stay on top of my workload, running errands and showing properties. She was doing great, and I was pretty sure she'd make a good agent if she felt like going through all the tests and certifications.

"I think you're like me," I told her. "Too ambitious to sit behind a desk all day. It's so much better to be out, doing things, making things happen."

She nodded but didn't look convinced. She'd had a haunted look in her eyes since she'd come back after talking to CJ the Friday night after we had dinner. That was a rough night for everyone, it turned out. I didn't like seeing Spider with another woman, but he was following directions, doing exactly what I'd told him to do. I couldn't begrudge him having a life just because I currently had none. I walled off the hurt and jealousy, the thought of him showering some other girl with that incredible smile or touching her with those perfect hands... None of that was mine anymore, and I couldn't hold it against him that he'd moved on. I vowed to do the same.

By the time the two weeks I'd been grounded were up, I was back to my old self. The tremor was largely gone, and Dr. Charles and I both felt that my new dosage was working. I was worried about the liver damage, and she clearly was, too, but it was easy enough to shove that concern to the back of my mind as I slowly moved back into my day-to-day life.

Work went well, and as we reached mid-October and T-shirts turned to sweaters in the city, I was back to a steady pace. Spider was still part of my daily thoughts, but I reached a point where I could think of him without feeling the deep longing that I'd let myself feel for a while. I even convinced myself that I was happy for him, that it was a good thing that he'd found someone else, forgotten me. We both needed that. It did neither of us any good to cling to a past that was gone. I found myself wondering whether he was even still in the city—he'd said he was here for me, but it sounded like he was actually here for his Poppy and that business was good. I wished Gaige Spydell and his meat sales the very best, and I hoped the pretty dark-haired girl I'd seen in the bar knew what she had.

Keeping myself on a regimented schedule—food, sleep, work, and visits to the doctor thanks to my now underperforming liver—kept me sane. The additional distraction of feeling somewhat responsible for Pepper's future helped too.

"So we're going over there today?" I was asking but not really asking. We were going to look at Catalina's place.

"I can't believe this is happening." Pepper looked glum. "This was supposed to be my year."

"Your year?" We were leaving my office, walking to the

east side where we'd grab the subway north to Catalina's. "What does that mean?"

"Everything was on track. It was supposed to get better, not worse. I was going to take decisions by the horns and stop letting other people determine my future. Now I'm your intern and I'm about to move in with my mortal enemy."

I stopped walking and stared at her. "You're not my intern. I'm training you to be an agent, and if it isn't something you want, then tell me now because it's a hell of a lot of work."

Her eyebrows shot up, and her face crumpled. "I do want it," she said, her voice softer. "I just... I don't know if I chose it. I just kind of stumbled into it."

"Pepper, it's in the way you think about things. Some things you see, and you go after, and you consciously tell yourself, 'I choose that.'" I glanced at her to see if she was following. "Like you moving to the city. You just did it. You decided, and you did it."

"Right."

"But a lot of the choices we make in life come as opportunities. I didn't know when I moved here that I was going to meet the best friends I've ever had. I didn't see you guys and *decide* to be friends with you. It happened. I had a chance to come out and get to know some girls, and I took it. The rest of it was a result of that choice. Sometimes our lives feel like they're just happening, but the events that sweep us along are all the result of a choice we made. You just have to look back to see it."

"I chose to kiss Bennett. And Damon."

This was getting old. "Pepper, you can also choose to keep beating yourself up over that and over all the things that came as a result or you can pull your head out of your ass and choose to move forward. If you want this to be your year, you're going to have to wake up. Take responsibility for yourself, and stop blaming the world and the circumstances for the things you don't like." My voice had gotten a little harsher than I'd intended, and I looked over at Pepper again, expecting to see her crumbling. She'd been such a mess for the last week or so.

But she wasn't caving in on herself again. Her chin was thrust in the air, and her blue eyes burned with a ferocity I hadn't seen in a long time. There were no tears, and her lips were set in a hard line. I wondered if I'd pushed too far and pissed her off. I hadn't seen angry Pepper before.

"You're right, Tam." Her voice was even and steady. "I'm tired of feeling like I'm not in charge, and maybe it's all in the perspective."

I nodded.

"I'm sorry if I've been whiny." She glanced down at me.

"It's okay."

"I'm not going to wallow anymore. In fact, I've been talking to someone about this. A therapist."

"That's great." I shot a look at her. "You're not pissed at me?"

"No. I'm pissed at me."

"Okay, just checking." We ducked into the subway station and reached the platform just in time to catch the train to 86th Street.

The shaking of the car and rumbling of steel wheels made it difficult to talk, so we each stared out the windows into the darkness, each with our own thoughts. I looked at Pepper a few times, wondering if she'd really been able to shake herself free of her own self-pity that quickly, but her eyes remained clear and sharp. It had been a long time coming. Maybe getting chewed out by one of her best friends was just the tap she needed to get to this point.

———

We'd all been to Maggie and Catalina's place before, so going to look was really a formality. I think both Pepper and Catalina wanted to see if they could tolerate being in the same room now that necessity might be forcing them together.

When we rang the bell, Catalina opened the door immediately, but she didn't seem quite herself.

She stepped back. "Come on in."

"Thanks," Pepper said. She was looking at Catalina closely, and I knew she was also trying to put her finger on what was different.

I put my purse down on the table next to the kitchen and then turned back around, realizing what it was. Catalina didn't have the dark eyeliner on, and she wore sweats. I'd seen all my friends on the weekends before, dressed casually and not trying to impress anyone, but I'd never seen Catalina looking anything besides perfect. I wondered if the constant shiny surface was part of what turned Pepper off to her. Maybe Catalina was savvy enough to realize that letting Pepper see her without her armor was a good strategy if she really did want her to move in. Maybe Catalina was a lot smarter than I'd given her credit for.

"Maggie's room is on the left. It's super clean. For some people, the vice is chocolate. For me, it's Lysol." She shrugged.

Pepper raised an eyebrow and then went in to look at the room. I followed on her heels, pointing out the ways in which it was better than her current studio.

"Look at all the light." There were two windows on the far wall, and an alcove with a built-in bookshelf between them. "Pepper, you know how rare built-ins are in the city." Most apartments were Spartan at best, in an effort to avoid any kind of personalization that would either result in additional maintenance cost or drive away potential renters.

"That is really nice," she agreed. "Look at the closet."

The wall opposite the windows was almost all storage. It was long and narrow, but that would make it easy to see everything hanging. "Nice," I agreed.

We checked out the bathroom and kitchen. Catalina said both had been renovated sometime just before she and Maggie had moved in. The tile was clean, and everything sparkled. "It's not a bad thing having a neat freak as a roommate," I whispered to Pepper.

She nodded, still giving Catalina a wide berth, as if she worried the other girl might suddenly attack.

We ended our tour in the living room, where Spartan furniture with clean lines made the room look larger than it actually was. "Someone favors IKEA," I said.

Catalina nodded. "The Swedes know what's up."

"My futon..." Pepper said.

"This is a pull-out," Catalina lifted up one of the couch cushions to show us. "But if your futon is nicer, I guess we could switch."

Pepper shook her head. "It's not."

My couch was ratted and old, a hand-me-down from the girl who'd been in the apartment before me, a friend of a friend. "If you didn't mind me using it, I could keep your futon," I told Pepper. It's nicer than my couch."

Pepper nodded. "Okay. I think the rest of my stuff will fit. I don't have much."

Catalina stood then, looking uncertain. "So it's eight hundred. And I should probably ask for first and last, too."

"I don't have it," Pepper said.

"So it's not a requirement, I guess," Catalina said. "More just an insurance policy." She shrugged.

They were both being remarkably reasonable.

"The lease is in my name only," Catalina continued. "So

there's no legal stuff to do. But that also means it's my ass, so my rules."

I felt the air chill around me as Pepper took a step backward. "Of course," she said, her voice only slightly less friendly.

"I think we can do this, Natalie." Catalina said. "And I think we both really need to."

Pepper nodded. "Okay."

"When's the move date?" I asked.

"Last weekend this month?" Natalie asked.

Everyone agreed, and the deed was done. As we left Catalina's building I waited for Pepper to say something horrible about Catalina or make some noise about regretting the way her life had gone. But she didn't. She was quiet until we got back to the West side, and then she surprised me.

"I feel good about this decision. I'll be saving money, and it will make it easier for me to find a job I like, instead of one that pays a certain amount of money."

I nodded. Pepper was sucking it up and moving forward. I resolved to do the same.

Chapter Twenty-Three

LIVING WITH THE ENEMY

Natalie

I HAD AN APARTMENT, but now I needed to find a job. Allan had turned up nothing of use, and I was discouraged. The Internet industry was still booming around me, but I was suddenly an outsider. At Sunday brunch, the whole table leaned in to help and our usual light-hearted recap turned into another strategy session.

"Can you go back to All Night?" Candace asked. She loved a good problem to work on, and I wished I'd brought her in earlier. She was a fixer who approached everything in her own life with a take-no-prisoners attitude.

"Hell no." The words came out more forcefully than I'd intended, and Andrew spit out his coffee, laughing. "Sorry, Andrew. It's just no. I worked with the most insane woman there. She literally pretended like she didn't know my name for almost a year while taking credit for every single thing I did. She'd never let me back in. Plus, I think I burned the bridge when I left."

"I doubt it," Candace said, "but I see what you mean. I forgot about psycho-Sally over there."

"I thought her name was Lanie?" Lulu looked confused.

"Fine, Loopy Lanie," Candace corrected herself.

"There are few women in international investment," Gregoire said, his dark brown eyes sincere. "Do you have a business degree?"

"That's nice," I told him, "but no. I'm liberal arts all the way."

"So you need a fuzzy job," Andrew said.

"No math, no science," Candace explained as Lulu's eyebrows went up in question.

I sat back and pushed my brioche French toast around on my plate. I wanted to be annoyed about being categorized as needing a "fuzzy job," but I couldn't deny that there was truth there. I'd fail miserably in international finance. "Thanks though, Gregoire. It was a good idea."

Gregoire smiled and toasted me in the air with his bloody Mary. I lifted my coffee in response. Sunday mimosas were no longer in my budget, and this way Tamara wasn't the only one not drinking.

"I still think you'd do great in real estate," Tamara said.

"And I like it," I told her. "But six months of studying and interning isn't really going to bring home the bacon, you know?"

She nodded. "I wish there was some way around that, but I don't know what it is. I asked if there were any paying jobs at the firm you could do in the meantime, but I guess my influence doesn't extend into HR." She smiled.

"Well," Lulu said, "I think you should make a list of your interests." She had recently taken a job in advertising sales and was doing very well. "What do you like?"

"I feel like I'm in the high school counselor's office again," I said.

"No, this is good." Tamara handed me a small notebook and a pen, which Candace immediately pulled from my hands.

Tom rubbed his hands together and leaned forward. "This is going to be awesome!"

"First interest?" Candace asked, pen poised to write.

"Burlesque?" Tom volunteered.

"Not yours," I said. "Mine." I turned back to Candace. "Books?" That was stupid. Books didn't make money.

"So, reading, writing, or selling them?" Andrew said.

"Any of the above, I guess. I have an English degree. I like books. I just like being around them." I'd always loved the way a new book smelled and had been guilty of sniffing books at the Barnes and Noble on the Upper West Side when CJ and I had gone there to browse. He'd caught me doing it and had never let me forget it.

"This is the right city for books." Candace added *publishing, editing*, and *selling* to the list. "What about writing?"

I nodded. "Maybe for a magazine? I mean..." I looked around, embarrassed. "If I get to dream." This exercise felt a little like opening my closet of deepest secrets and inviting everyone inside, but these were my closest friends. In a way, the dreams I held dear felt just a tiny bit more possible when I shared them.

"Are we ruling out the Internet industry?" Tamara asked.

I shook my head. "I don't have any special Internet skills, but it pays well and that's where I've got experience."

"Marketing experience," Candace pointed out. "That applies to everything."

We brainstormed for another hour, the entire group weirdly focused on my joblessness, even Andrew and Gregoire. At one point, I found myself watching my best

friends debate my options and felt a deep sense of security
spread through me. These were my people, my family away
from home. They cared enough about me to focus on my
problems for hours at a time. I was flattered and touched, and
more than anything, I realized how lucky I was. These people
would never let me fall. No matter what stupid things I did,
or who I mistakenly kissed, these people would make sure I
was okay.

I wished for CJ at my side, but from what Andrew said,
he had his own worries right now. I needed to focus on
getting back on my feet, and then I would figure out how to
win CJ back. One step at a time.

———

Brunch left me with a list of jobs to investigate and a strategy
to fill the in-between time with an income. So basically, my
friends loved me enough to give me homework.

I explored job listings on the Internet in the different
industries we'd identified: publishing, branding, education,
and art. I took a typing test and submitted an application
with a temporary firm. As long as they didn't send me to
temp at All Night, AdTrack, or Irene's firm, I figured I could
work just about anywhere. It'd be interesting to see lots of
different places, and maybe I'd find a job that I really liked.
The woman who interviewed me told me that she thought
they'd be able to place me immediately but to expect to be
working as a receptionist or personal assistant. I thanked
her and moved on to my next assignment: setting up my
move.

By the time moving day arrived, I had packed my few
belongings into boxes and had Gregoire, Andrew, and Tom
prepared to drag my heavier items downstairs. Tom insisted
that he could drive the truck, so I thanked him and promised

him a nice dinner at my new place in return. I hoped Catalina wouldn't have an issue with that.

She and I hadn't spoken since I'd toured the apartment except to confirm that keys would be ready for me this morning. She told me that she'd stay out for the day to make it easier for me to move, but I suspected she just didn't want to break a nail by having to help move a box or two. She'd been perfectly civil when I'd visited, but I wasn't ready to change my opinion about Catalina. Not without a hell of a lot more evidence.

As Gregoire and Andrew struggled to get my futon down the stairs, I stood at the back of the truck, biting my nails. This whole endeavor had me on edge. There was something so unnerving about having everything you owned dragged across a New York City sidewalk. Since I was nervous and a little out of sorts, I thought I was probably just seeing things when a familiar blond-haired figure turned the corner and walked toward where we were hustling boxes and furniture. I convinced myself that the long confident stride and football physique could not be CJ, although everything about the man walking toward us screamed that it was. It was only when Tom stepped away from the truck, calling, "CJ! Good to see you!" that I realized it was really him and not just my wishful imagination.

I walked to the middle of the sidewalk but found that I couldn't approach him. My feet were frozen in cement, and I just stared. I'd wished for him to come for weeks now but had given him the space I thought he needed while I sorted through the debris of my own disastrous life.

"Hi, Natalie." He walked toward me and took me in his arms then released me. A friendly hug.

I tried to make my body stop humming where he'd touched me. "Hi." There. I did have a voice.

"Heard you were moving today. I thought you might need

a hand." He grinned at me, took the steps to my front door two at a time, and disappeared inside my building.

What was happening? I couldn't put the CJ who had told me he was angry and hurt and needed space into context with the friendly guy who had just showed up to help me move. I might not understand it, but I wasn't going to question it.

"Hey, Pepper, just because you have all these strapping handsome men around doesn't mean you don't have to help," Andrew called down from the fire escape.

I smiled up at him and went inside, steeling myself for CJ's confusing presence.

CJ passed me on the stairs, carrying my bookcase down by himself. Despite the clear strain on his face, he flashed me a thumbs up and my heart raced.

Inside, Andrew waited. "I hope it's okay that I called him."

I nodded. "I'm just... I thought he didn't want to see me."

"He's miserable without you. I thought this would be an easy way for you to see each other. You won't be alone, and he can feel like he's helping you with something... Maybe you can get him talking about whatever is going on with him. He won't tell me."

I shook my head. I wasn't going to push. I was happy just to have CJ nearby, to know that he wasn't gone completely. There was no way I would push him away by digging too deeply into whatever was going on with him.

———

It didn't take long to load my life into the back of a small moving truck, and it was unsettling to see my life reduced to that tiny space.

"Is this really my whole life?" I asked Tom as we drove away from my building. "In this tiny truck?"

He shook his head. "No, honey. Your whole life is those people sitting around the table at Cafeteria, helping you figure out what to do next. Your whole life is those guys who came to your house on a Sunday to help you move your furniture and books. You have way too many books for a girl living in the city, by the way."

"It's an addiction."

"I know." Tom managed the drive well even though it took almost an hour to get through traffic and find a place to double-park the truck outside the building. Luckily, the doorman was very helpful and had some cones he put out in the street to help us.

Andrew, Gregoire, and CJ met us on the Upper East Side, having taken the subway since we wouldn't all fit on the bench seat in the moving truck. We had dropped the futon at Tamara's on the way over, the three of us barely getting it up her stairs. It would have been good to have one of the other guys ride in the truck. We rested and sweated for the remainder of the drive over.

As we hauled boxes and furniture up to the new apartment—a process made easier by the fact there was a freight elevator—I thought about what Tom had said, and I knew he was right. Even though moving was terrible in the best of circumstances, I knew I was going to be okay because the life I'd built here was strong enough to weather the trials that might come.

"People who are moving don't smile this much," Andrew quipped as he pushed the mattress back onto my boxspring.

I helped him from the other side. "I can't help it. I'm just so glad you guys are here."

"Yeah, this would've cost you a fortune."

"No. I mean, I'm just so lucky to have so many friends. People willing to go out of their way to help make sure I'm okay. I really appreciate it."

"It's no problem. And I take payment in beer." He winked.

I turned around to make another trip and nearly crashed into CJ standing in the doorway. He was watching me with a thoughtful expression on his face. When our eyes connected, I immediately looked away. My stomach was jumpy and I couldn't figure out how to act.

"You seem like you're doing well," he said as we rode the elevator back down for another load.

I nodded, not sure how to feel about being so close to him and still having this icy distance between us. "Things are getting better, I think. How are you?"

He shook his head. "Things have been better." He gave me a smile as the elevator doors opened, but the light was gone from his eyes and my chest clenched. Had he come back because he needed me?

I didn't get another chance to talk to CJ that day, and Catalina arrived just as we were finishing, with more beer than I would have thought she could carry in her frail bird arms. I guessed that was the advantage of a doorman and an elevator building.

"Thought you guys might be thirsty after all the heavy lifting," she said. The ballet flats and cardigan were back, her dark hair swept back and makeup in place, but this thoughtfulness was new and unexpected.

"That was really nice of you," I told her.

The guys all dove for the beer, and I picked one up as well.

"How did it go?" She looked around, her eyes pausing on the cluttered additions to her previously clean space. "All done?"

I nodded. "I promise I'll get it all cleaned up. And most of my stuff will stay in my room."

She raised an eyebrow, and I prepared for a sarcastic

remark. "Natalie, you live here now too. Your stuff can be out here. You don't have to stay in your room all the time."

It was my turn to raise an eyebrow. Was Catalina really this reasonable? I wasn't sure what to make of it, but at least she wasn't being openly hostile.

The guys stayed for another hour once Tom returned from dropping off the truck, and it was late when everyone finally rose and moved for the door. I thanked them each, almost finding myself in tears with gratitude.

Tom gave me a long hug and then held me in front of him, looking into my eyes. "Don't be a stranger, Peppercorn. I'm going to miss you stomping around upstairs, you know."

"I know, Tom. Me too." I watched the guys leave, feeling luckier than I had in months.

CJ stayed until everyone else had gone, lingering near the door.

"Thank you so much for coming to help," I said, not sure what to do next.

"I don't think you needed me. You've got good friends, Natalie." There was a wistfulness in his voice that pulled at my heart. CJ looked so sad suddenly.

I nodded. "Hopefully you're one of them." There. I'd said something that poked at the strange relationship between us. Something that asked the question I couldn't ask.

He tilted his head and nodded. "I miss you." His voice was a whisper.

"Me too." Was this it? Would we get through all of this and find our way back together?

"Bye, Natalie." CJ stepped away from me and pushed the button for the elevator.

I stood in the open door and watched him. "Bye, CJ."

He got into the elevator, and the doors slid shut. Just like that, CJ was gone again. I was really starting to hate elevators.

Chapter Twenty-Four

I'M THE ASSHOLE

Tamara

NATALIE CALLED SUNDAY NIGHT, letting me know the move had gone smoothly and that Catalina was being tolerable, if not downright friendly. "I don't trust it," she said. "I think she has some kind of plan."

"Yeah, I think it's called 'paying the rent.'"

"Are you okay on your own? You're taking your medication?"

"Yes, Mom. It's a good time for you to be gone. I have to do another twenty-four hour pee test."

"Oh, fun. Well at least now there's no danger of anyone mistaking it for lemonade."

I laughed. There wasn't much about collecting pee for twenty-four hours that was amusing, but watching Natalie investigate the multiple containers in the refrigerator last time had been pretty funny. I had to turn in one big orange bottle, but since it was too big to fit in the refrigerator, I had my own system. Usually there was no one around to complain.

"You feeling okay?" Natalie sounded like she was pacing. She did that when she was nervous, and I knew she had been nervous about the move.

"I'd be better if everyone would quit asking me that."

"I know you hate it, Tam, but we are going to worry about you. It's our job as your family away from family."

"This is why I left my family."

It was true, though Pepper's statement had the strange effect of reassuring me. The last thing I wanted was to have my friends pity me, but knowing they cared about me was nice. Maybe you didn't get one without the other. I'd have to spend some time thinking about that.

"You coming to the office tomorrow?" Pepper had been learning the ropes and helping me, but after the brainstorming session at brunch, it was pretty clear she wasn't destined to follow in my footsteps.

"I'm supposed to report to the temp agency and get my first assignment. I have a job tomorrow but no idea what it will be. It's kind of exciting, actually."

"That *is* exciting." The uncertainty of it all would bother me, but Pepper seemed legitimately excited about having no idea what her week would hold. I flopped back on my bed and closed my eyes.

"So, CJ showed up when the guys were helping me move."

"You're kidding." Natalie hadn't seen CJ in weeks. "Did you ask him to help?"

"No. Andrew mentioned it to him."

"So that's good, right?"

"It was definitely good to see him," she said. "Weird though. I didn't know how I was supposed to act."

"Was he still mad?"

"I don't think so. More sad. Andrew said there was something going on with him, but I doubt I'm the one he's going to talk to at this point. I guess he's not telling Andrew, either." Pepper's voice had gotten lower.

I stared at the walls around the window, tracing cracks in the paint with my eyes. It was chilly, and the radiator had creaked to life the day before, clanging and hissing and scaring me to death before I realized what it was. I shivered. "Well, I'm glad he came. It seems like a first step to getting back together."

"I hope so. I don't want to push it."

"Yeah." We were both silent a moment, and I tried to picture Natalie in her new apartment, living with someone she had previously despised. I would have to see it for myself.

"So Bennett has called a couple times," she said.

"What for? He doesn't think there's anything between you, right?"

"No, he knows. I didn't say goodbye when I left AdTrack. I think he's just trying to figure out what happened. I want to talk to him, but I'm scared to call him back."

"Why? Are you worried that something will happen again? Do you have actual feelings for him?"

"No." She sounded certain. "I guess I just feel like it's disloyal to CJ to even call him."

"Um, you already kissed him. I think talking on the phone would be slightly lower on the disloyalty scale." I rolled over, trying to relieve the ache in my stomach that had started earlier in the day.

"Yeah, I guess you're right."

"Then again, I mean, why do you care? You don't work with him anymore, so you don't have to see him."

"He's a friend."

I shrugged, pulling a blanket around me. "Okay."

"Okay. I better go. I'll talk to you tomorrow?"

"Goodnight, Pepper." I put the phone on my dresser

and burrowed down into the blankets on my bed. I was tired of feeling crappy, but a good night's sleep couldn't hurt.

The city wailed and sang outside my window and the strangely soothing hiss of the radiator lulled me to sleep, signaling the fact that winter was on its way to New York.

———

I dropped off my sample with the lab in the morning and took a cab to work. I was still tired, and the thought of shoving myself into a subway car with everyone else in the city held no appeal at all. When I got to my desk, the phone rang almost immediately.

"Why haven't we planned anything for Halloween?" Candace asked.

"Is it Halloween?"

"This Sunday."

"Maybe because people don't celebrate Halloween when it falls on a Sunday." I wasn't excited about celebrating it this year. I didn't have the energy to brainstorm an outfit, and the thought of wearing something that would undoubtedly leave skin exposed to the quickly cooling air outside made me shiver.

"People celebrate on Saturday. There's a party. What should we be?"

"Can we be girls who don't want to go to a party?"

"No. Why are you being a buzzkill?"

"Oh, I don't know. Maybe because I had a seizure and collapsed the last time I went to a party?" It just slipped out. In a venomous voice.

The point was made, because Candace was silent, and that rarely happened.

"Sorry, Tam," she said after a moment.

"No. I didn't mean to say that." I was an idiot. I leaned back heavily in my desk chair.

"I don't know how to talk to you," she said softly. "You get mad if I ask you about your disease, and then you bring it up like that and make me feel like I should be more sensitive to it."

"I know," I moaned. "I'm an asshole."

"No, but you're sick and I get that."

"I'm not sick," I complained, my stomach turning. I actually did feel pretty sick today. I hadn't eaten breakfast because I was so nauseated when I woke up. I needed to eat something, though, and the girl with the bagel cart had just wheeled by. "Hey, Candace, I have to go."

"Okay. So Halloween?"

"I'll think about it."

We hung up, and I followed the cart down the hall and got a bagel with cream cheese. I managed to eat half the bagel at my desk and then dropped my head on my arms for a few minutes, feeling like I'd just thrown a lead weight into my gut.

The phone rang again, and I realized I'd been in that position much longer than intended. I hoped no one in my office had walked by and seen me that way. Had I fallen asleep? What the hell was going on with me?

The call was to confirm one of the appointments I'd set up for this afternoon. I hung up and stared at my calendar, daunted by the schedule I'd built myself. I wished Natalie was still playing assistant. I could have used some help, but I'd have to handle things myself.

By the time I got back to my apartment that night, I was feeling much worse. That was why it didn't surprise me when Dr. Charles called.

"Tamara, how are you feeling?"

"Honestly? Not good."

"Well, I'm not surprised. Your test results aren't good. I need you to check in at the hospital."

I shook my head. "What?"

"The hospital. Tonight, Tamara. Your urine test suggests that your kidneys are failing. We need to run more tests, and I want you here where I can keep an eye on you."

As soon as the words were out of her mouth, my stomach clenched again. I pulled my knees into my chest, every muscle in my body tensing until the pain had lessened. There was definitely something wrong. "Okay. I'll come."

"Tonight. Immediately."

"On my way." I hung up and stayed where I was, curled up on the futon I'd gotten in Pepper's move. I knew I needed to get up and get myself downtown to the hospital, but the idea of moving was exhausting.

The other thing stopping me was simple: I didn't want to go. Beyond the cold sanitized rooms and the tests, which were no one's idea of fun, the thought of taking myself to the hospital made me feel horribly sad. Although I'd ended up at the hospital before, I'd always found myself there surrounded by my family, or my friends. If I went there now, tonight, no one would know unless I made a point of calling to tell them. I'd done such a good job keeping people away, out of my business and in the dark about my disease, that I was alone with it now. My kidneys were failing, and there was no one here to tell—I couldn't drag my friends back to the hospital again. Maybe the doctor was wrong. Maybe I could just go in, and call them later if it was something serious.

I hadn't turned on the lights in my apartment when I'd gotten home at dusk, and now true darkness was settling in around me as I lay in a ball on the futon. I dialed a car service and waited, alone in the dark.

———

On the way to the hospital, I felt truly miserable. The driver kept glancing in his rearview mirror at me as I leaned my head against the door. He looked suspicious, and I wondered how may drunk and overdosing idiots he'd driven around before.

"You okay, miss?"

"Uh, we're on our way to the hospital. So not really." Dammit. Being a bitch wouldn't help.

His gaze held mine for a second, and then he shifted his weight, his face leaving the mirror.

"Sorry, no. I'm sick, and the doctor has some tests and wants me to come in right away. So no, not really very okay."

The driver said nothing else, and we moved south down Seventh Avenue. I felt alone and very small as I huddled against the window. I wasn't some ball-busting executive like I'd been pretending to be for so many months, making her way in the big city. Really, I was just a sick girl trying to run away from her problems and pretend to be someone new. I hadn't left my problems behind at all. Instead, I'd left my family behind and pushed away anyone else who had tried to care about me. I squeezed my eyes shut and finally let myself admit something else: I was terrified. Ever since the tremor had started coming back, I'd been pretending I could handle this, that I could take it in stride. That I was strong and fearless and tough, that I didn't need anyone. Collapsing at Maggie's party had been a wake-up call, but I hadn't listened to it. I didn't know what was going to happen to me.

We neared the hospital, and the fear gripped me. I pulled my phone from my purse, scrolling through my contacts. There was one person I wanted to call, but I couldn't do it. I'd let him go, and he didn't deserve to get hauled back into my mess just because I was scared. I put the phone away as the car pulled to the curb.

"Do you need help getting inside?" the driver asked.

I started to say no, but then I pushed open the door. I wasn't sure I'd be able to walk all the way in on my own. Pain gripped at my insides, making my back hunch and my legs wobble. "If you don't mind," I said.

Tears slid down my face as the driver—a man I didn't know and whom I would never see again—put an arm around my waist and helped me to a chair in the emergency room. He even walked up to the nurse at the desk and said a few words, pointing at me as I curled into myself in the chair. I needed to check in, but I couldn't even do that. All I could do was cry.

The nurse came to talk to me, and I managed to tell her what she needed to know. They brought out a wheelchair a few minutes later and took me into the bowels of the hospital. As much as I hated hospitals, they all smelled the same and the scent was oddly comforting, because that familiar antiseptic stench was the closest thing I had here to anything like home.

Chapter Twenty-Five

UNEASY ON THE UPPER EAST

Natalie

WAKING up that first morning on the Upper East Side was strange. No less strange was seeing Catalina in the morning, standing at the kitchen counter, drinking coffee with her hair sticking out in all directions.

"Good morning," I ventured.

"Maggie and I had an agreement," she said, her voice flat and dull. "No talking in the morning."

So Catalina wasn't a morning person. That was okay with me. I was never quite human until after ten anyway. "Works for me."

Despite the relative silence as we moved around each other getting ready for work that first morning, it worked out okay. Catalina wasn't friendly, but she wasn't hostile. In the past, she'd definitely been hostile especially to me. None of the other girls seemed to mind her, and Maggie had lived with her, so I guessed she actually liked her. I'd have to call Mags and see if she had any insight that might help, although understanding Catalina wasn't high on my list of goals as long as she remained civil.

Sharing a bathroom as we got ready for work took a bit of coordination, and we both stood at the bathroom door looking at one another, evidently hoping to shower at exactly the same time.

"How'd you and Maggie handle this?" I asked.

"She left for work at like seven."

"What time do you need to get in?"

"Around nine."

That could work. "I'm supposed to report at 8:15, at least today."

"Where?"

"Midtown. Where's your office?" Catalina worked in PR.

"Midtown East. Easy commute. You go first." She turned on her heel and went back to her room, the door closing behind her.

I didn't see her again that morning but was grateful not to have to dance around each other in the mirror. I'd lived alone for a while now and was used to doing what I wanted when I wanted. That said, it worked out fine and I was at the temp agency on time, ready to go.

My first assignment was as a receptionist for a major investment bank downtown. Since it was a bank I'd heard of, I knew it was kind of a big deal, but all I did that first day was answer one particular phone line.

"You'll sit here," the woman showing me around said, walking me into a circular reception desk where I would sit in an elevated chair to see over the counter. "I'm Sarah, the office manager. Here's how the phone works. The first line is the main line. That's the only one you need to worry about.

You answer with the bank name and then transfer the calls as necessary. Here is a list of extensions." She pointed to a long list, showing names and four digit extensions. "Transfer by hitting the 'transfer' button and then dialing the extension. Introduce each caller before you hang up. If there is no answer after four rings, take a message. Messages go here." She pointed to a series of cubbies under the counter with names next to them. "You'll be busy, Natalie. Think you can handle it?"

"Sure." I settled myself in. The phone in front of me had about sixteen lines on it, all of which seemed to ring constantly, but the only one I was responsible for was the main line coming in. The pace was fine, but when Sarah came out to relieve me for my lunch, I was tired. Who knew answering calls could be so exhausting?

Since I was in the financial district, I got a sandwich and wandered to Battery Park to eat. It was beginning to be cold, but there was still sunshine bouncing off the water, and it buoyed my mood. It felt good to be doing something, to be working toward a goal again. I'd hit rock bottom, and I was making my way back out. I had a place to live and a job—at least for now. The only thing still missing was CJ.

I spent the hour staring out at the Statue of Liberty standing in the harbor and pulling up old memories of the times I'd spent with CJ. I let myself see his eyes, his smile. I pulled up a memory of his voice. Thinking of him, now that I knew he wasn't still angry with me, was a little bit like being with him. When I returned from lunch, I felt happy. It was almost like I'd had lunch with CJ.

———

Catalina was already home when I got back to the apartment. She switched off the television and stood as soon as I walked in. "How was your first day?"

"It was fun," I told her. "Not too difficult. Just answering phones. They want me for the next two weeks, so I guess that's good."

"Isn't it kind of boring?" Catalina's face showed the disdain she clearly felt for answering phones.

I nodded. "I think it will be after two weeks." I poked around in the refrigerator, pulling out a yogurt just as my phone rang in my bag. "Hello?" I pulled the phone out and tried to balance it on my shoulder as I opened the yogurt.

Catalina lost interest in me and went into her room. She left the door standing open, so I didn't interpret it as unfriendly.

"Natalieeee," it was Lulu. She had a habit of extending my name.

"Hi, Lu, how are you?"

"Andrew just called. Tamara is back at the hospital."

My heart sank, and a chill ran through me. "Oh no. Is she okay? What happened?" I imagined Tamara collapsing again and cringed, wondering where she had been, if she had been alone.

"I don't really know, but he said we should come down. Do you have any numbers for her family?"

"No, I don't think so."

"She doesn't want to call them, but Andrew says she really needs someone to come. He won't tell me very much. I'm going now."

"I'll meet you down there. It'll take me a while to get there," I said. My mind was spinning. How could I get numbers for Tamara's family? "Why can't Andrew ask Tamara for a way to contact her family?"

"I don't know. I think she isn't close with them." Lulu was slightly out of breath.

"Are you running?"

"Walking to the hospital. It would take longer to try to get a cab."

I missed being so near the village. "I'll be down there in forty minutes."

"Okay."

"Call me if you get a room number or anything. Should I call Candace or Tom?"

"I'll call Candace now."

"I'll call Tom. See you in a bit."

I put down the phone and stuck my head in Catalina's room. "Tamara is back in the hospital. I'm going now. Do you want to come?"

Catalina was sitting in the center of her bed with a book. Her big eyes widened, and she nodded, scooting off the bed without saying anything.

"I'm going to change, and then we'll go." I dashed to my room, changed into jeans, and pulled my hair up into a messy knot. We were on the subway heading south five minutes later.

"What happened?" Catalina asked me as we sat side by side in the plastic orange and yellow subway seats.

"She's sick. I don't know exactly what happened this time. She has some kind of genetic liver disease. She won't talk much about it, but I learned a little bit when I stayed with her. I guess her brother has it, too."

"Did you call him?"

I wished I could. "I don't have his number. I don't know anything about her family, really. I don't even know her hometown, so I'm not sure how to look them up."

I hoped it wasn't serious enough that her parents needed

to know. My dad would want to know if I went to the hospital, I thought. Even if it was just for a stubbed toe.

"Didn't she grow up with that hottie cowboy?" Catalina asked.

"Oh my gosh, Spider! Yes!" I could call Spider. He knew her family, and he should know where she was anyway. He seemed to really care about Tamara. "Do you remember his real name though? How do I get a number for a guy called 'Spider'?"

Catalina shook her head, her dark hair falling around her shoulders and brushing the top of the light blue cashmere cardigan she wore. "It's probably in her phone. Maybe we can find that when we get there."

That was a good plan. I felt a little less panicked, knowing there might be something I could do to help. Catalina was staring out the subway window. "Thanks, Catalina."

She looked at me, surprise showing in her dark eyes. "You're welcome, Natalie."

———

When we came up from the subway, I had a message from Lulu giving me the floor number where Tamara's room was located and telling me that we couldn't see her because she was in intensive care. We rushed off the elevators to find Lulu, Gregoire, Candace, and Tom already sitting in the waiting area, worry and fear scrawled across their features.

"What's going on?" I asked, hugging Lulu.

"Her kidneys are failing," Lulu said, tears in her eyes. "We have to call her family."

"Is she awake?"

"Off and on," Lulu said. "She refused to give Andrew their information. He says we can't make her because she's not a minor."

Andrew came through a set of double doors nearby, Gabe close behind him. Both men wore blue scrubs, and it was hard to put this very institutional image in line with the casual guys I hung out with on the weekends.

"How is she?" Lulu asked as everyone stood.

"Not good." His fingers pulled nervously at each other. "Listen, Dr. Charles has been caring for her for a while, and she is here with her. She put her on the transplant list a few weeks ago for a liver, but she needs one now."

We stared at him, and Lulu made a little sound of surprise.

"A live donor can donate part of their liver," he said, "and the rest will grow back."

"Like a worm," Candace said.

We all stared at her.

"Didn't you ever hear that? Or a starfish. It'll grow its arms back." She shrugged and looked back at Andrew.

"Yeah, like that, Candace. Anyway, it's not a small thing to donate a liver. There are risks for the donor as well as the recipient, but you could save Tamara's life. I just wanted to throw it out there. We'll look for a match through the hospital system, but it could be a few weeks or more before we find one. We usually recommend that friends and family get tested for a match, too."

Candace nodded and stepped forward. "Show me the way. I rock every test I take."

"I'll do it too," I said, not even really considering that we were talking about open surgery and a hospital stay.

Everyone else nodded and volunteered as well, and while I was terrified for my friend, it was wonderful to see everyone coming together as a family.

"Did you get in touch with Tam's parents?" Gabe asked.

"I don't even know where they live in Indiana," I said, frustration making my voice darker. "Is there any way to get

Tamara's phone? I could call them if they're in there or look for Spider. I'm sure he knows how to reach them."

Gabe nodded and disappeared through the double doors again.

Andrew gave each of us a form to fill out. "I'll be right back with the transplant nurse, who will tell you what you might be signing up for. This evaluation is the first step. If everything looks good there, we'll do a quick blood test to see if you're a blood match, and then there are x-rays and other tests to look for liver compatibility."

"Is Tamara okay until then?" I asked.

Andrew nodded. "She's stable for now, but things could change pretty quickly, so this has to happen fast."

We all dropped our heads, filling out the health questionnaires he'd given us.

A few minutes later, Gabe came back out, holding Tamara's phone. "She doesn't know I took it," he said, looking guilty. "If this ever comes up, I didn't." He glanced around and looked relieved that no one from the hospital was nearby. He could probably get in trouble for taking a patient's phone.

"Thanks." I took the phone and scrolled through her contacts. It was all first names, and there was no "mom" or "dad" listed. I couldn't remember her brothers' names and felt like hope was slipping away. I'd have to just call every number and ask enough questions to find the right ones. I checked her call log as a last ditch effort and found a call from a couple weeks ago at the end of the list. Gaige. The name was vaguely familiar, and I took a chance that Gaige might be Spider and dialed.

The phone rang once, and then a languorous deep voice answered, "Tamara. I knew you'd come to your senses eventually and realize you can't live without me."

Okay then, that was one way to answer the phone. I'd

have to mention that to Tamara when this was all over. This was one cocky cowboy. "Is this Spider?"

"This isn't Tamara." His voice had changed. He was serious now, businesslike.

"It's Natalie Pepper, Tamara's friend. Spider?"

"Yeah. Is she okay?"

"No. We're at St. Vincent's. Third floor."

"On my way." He hung up.

I put Tamara's phone in my purse. I had no doubt she'd be pissed if she knew I'd called Spider. And I had no doubt that I'd done exactly the right thing for once in my life.

Chapter Twenty-Six

A ROOM OF MIRRORS

Tamara

MY DAYS WERE confusion and blackness. Were they hours? Were they weeks? I was in the hospital. I knew it by the smell. I saw Gabe, and I saw Spider. I saw Hal and Brody and Trask and Jeff, all my brothers, gathered around me. They were swimming, and there was a light in the sky that blinded me and made every image surreal and confusing. They weren't really there. I knew they weren't.

And I knew I was dying.

"Hang in there, Tam..." Spider's voice floated through darkness, and I grasped it with every ounce of energy I had, dangling from the small refuge it offered and clinging to it as I hung out over the dark tumultuous emptiness.

"She's not awake." Another familiar voice.

"Baby! Oh God..." Mom?

I wanted to reach out to her. Why was my mom here?

"Honey." Dad. Strong, stoic. Was he talking to me? Or to Mom? I heard sobbing.

Oh shit. If my mother was here, I was surely dying. I struggled for consciousness but gave up, acknowledging the fact that the cavalry had been called in. This was some kind of last-ditch effort, and I probably didn't have a chance. This wasn't how I imagined it happening. Even with this shitty disease, I'd imagined myself leading a long life. I didn't want to, but I thought my brothers and I would bury our parents. I'd get married. If I was honest, in every single one of my visions of married life, it was Spider by my side. Maybe I couldn't have kids, but I'd live a good life. I would beat this stupid disease, or at least come to some kind of truce with it. It wasn't going to get me—that's what I'd always told myself.

Yet I was here, in this cold empty room with water all around me. Where the hell was I? No, not water... Mirrors? With moving images of my past. I tried to turn around, but it was like an invisible force was holding me still, forcing me to look into the windows that reflected my past to me.

I was leaving home.

I was laughing with my brothers, rolling on the floor of our living room.

I was kissing Gaige in the barn, and the Indiana sky was bursting with stars outside as the cicadas screamed louder than my crazy heart.

I was dying.

Chapter Twenty-Seven

A COWBOY CIRCUS

Natalie

SPIDER ARRIVED within an hour of my calling him, all long limbs and sexy blue eyes in a whirlwind of action. He stormed around, demanding to be let in to see Tamara. He had Andrew and Gabe paged and threatened to tear the hospital to shreds if they didn't let him past the double doors that led to the intensive care wing where Tamara lay, unconscious, according to Andrew.

Dr. Charles appeared after a few minutes of Spider's fury caused a ruckus in the waiting area, and he darted to her side. "I'm not fucking around. Tam is my family and I want to see her."

"Look. Gaige?"

Spider nodded, confirming his name.

"No one is allowed in there right now. We've just gotten her stable, and she needs to rest. If you could help us, though, we'd appreciate it."

"I'm trying to help!" Spider was running his hands through his hair, practically shaking with frustration and energy. "All I want in the world is to help, and I can't!"

Dr. Charles stared at the man who had just screamed at her in the intensive care waiting room, as if she knew that he would eventually come to his senses and pull himself together.

"I'm sorry," he finally said.

She stood still, watching him.

"I can help. I'm sorry. I'm a friend from childhood. I just... I've known Tam my whole life."

"Okay. Well, we need you, then. Can you please call her family?"

Spider whistled, long and low. "She won't like it."

"I understand, but is the relationship with them one that you think matters to her at all?"

Spider's mouth tightened. "Yeah."

"Then we'd better get them here if they can come."

"Okay."

Dr. Charles turned to go.

"Doc?"

She turned back around.

"What do I tell them? When can we see her?"

"Tell them that she's in critical condition awaiting a liver transplant from a living or cadaver donor. Tell them that her kidneys are failing, but that we can keep her alive for a few days. Tell them to get here as quickly as they can and that we're doing everything in our power to save her life. You can see her when I'm confident that she's stable."

Spider stared after the doctor when she'd gone through the doors at the end of the hallway, and I moved to his side. "Do you want help making the calls?" I asked.

My voice seemed to bring him back to the present. "Nah."

He smiled at me, cocky cowboy facade back in place to some degree. "I got this."

He wandered to the other side of the waiting room and I heard him talking in a low voice, repeating what the doctor had said as I waited with everyone else for the initial blood results.

"Natalie Pepper and Catalina Greaves?" A nurse stood near the elevators.

We both stood and approached the nurse.

"You are both blood type matches for Tamara Hunt. We'll take some more blood and do some X-rays to see if either of you might be a donor for your friend."

We answered in unison and followed the nurse through another set of doors on the other side of the waiting area, glancing at one another. I wondered if I looked as frightened as Catalina suddenly did.

Over the next few hours, I felt like a lab rat, even though everyone I dealt with was very nice. They put me in a gown and took Catalina in the other direction. After that I waited. First, I waited in a small examining room and then in a lounge with a television and magazines. They did some X-rays, and then I waited some more. They drew more blood, and there was more waiting. I have no idea how long the entire process took, but in the end, they had me dress again and then rejoin my friends to wait more.

"What's going on?" Candace asked when I came back out to the waiting area.

By now, it was after midnight. Everyone was still there, sprawled in stiff chairs around the intensive care lounge. Lulu had a little bit of pull with the nurses as "Dr. Barton's girlfriend," and she'd managed to score some blankets and pillows. Although Andrew was an ER doctor, he checked on Tamara regularly and came out to update everyone as often as he could.

"I don't know," I told Candace. "They just sent me back out. They took X-rays and a ton of blood. I guess they'll have to put it through the lab and everything…"

Catalina wandered out the doors I'd just come through, looking traumatized with her hair sticking up on one side and her makeup smudged.

"Hey," I said.

She smiled at me and sat down in the empty chair at my side.

"That was terrifying," she said. "I hate having blood drawn."

I nodded. "Me too."

"I hope one of us can help Tamara," she said.

I nodded again, looking at her. It felt strange to sit next to Catalina and not be on edge. I still didn't trust her fully, but I was no longer worried that having me move in was part of some greater plot to ruin my life. Plus, since I'd managed to pretty much ruin my life all on my own, it wasn't a great risk even if that was her plan. I still didn't understand the way she'd treated me prior to this, though, and needed to find out once everything with Tamara had calmed down.

Spider sat next to Gregoire, still high strung and fidgety.

"Did you manage to talk to Tamara's parents?" I asked him.

"Yeah. Her dad isn't my biggest fan. I had to convince him that this wasn't somehow my fault."

"Did he know she was sick?"

"Yeah, but he always thought that spending time with me was bad for her condition, that I was distracting, and we were out running around when she should have been resting."

"Weren't you friends with her brother too? Doesn't he have the same disease?"

Spider sighed. "Hal. Yeah, he does. Tamara's father is old-fashioned though. Hal's a man. He can take care of himself, right?"

I shook my head, glad my own father wasn't the type to thrust me into a stereotype just because I was a girl. He assumed other things about me that weren't true—that I was flighty and irresponsible. "Are they coming?"

"Yeah. You're about to meet the whole Hunt clan. Prepare yourself." He grinned, stood, and paced around the waiting area.

"Have you gotten to see her?" I asked as he strode by.

"No, and it's killing me." His voice was a harsh whisper now, and his hands were in his spiky dark hair. "She needs to know I'm here. That she's not alone."

"Andrew will tell her." I was trying to make him feel better, and myself, too. I hated that Tamara had brought herself here alone, that she hadn't called me when she started feeling bad.

"She's out. He can't tell her anything. But if I could hold her hand and talk to her, she'd know I'm here. She'd feel me here, and she'd know that I came." His voice was a ragged thread of emotion, and his eyes shone with tears on the edge of falling.

Spider was definitely still in love with my friend. I hoped she'd pull through this and give him a chance to tell her. I hoped he'd be brave enough to say the words.

After an hour of silent waiting, Dr. Charles came out and asked Catalina and I to come with her. We followed her to a small sitting room, side by side, our eyes wide. She waved us into chairs and took a seat across from us, spreading a folder open on a round table.

"Natalie, you are a match," Dr. Charles said. "Actually, Catalina, you are too. This is a very rare situation. In most cases, it's difficult to find one living donor who is a good match for a patient. Tamara's extremely lucky to have two.

Having the most common blood type helps, too, but there are so many other factors that this is really a unique occurrence."

Catalina and I looked at one another.

"You are both in good health, and you're both close enough to Tamara's physical size that either one of your livers should work, at least as far as we can tell at this point. There is always a chance her body will reject the transplanted organ, but all of the external factors are right.

"The question at this point needs to be settled between the two of you. I'd suggest that whoever has family closest might be the best match. We'll need to begin working in the morning, and you'll want to have someone here for you. You'll be in the hospital for a minimum of five days, and you cannot go back to work for at least six weeks. We usually recommend eight. You should check with your insurance and your employers in the morning to see if this is even feasible."

I sat up straighter. Though I had benefits with the temporary agency, they wouldn't kick in for another two weeks. I had elected continuing coverage from my previous job, but I didn't know how that worked in a situation like this. I'd have to make calls in the morning.

"I have excellent insurance," Catalina said, "through my employer and then a secondary through my father's business."

I turned to look at her, my mouth dropping open. Was she volunteering?

"And my parents live in the city."

Another shock. I realized I knew almost nothing about Catalina's family. "They do?"

She nodded, her deep brown eyes on me. "I'll do it, Pepper. You just started a new job. There's no way you can take off for eight weeks right now."

She was right. As much as I wanted to be the one to help Tamara, there was almost no way I could, and still take care of myself. I could think of nothing to say, so I just nodded back. "Thank you," I said.

"Well, I wouldn't settle anything until you've had some sleep," Dr. Charles said, standing. "Please be here at eight o'clock, and we'll go from there. You should all go home for the night." She nodded toward our gang of friends out in the waiting area with a little smile. "There's nothing you can do for Tamara here tonight, and I don't expect any changes in her condition at this point."

We returned to the waiting room and gave our friends the news. Everyone agreed that sleeping and then returning in the morning would be the best plan. Everyone except Spider.

"Nah," he said. "I'll camp out here. I brought a change of clothes, and I bet I can talk my way into a shower around here somewhere. Lots of cute nurses here who won't be able to resist my country charm." He shot us a grin and stretched himself out on a couch, pulling one of the blankets over his legs. "See y'all in the morning. I'll call you if there's anything going on."

We went outside to the curb together and hugged our goodbyes. Candace and I both needed to at least check in at work. Everyone else made plans to return early. Although I had a million questions for Catalina, I was practically asleep by the time we got home. The questions would wait.

———

The next morning found Catalina and I sitting across from one another in the bleary early hours, eating cereal and drinking coffee.

"Are you scared?" I asked her.

She raised one shoulder. "I guess so."

"What did your parents say?" She had called them first thing this morning, despite the hour.

"I guess they were surprised. They're going to try to stop by the hospital."

My mouth dropped open. "Try?" I said softly.

She nodded, taking another bite.

"They're pretty busy?" I suggested.

"Something like that. Or they don't give a shit. Might be that." She lifted one shoulder and let it fall, dismissing the entire issue.

I didn't say anything else. It was too early for deep conversation, but I understood something in that moment that I hadn't before and felt as if I knew Catalina as I never had. She tried to look like she didn't care, but it was clear in the sad set of her mouth that she did. Her parents lived right here in Manhattan, and they might be too busy to stop by the hospital where she was donating part of a vital organ to a friend they'd never met. I had dreaded telling my dad when I thought it'd be me making the donation but only because I knew he'd get on a plane and fly out here immediately and possibly never leave.

"Well, I'll be there as soon as I can be. Do you need any help packing or anything?" I had no idea what to offer, but despite our past, Catalina needed someone to stand next to her today.

She shook her head. "No, go to work, Pepper. I'll see you a little later."

I put away my cereal bowl and picked up my things. Today I was to go directly to the bank, which meant arriving by eight a.m.

The day was long and boring, punctuated by frequent phone calls from Lulu with updates.

"Tamara's family just got here," she told me around two. I could hear excited chatter and lots of masculine voices in the background. "The hospital has turned into a cowboy circus."

"I don't think that's a thing. A rodeo?"

"Yes. A rodeo. Tamara's brothers are all big and cute, and they all have on the biggest belt buckles I've ever seen."

I tried to picture four more cowboys sitting around the waiting room at St. Vincent's, kicking long Wrangler-clad legs out before them and wearing huge hats. Spider was the only honest-to-goodness cowboy I'd ever met. If they looked anything like him, lower Manhattan was in trouble.

"What are her parents like?" I asked.

"They seem very sweet. They are worried, of course. Her mother has decided to be in charge of everything. She moved all the furniture around."

"You're kidding."

"Not kidding."

That was new. I looked forward to meeting this woman. "Have they gotten to see her? How is she?"

"They let the family back when they got here. They said Tamara has been awake part of the day, so I think she got to see them. Spider went, too. I think the hospital staff is confused how many cowboys are actually her brothers, and he just slipped in."

I smiled. I knew he'd find a way to get back there.

When it was time for me to go, I'd learned that Catalina had been taken back to a room and that the transplant would happen the following day. Lulu had been back to visit her, but she said that she didn't think Catalina's family had been by to see her. My heart ached for her. It had been a long lonely day for her, and she was probably scared. I stopped through a bodega on my way to the hospital and picked up some flowers.

And then, as I walked, I did something I wasn't sure was right. I called CJ.

"Hey," he said, recognizing my number. "How are you?"

"Things are a little weird," I told him. "Tamara's in the hospital again. Catalina is donating part of her liver."

"Holy shit. Are they okay?"

"For now. Tamara's whole family got here today, I guess. I had to work. I'm on my way over there now. I thought maybe Andrew had told you."

"I've been really busy. I think he might've called, but I didn't get time to listen to messages." CJ sounded different, his voice ragged and thin.

"Are you okay?"

"I'm coming down there. We can talk then." He hung up.

I couldn't help but smile. I was going to see CJ. I didn't care what had happened between us before. I felt like we might be able to start over, and despite all the bad feelings, at this moment, all I wanted was to see him. My stomach fluttered, and everything inside me reminded me of the very beginning of our relationship—before we even had one—when I was excited just to be in the same room with him, when I thought there might possibly be a chance for us some day.

I rushed to the hospital, arriving at the third floor waiting room to find a state of utter chaos as Tamara's family took over.

TRANSPLANTS FOR ALL MY FRIENDS

Tamara

I WASN'T DYING. Not yet.

I could tell my mother was nearby before she burst through the door into my room. Even before she appeared, the atmosphere around me had changed, had energized and reorganized. Even in my half-dead super groggy drugged-out state, I knew it was Adelaide Hunt. No one else could take charge of things the way she could. I swear, my mother could force oxygen to change its structure if she wanted it to. It just took the right amount of force and sugary sweetness.

"There's my darlin' daisy." She picked up my hand and leaned in to kiss me through the paper mask they'd made her wear. "Oh, honey." Tears rolled down her cheeks, and she shook her head at me.

"Hi, Mom."

"Tamara, honey..." Here it was. She didn't even have to say

it, but she did. "Why did you have to drag yourself to this Godforsaken city so far away from home? This would never have happened if you'd stayed where you belonged. I could have looked after you, made sure you were resting—"

"Mom." I could barely summon the energy to lay here and be awake, but I found the force I needed to interrupt my mother's wailing rant.

She stopped, her eyes widening.

"This is my home now. I'm glad I left. I missed you, but I have a life here."

She shook her head. "Oh, honey..."

"No. Listen." My voice was raspy, and I took the sip of water she offered. "I get to be my own person here. It's been good. Really good. Even if this is it, I'm still glad I got to find out who I am outside of Indiana. I love you, Mom, but you fill all the spaces you're in 'till there's no room for me. You all do."

Her eyes narrowed as she visibly thought about my words and tried to decide if anger would be the right response. She must have settled on disappointment instead, because she tilted her head sideways and patted my hand. "Well, none of it matters now. You'll get better, and we'll take you home."

Anger bubbled inside me, but I was too tired to give it a voice. I'd handle this later.

The door opened again, and all of Indiana filed in, wearing thin blue paper masks and blue jeans. My brothers and father circled my bed, and Spider appeared opposite my mom, taking my hand delicately between his big warm ones as if he worried he might break me. The boys all talked, joking and shifting their weight, glancing around the room and making ridiculous jokes.

"Hey sis," Hal said from the foot of my bed.

"If you wanted us to come visit, you could've just asked,"

Trask joked, his strawberry blond stubble making him look rougher than his baby face usually allowed.

Jeff leaned in. "It'd a been a hell of a lot cheaper to fly you back instead of us coming here. Plus, I don't think LaGuardia airport will ever recover. Mom rearranged their entire luggage-return system."

"I just made some suggestions so it could run a little quicker," Mom said, her face crumpling.

"She's got ideas about food service on planes, too," Hal said under his breath. "I think we're banned on American now. We might have to come live with you."

My dad smiled down at me but didn't speak. Brody did the same, the two of them looking like a mirror image of the other as they always had.

I couldn't speak anymore, had used all my energy on Mom, but seeing my entire family around me, with Spider silently holding my hand, I felt like it would be okay if I just slipped away now. They loved me. They were all here, and I was just so tired.

The nurse came in and whisked them all away again, but my heart felt lighter than it had. Before she could pull Spider from my side, he leaned in and whispered, his breath hot in my ear,

"Don't you dare leave me, Tamara. I have big plans for us. I love you, and I know you love me, too. Life is way too short to play it cool anymore. I'm waiting for you long as it takes. I'll be right here. Just like forever." He put two fingers over my heart and kissed my cheek, moving his mask out of the way to do it.

"Sir," the nurse said, having waited patiently although I was sure she was probably breaking some kind of rule in letting him kiss me.

"Coming." He held my gaze as he stood. "I'm coming. I'll be right outside, Tam."

Time moved like liquid, thank to the drugs being pumped through my IV for pain and to try to stabilize my struggling kidneys and useless liver. Light flew from one side of my room to the other, shafts of sunlight chasing each other around the walls as I watched. My family had come in, Spider had come back once before being shooed out again by a different nurse, and Dr. Charles visited now and then. It might have been days, or hours, I wasn't sure. I felt like I floated in some kind of in between space between waking and sleeping, between living and dying.

I understood that someone had a liver for me, that I would be receiving a transplant. At times, I wasn't sure if that had already happened. From the way the air around me dampened time and emotion, it was possible that I'd been in surgery and just not realized it. Or forgotten.

Either way, I had no control over anything, and there was something freeing in that knowledge. I'd given up struggling. What would happen would happen, and I was happy to have my family around me, to have Spider holding my hand and telling me he loved me.

If this came to an end, if I ever came back to myself again, I would tell him I loved him, too. I would stand next to him, on a box if necessary, so that I could whisper right in his ear and be there by his side. Spider, I realized, had never tried to stop me from doing anything. He'd worried about me. He'd cared for me. With Spider, I'd been free to explore the world on my terms, knowing he would be there to catch me if I fell down.

I used to think it was limiting, having a pair of arms right there, ready to pick me up, ready to push me out of the way if something looked too challenging. I used to think having

Spider there meant he expected me to fall. Instead, it meant he loved me enough to let me fall, to let me take on the challenges that came across my path. It meant he would always be there to cushion the landing and help me back up. I finally understood there was a difference.

Chapter Twenty-Nine

FAMILY TORNADO

Natalie

THE ENVIRONMENT of the hospital waiting room had changed entirely, and so had the layout of the furniture, as Lulu had warned.

Adelaide Hunt was clearly the queen of her castle, and there were five plaid-clad men scattered about the room on call to do her bidding. When I first walked in, she embraced me into her strong arms. The scent of rosewater and baby powder flooded my senses for a moment, and I had a fleeting image of what Tamara's childhood might have smelled like.

"Natalie Pepper," she trilled. "I have heard so much about you. Lord, I'm glad you were there to take care of my little girl when she needed you. You are a true friend, darlin'. It makes my heart happy to know there are genuine human beings in this mean old city."

One of the Hunt boys leaned in over his mother's shoulder, rolled his eyes, and shot me a grin. He had strawberry blond hair and a bright smile that reminded me of Tamara's.

I met each of the brothers in turn—Trask, Jeff, Hal, and Brody—and then met Tamara's father, who was as soft spoken as his wife was loud and commandeering. Once everyone had settled back into chairs, I asked Lulu if she could help me find Catalina, and we got in the elevator together.

"Those people are like a fucking tornado," Lulu said. There was both irritation and admiration in her voice, and I turned to stare at her. "What?" she asked.

"I can't figure out if you're jealous or angry."

She squinted her eyes. "I'm jealous. I can't imagine having enough family to literally take over a hospital."

"Well, just the one floor."

"Pepper, in comparison, I have no one." She stated it as a fact, but her eyes were sad. Lulu's family life had not been a happy one.

"We make our own families here," I said, really believing it was true.

Lulu nodded. "It'd still be nice to have thirty cowboys ride to my rescue whenever I needed them."

"Don't forget they were part of the reason Tamara left to come here."

The elevator doors opened, and Lulu pulled me down a hallway past several open doors. "Do we need to ask directions?" I asked her while she hauled me along.

"I was just here. I know where I'm going."

I followed obediently and Lulu led me into an open door. A very fat bald man lay sprawled in the bed inside the room, and both he and the woman at his side looked surprised to be interrupted by two tall women who were clearly lost.

"Wrong," Lulu declared, turning on her heel.

"Feel better," I offered, the heat in my neck telling me that I was turning bright red.

I stopped Lulu in the hallway. "Did they move her?"

She shook her head. "All the hallways and doors look exactly the same. Let's call Andrew." She pulled out her cell phone.

"Or we could just ask," I pointed to the nurses' station as I approached it.

The nurse behind the desk gave me the room number at the same time Lulu reached Andrew, who had probably been pulled away from a patient to speak to her. "Never mind," she sang. "I love you!" She hung up before Andrew could have possibly said a word and followed me to Catalina's room.

I stepped in cautiously, knocking on the open door first to let her know we were coming in.

"Come in," Catalina's voice floated to us.

We walked to her bedside and Catalina wiped at her face. She looked small and frail, lying in the hospital bed with her hair pulled back in a headband and no makeup on.

"These are for you," I said, finally putting the vase of flowers down.

She smiled, but the sadness on her face remained. "Thank you. That was sweet."

There was another vase of flowers near the far window, roses and orchids and baby's breath overflowing an extravagant vase. "Look at these," Lulu gasped, petting them as if they were delicate kittens. "Pepper, I think you have been outdone."

"My parents," Catalina said.

Lulu was already reading the card out loud. She rarely worried about invading the privacy of others. "Get well soon. Mummy and Dad." She lifted an eyebrow. "You call your mother 'mummy'?"

Catalina shook her head, and the sadness in her eyes grew deeper. "I don't call her at all. And she doesn't call me, so it works out."

"They're not coming by?" I guessed.

A tear leaked out of the corner of Catalina's eye. "No. I didn't expect them to."

Lulu and I sat on opposite sides of Catalina's bed. "Oh, honey," Lu said. "I'm sorry. But we're here for you."

How could any parents be too busy to cross town to see their daughter when she was about to have a vital organ removed from her body, cut in half, and replaced?

"Do you want to talk about it?" I didn't know my new roommate well enough to pry.

"It's simple, really. I didn't marry the boy they'd arranged for me to marry. I didn't ensure the future wealth of my family and our future offspring and decided to go off and live in a squalid apartment with rabble like Maggie instead."

My eyebrows shot up. "Seriously?"

"People still arrange marriages here?" Lulu sounded shocked.

"My people do," Catalina said. "It's a wonder they didn't cut me off completely, but money is like water to them. They just quit acknowledging me instead. They still pay me my allowance and provide any little thing I might need. Except their presence."

I nodded, even though I had only the smallest understanding of what she was talking about.

We stayed in Catalina's room for an hour or so, until a nurse told us that visiting hours had ended and ushered us out. Catalina looked better when we left, smiling and even laughing as we told her about Tamara's family.

"I'll see you tomorrow," I told her as I left. "I'll be here the whole time, okay?"

She nodded and whispered, "Thank you."

———

A game of five-card stud had been set up in the intensive care waiting room and was in full swing when we returned with snacks from the cafeteria. CJ was in the midst of it, sitting next to Spider and laughing with Tamara's brothers. He looked out of place in his tailored shirt and dark pants, but he looked amazing.

As soon as Lulu and I put the snacks on the table in the center of the room, CJ stood and walked over, pulling me into his arms and hugging me. There was something more than friendly in the hug, and I allowed my hands to cling to him, to feel the warmth of his back and to remember what it felt like to be pressed up against him like this with nothing between us. No clothes, no misunderstandings, no mistakes.

"I'm glad to see you," he said.

"Me too."

His face was drawn, thinner, and there were lines around his eyes. I couldn't imagine that I was looking my best, given the late nights and worry about Tamara, but I hadn't expected to see such a change in CJ.

"What's going on?" I asked him.

He took my arm and pulled me to a corner of the waiting room. I glanced up as we walked to see Adelaide Hunt's eyes following us while she doled out the food I'd set out. I got the sense she didn't miss much.

"You're freaking me out," I told him as we sat.

"I'm pretty freaked out, too."

What the hell was he talking about?

"You were always worried that Irene had some ulterior motive when it came to me, right? Well, you were right. But it wasn't what you think."

I watched his face as emotions crowded into his eyes and he paused.

"Natalie, she's my mother."

Surely I hadn't heard him right. The raucous laughter coming from the other side of the room was too distracting. "What?"

"She's my mother."

"How is that possible? Your mother lives in Buffalo. You've told me that a million times."

He shook his head slowly. "I was adopted. They just told me, but only because they had to. Because Irene was about to tell me and they wanted it to come from them."

"Oh my God, CJ." I leaned forward and took his hand. "Why didn't they tell you years ago? When you were little?"

CJ shrugged and left his hand between mine, squeezing my fingers gently. "When we were little, I think parents just wanted to pretend that the children they adopted were really theirs. The birth mothers usually didn't get any rights, and the kids never found out."

"I don't know what to say. Are you okay? What happened when they told you?" I couldn't believe so much had happened in CJ's life since we'd talked last—so much important incredible stuff.

And that I hadn't been there.

"I don't know how to feel about it. I was angry at my parents at first, for not telling me." He stared at our hands. "And then I got really mad at Irene. She's known for years since I was a little kid. It's like she basically plotted a way to get back into my life."

I thought about that. "In a way, I don't really blame her."

His head snapped up, and his eyes caught mine. "You're going to be on Irene's side *now*?" He was incredulous, and it wasn't a surprise.

"I'm not on her side, but I could see why she'd want to stay close to her child, to try to be a part of your life."

"She was totally dishonest about it the whole time. She's

been weaseling her way into my life since I was in graduate school. And she told me that she's watched me since I was a baby!"

"That's a little creepy."

"You think?" He shook his head. "I quit. I went back to All Night and took my old job back. I told Irene I never wanted to see her again."

I blinked. That seemed over-reactive, even if she had been dishonest. "How are your parents? Are you still angry with them?"

He shook his head. "No. I spent a couple days at home, and we talked a lot about everything. They told me they'd considered telling me and about how they'd decided not to. They told me how happy they were when they got me, how long they'd wanted a little boy. I know they love me. They didn't do anything wrong. They gave me a home and a fantastic life. They're good people."

"So where does this leave Irene?" Why did I feel sad for the vulgar cougar who had caused so much trouble in our lives?

"I don't know."

"Are you really just never going to see her again?"

He sighed. "I don't know."

We sat together in silence for what felt like hours, holding hands in the corner of the waiting room. There were so many things that I wanted to say, to ask, but it felt more right at that moment to just be. To just be with CJ. To be there for him.

I should have gone home that night, and CJ looked uncomfortable in his work clothes, too, but neither of us seemed ready to break the moment we'd found where we were together again, not discussing the people who had come between us or the mistakes I had made. We held hands and stayed in the corner as the waiting room circus settled down around us. The Hunts had a hotel room at the Washington Square Hotel, and throughout the night, they came and went in shifts.

When the first yellow sparks of light gleamed across the waiting area, my eyes were already open. CJ's head was in my lap, and I'd been sitting for hours just watching him, wondering how long this second could last, how long it would be before all the things that had come between us sprouted arms and legs and voices again. For hours, I'd rubbed his head, let my hands feel the coarse softness of his hair and watched the peaceful rise and fall of his chest as the heart I loved beat within it. For a little while, I'd been peaceful and happy, despite the difficult scene unfolding around me.

But when morning officially arrived in the form of Adelaide Hunt shepherding along a girl pushing an enormous coffee cart, CJ woke up and lifted his head, and the quiet hours ended.

"She said she don't normally come up to this floor, but I assured her there were plenty of hungry and thirsty folks up here to make it worth her while," Mrs. Hunt explained as she helped the girl maneuver the cart out of the elevator.

"I can't stay up here long, though," the girl said, looking like she'd been given absolutely no choice in the situation.

We all bought breakfast, and the noise level steadily increased as the Hunt brothers came back to life, coffee and doughnuts infusing their bloodstreams. Although they were noisy and perhaps not entirely refined, the Hunt family seemed to stick together. They brought a certain amount of good humor to a dire situation. While Adelaide was pushy and bossy, having her around made me feel like the situation was well in hand.

Once the coffee cart had returned to wherever it belonged, I realized I needed to do something about work. I couldn't risk being fired again. "I have to call into the office and see what I need to do," I told CJ. I pulled my phone from my bag, but it was dead. I might have to give in and update my cell soon. CJ handed me his sleek black flip phone. "Thanks."

I called the temp agency and explained what was going on.

"You should call into the client and see what they want you to do," the girl told me. "We can send someone else over for today, but they might just decide to keep whoever replaces you, and then you'd have to find another position."

"Thanks." I hung up, called the bank, and explained what was happening to my manager, Marc. I'd told him a little bit about it yesterday, so he wasn't surprised.

"We'd like to have you back when you can be here," Marc said. "We've never had a receptionist consult on our branding before, and the marketing people actually really liked some of your suggestions on the website."

I'd been a little bored, and in my free time, I had edited the firm brochure they'd handed me when I'd come in the first day.

"Oh," I said, surprised. "Well, that's good." I hadn't actually intended anyone to see my suggestions, but I must have left my notes on the desk.

"Just keep me updated, okay?"

"Okay," I hung up.

"You're not at AdTrack anymore?" CJ looked confused as I handed his phone back to him.

"I got fired," I said.

His eyebrows shot up, but he didn't ask why. I was glad. There were a lot of things we needed to talk about, but now didn't feel like the right time.

Dr. Charles appeared at eight-thirty to tell us that both Catalina and Tamara were being prepped for surgery and that we could quickly say hello to them. "But you cannot all go in to see Ms. Hunt," Dr. Charles said.

"Of course we won't all go," Adelaide agreed. And then the entire Hunt family, with Spider, Lulu, Candace and Gregoire followed her through the swinging doors.

CJ and I went to see Catalina.

Her eyes widened when she saw CJ at my side. This was one topic she and I had not discussed.

"Hey, Catalina." CJ gave her a kiss on the cheek. "This is such an amazing thing you're doing for Tam."

She smiled. "I'm just glad I can help."

"Do you need anything?" I asked her. "Should I check in with your work, or is everything all set?"

"All set." She reached out a hand, and I offered her mine, surprised at the gesture. "Thanks, Natalie. It's nice to have a friend here. This is a little scary."

"Of course it is," I said. "But you don't need to worry at all. Andrew says the transplant team is awesome. I'll be waiting for you to get out, okay?"

"Me too," CJ said.

"Thanks, you guys." Catalina looked tiny and young, and just as beautiful as ever, even in the paper cap they'd used to cover her hair.

As we left her room, anger at her family bubbled in my chest. How could they let her face this alone when they were just a few miles away? How could they not be worried, be terrified, for her?

"There's nothing you can do about that," CJ said when I told him. "All you can do is be a friend."

I nodded.

"And Natalie?" He looked unsure whether to continue his

thought, his dark eyes holding mine as he paused. "I'm proud of you."

I didn't know what to say, so I just held his gaze. We returned to the waiting room to sit side by side with our friends—our family away from family—to wait.

Chapter Thirty

JOY AND PAIN

Tamara

I DIDN'T MAKE the choice to slip away. I didn't follow the light or hear strands of soft music beckoning me. I saw my family, a mass of smiling worried faces looking down on me as they wheeled me to surgery. I felt the pressure of Spider's hand, heard his voice through the others, heard him say he loved me. And then I let go. I breathed in, breathed out. I didn't hurt, didn't think, didn't care. I just floated in a blissful calm where no will weighed on me, not mine, not Spider's, not that of the indomitable Adelaide Hunt. It was fine. It was comfortable. It was easy.

It was nothing like the pain that followed.

When I opened my eyes next, it was because I wanted to stop the evil madman who'd evidently snuck to my bedside to rip out my guts with a rusty butter knife, but when my heavy eyelids finally lifted, I was alone. Alone with the unendurable pain that pulsed through me, turning me inside out, threatening to drive me from my mind for once and for all. It took every ounce of effort I could summon, but slowly I managed to lift my hand to the side of the bed where a button was mounted. A red button. As a searing burn ripped through my side, I pressed it.

Chapter Thirty-One

NOT THE PIE-MAKING KIND

Natalie

WE HAD eight hours to wait while Catalina and Tamara were in surgery and recovery. The Hunt family continued its rotation through the one hotel room they'd reserved, sleeping and showering in shifts. Even though this had to be trying and frightening, there wasn't a single member of the family who didn't seem to take the whole thing in stride. I attributed a large part of that to Adelaide, who seemed to be confident and in charge everywhere she went. I marveled at her strength and energy as she bustled about, chiding her boys to take their boots off the tables and reminding everyone to drink water and stretch their legs. Brody, Tamara's oldest brother, must have been at least thirty-five years old, but he took orders from his mother just like the rest of them, letting her push him around like a child.

CJ eventually left, promising to return after a shower and a change of clothes, and after checking in at work. I didn't want to go far, so I let Lulu drag me to her apartment to borrow some of her things, since she lived in the Village just a few minutes from the hospital. When we returned, I excused myself to the restroom before heading back to the waiting area, which was now practically the Hunt family living room. They had piles of books and magazines, cards, and coolers of food stuck in various places. They were in this for the long haul.

The bathroom was cool and sterile-feeling, and every time I'd been in here, I had been alone. This time, a gentle sobbing greeted me as I entered, and I stopped in surprise to see Adelaide Hunt slumped against the counter at the far end of the room, her head in her hands. She looked up, clearly surprised to see me, and wiped at her eyes.

"I guess it'd be downright silly to pretend I hadn't been crying," she said, turning to the mirror and tending to the long dark hair that had escaped her swept back knot.

"I wondered if there were any chinks in that armor, actually." I smiled. "It's a bit of relief to see that you're human."

Her face crumpled again, and her shoulders slumped. Her gaze caught mine in the mirror. "It's a reflex. Controlling everything. If I control everything, nothing bad can happen, right?"

I shrugged. "I never manage to be in control of anything, so I don't think I'm the best person to ask." I took a few steps toward her.

"It's just... Tam's been sick since she was a teenager, you know? And this hospital routine... well, you can see, the boys are used to it. We all are. We've done this kind of thing before, with Tam and with Hal." She shook her head. "You have these tender little babies, and you do everything you can for them. Then the world just takes them from you and tosses them around, and you can't do anything." Her gaze dropped to her hands, and she continued shaking her head back and forth. "I just can't do anything at all to stop it."

I crossed the room and put my arms around Adelaide. "It's going to be okay," I said, having no idea what other wisdom to offer.

"Or it won't be," she whispered. "Nothing we do will make a damned bit of difference either way."

I stepped back. "I don't believe that. I think Tam knows you're all here. She knows you love her and you're pulling for her. That's gotta count for something. She knows she matters to someone. It gives her strength, something to remember."

Adelaide nodded and tilted her head at me. "She's the only girl, you know. My fifth baby. I would have tried four or five more times, but poor Hamill, he only ever wanted two. He would have been happy with just Brody and Trask, but I wanted a little girl. I wanted bows and frills and someone who would be inside with me while those boys ran the cows around out there and farmed. I wanted a little girl to keep me company..." Her eyes filled with tears again. "All Tamara ever wanted was to get away."

I shook my head. "Ma'am?" I'd never used that word before in my life, but it felt right. "I don't think that's quite right. Tamara talks so fondly of life with you and her brothers, and Spider. She did want to get away but not from any of you. She just wanted a space where she could define herself." I didn't know how much more philosophy I should spew at a woman whose only daughter was currently open on a table in the hospital. "It didn't change her love for her family."

"But she didn't want to be with me, making pies and taking care of the boys."

I raised an eyebrow. "Forgive me for saying this, but I have a feeling you knew when Tamara was four or five that she wasn't going to be the pie-making type."

A smile flickered across Adelaide's features. "I did. I just hoped maybe one day things would be different."

"I think there's still time for pie. Maybe while Tam gets better? She's going to have a lot of down time."

"You are right. Perfect time for baking lessons." She pulled herself tall again and turned toward the door. "I'd better go make sure those boys haven't torn this place apart while I've been gone."

I smiled as her tall thin form moved out the door and felt a deep longing for my own mother. I wondered if Tam's mom would be willing to teach me to make pie, too.

———

Dr. Charles came through the double doors, Andrew on her heels. They both looked grim, and for a moment my heart dropped. I considered the things they might be about to say. Their faces sagged with weariness and the gravity of the whole situation hit me yet again.

"The surgery went fine," Dr. Charles said.

Tamara's brothers hooted and high-fived one another, while Adelaide slumped into her husband's arms.

"There are still a few days of uncertainty ahead, particularly for Tamara, since we need to see how her body takes the new liver," she continued. "Catalina did great. In the morning, they should both be ready for visitors."

Candace and Gregoire hugged everyone goodbye and made their way out, promising to return tomorrow, and Lulu followed close behind them with Tom at her heels.

I waited a little longer. I had promised to be there when Catalina woke up. The nurses at the station assured me that she couldn't receive any visitors before eight o'clock the following morning, so I hugged the Hunts goodbye and wandered out into the chilly air. I'd given Adelaide my number in case there were any changes.

It was late Thursday night, and there were pre-Halloween festivities going on around me in the Village as I walked to the east side to catch a train from Union Square. The Village is famous for celebrating Halloween with a certain glam-sham fabulousness that I didn't think happened in just the same way anywhere else. Boys and girls cross-dressed, and there was plenty of neon, spandex, and lots of feathered boas everywhere. It wasn't in full force yet, and I was sure it would be Saturday, but there were groups of people here and there that made me marvel at the way the city marched on despite the drama in our lives. Halloween in the Village lived and breathed, and New York City would continue to live, to evolve, no matter what events big or small might be wrought in the shadows of its tall buildings. At that moment, I was glad just to be a part of it.

Once I was back inside the quiet apartment Catalina and I now shared, I sat down on the couch and dialed CJ's familiar number.

He answered on the first ring. "How are they?" He sounded worried. "I almost came down, but I was at work so late, and you hadn't called so I figured they were still in surgery."

"They're both fine. They have to keep an eye on Tamara. I guess her body could reject the transplant, but they said we can visit Catalina in the morning, and Tamara too, probably."

He exhaled. "That's great. That's really good news."

"It is."

We were both quiet, each of us sitting on one end of the tenuous connection between us. I wasn't sure what to say next, how to reinforce that bridge we'd begun building again. Was our relationship repairable? Or had we had a reprieve due to the stress and fear that had come with Tamara's illness and the suddenly dire situation we all faced?

"Do you want me to come over?" CJ asked finally.

"Yes." I didn't hesitate. "But only if you want to."

"Of course I do." There was still something uneasy between us, but long days and nights spend focused on matters of real gravity, life and death, had made us both realize it could be overcome..

"I'm going to go back to the hospital pretty early."

"I know. I'll go with you."

"Okay." I waited. This was unfamiliar territory. Everything between us had evolved so easily, so naturally. If we were going to rebuild it, it seemed we would be doing it from scratch. And I wasn't sure how to begin.

"I'll see you in a bit."

"Bye."

We hung up, and I waited, adjusting chairs and fluffing pillows for no reason at all. When CJ arrived, the doorman buzzed up and I stood nervously by the open door for the elevator to arrive at our floor. CJ stepped out and walked toward me down the darkened hallway, and I felt like everything I wanted in life hinged on that moment. On that man. I'd spent so long trying to work out who I was supposed to be, trying to grow up and learn to make decisions on my own. Ronnie was always telling me to consider why I wanted something, to think about the alternatives to that thing, that choice. As CJ walked toward me, I felt like every choice I ever made had led me to this point, to standing in an open doorway, hoping CJ might walk through. It felt strange and momentous and surreal.

"Hey." He grinned at me and took me in his arms as he dropped his bag at our feet. He hugged me tight and then stepped back, picking up his duffle bag. "Want to go inside? I mean, it's a cool hallway and all..."

"Sorry." I stepped back so he could come inside, still not recovered from what had felt like a revelation in the hallway.

"It's pretty late." He put his bag next to the couch and looked around as if he'd never been here before. "Hey, the place looks nice."

"Yeah, it's working out okay." I walked into the kitchen, peering at CJ over the counter. It was strange feeling awkward with him, but he was here and that was the first step. I just wasn't sure what should happen next. It was already midnight, but I couldn't imagine just going to sleep now. Or going to bed and... not going to sleep.

"Think it's too late for a drink?" he asked, his bright eyes hopeful.

"Not at all after this week." I smiled as I turned to pull some things from the liquor cabinet. "What do you feel like?"

"Scotch?"

"We don't have scotch. Rum?"

He stood and came to rifle through the cabinet at my side. "Do you have any olives?" CJ pulled a bottle of vodka down and set it on the counter.

"We don't have much." Neither Catalina or I seemed to have taken on the role of lead grocery shopper, and since she'd been gone almost since I'd moved in, there wasn't much in the refrigerator. I pulled it open for CJ to inspect, leaning toward him.

"Let's see. Yes, you've got all the New York City staples. Mustard. Strawberry jam. A takeout container full of God-only-knows-what or how old it is... Relish... Kudos on the enormous block of Jarlsberg cheese." He grinned at me. "And olives!" He pulled out a jar that was half full, green olives floating in briny liquid. "How old is this?"

"I just moved in." I shrugged.

"The alcohol will neutralize any harmful bacteria," he said, sounding confident.

I raised an eyebrow.

CJ made two dirty martinis, and I followed him to the couch. We touched the rims of our glasses together and drank in silence for a few minutes.

"This is perfect," I said.

"The martini?" CJ asked.

I smiled. "Yes, but also... having you here. Just getting to sit next to you again. Feeling like maybe we are okay?"

I was asking. I needed to know if we were okay. I needed to know if he had forgiven me, what I could expect going forward. Were we headed back to solid ground? Were we back together tonight just because our friends were in trouble and we were showing some kind of solidarity?

CJ simply nodded. "It is," he agreed.

After a few minutes more, I couldn't sit and drink and not know what might happen. As much as I wanted to enjoy my time with CJ, I also needed to know where we were headed this time. If we were still together, if I could relax. "CJ? I asked.

His golden brown eyes found mine, and the deep warm depths of them steeled me for what was to come.

I wanted to just fall into his arms, but I needed to talk to him first. "What happens now? With us? I don't know how to think about this. I know I hurt you..."

He looked down into his drink, leaned forward, and set it on the table. "These last couple weeks, Natalie...I've done a lot of thinking." CJ's face remained calm, only a glimmer of stress in the tightness of his jaw. "I've thought about family and what that means, and I've thought about love. I thought a lot about us, about the choices you made, about the ones I made."

I nodded, not sure where he was going but relieved that he didn't seem angry or upset at least.

"And I decided that people screw up. People who love us

screw up and hurt us. Look at my parents. They did what they thought would protect me, and it ended up hurting me in the end." He shook his head lightly. "I don't know why you kissed someone else, really. But I think you just screwed up. With my parents, it didn't matter. Finding out they did something I didn't agree with didn't change the way I loved them. Finding out what you did... it didn't change the fact that I loved you."

My breath caught in my throat and tears gathered behind my eyes, but I wouldn't blink. I didn't want to cry—didn't want to move even, for fear he would change his mind suddenly.

CJ continued.. "But you and I have to be different. We have to trust each other. We have to be able to believe in each other. I know you're a good person, Natalie. I love you." His arms reached for me and I fell into them, burying my face in his shoulder. "I'm willing to trust you again. We don't have to drag out the details of the whole thing over and over. But I need to know that you love me, and that you won't hurt me like that again."

I wrapped my arms around him, feeling the warm solidity of him seeping into my body. He was really here, he was really back, and I could almost relax. "I won't. CJ, I'm so sorry. It was so stupid. I was stupid..."

"No. We're the same. We're just trying to figure things out as we go along. It isn't always going to be easy, but I had a chance to see what it was like without you in my life for a while, and I didn't like it." He pulled me close and I turned my head up to see him, his eyes darkening just before his mouth found my jaw, sending shivers skittering over my skin. "Please don't hurt me again, Natalie."

I shook my head, my hands finding the strong muscles at the back of his shoulders. My arms pulled him closer and I felt his heart beating against mine. "I won't," I breathed.

"I love you, Natalie."

"I love you too." I let myself be pushed back into the soft warm couch while CJ's mouth explored my neck, kissing my jawline until he found my mouth.

"I've missed you so much," he said.

After that, we didn't talk very much, but we said everything else that needed to be said.

Chapter Thirty-Two

HELL AND HIGH WATER

Tamara

THE NEXT TIME I opened my eyes, the pain wasn't as bad. There was a throbbing ache with a knife's hot edge somewhere under the bandages on my stomach, but it was manageable. I cleared my throat and opened my eyes, and heard movement in the room as the world tilted into focus.

"Tamara," my mother was by my side in a second. "My baby girl, there you are." She held up a straw, and I sipped at it, the cool liquid soothing my throat.

My dad jumped up from the chair behind her as if he'd just been shaken from sleep. "Hey, pip," he said. Dad referred to me as a pipsqueak since I'd been tiny. When all my brothers passed six feet and I remained barely over five, the name stuck.

"Hey, guys," I said. Although I'd fought the idea of calling them, it was good to see them here, and I knew it had to have been a rough few days. "How long was I out?"

"You had the transplant two days ago," Mom said. "We hoped we'd get to see you yesterday, but you needed to rest a little longer."

I'd been unconscious that long? No wonder I was so disoriented. I gazed around the room, and something in me crumpled in disappointment to find that Spider wasn't there. I knew it was ridiculous. I couldn't expect him to be by my side every minute of every day, and yet, that was kind of what I'd expected from him.

"I hope you know that boy Gaige wouldn't give you two minutes of peace if I hadn't sent him away," Mom said, puffing her chest out.

"What?" I said, my voice a rasping shriek.

"Oh, just for the morning. He hasn't left this hospital in five days. Not since you were admitted! That waiting room was becoming his own personal space. He was working from there, sleeping on the couch. I finally had to send him home for fresh clothes, honey."

My heart rate slowed again. He would be back. Mom had made him leave. I smiled at the thought of Spider refusing to leave the hospital. That was more in line with the Spider I knew.

"Your brothers are all here, Tam," Dad said. "And your friends. You've got a good group here."

"I do." I hoped my friends hadn't been too worried. "How is Catalina?" I still couldn't believe she'd donated part of her liver.

"They moved her out of intensive care this morning and she's doing great," Mom said.

Dr. Charles came in a few more minutes later and took all my vitals, telling me she was pleased with the results. "You know," she said, "once your new liver has grown to it's regular size and is working at full function, you won't have Wilson's Disease anymore."

Shock made me lift my head from the pillow. "What?"

"The defect is in the liver cells. New liver, no defect. No disease."

"Really?" I hadn't thought of that. I hadn't had time to think of it. "That's amazing."

"You'll still have to take medication every day, but life should get a little less complicated for you." She smiled and patted my hand. "You need lots of rest, though." She raised an eyebrow. "I have tried to keep your family in check, but I have to say they're a handful."

"They are," I agreed.

"I like your boyfriend though," she added. "He's definitely the hell or high water type."

"I think he's been through both with me." It felt natural to have Spider referred to as my boyfriend. Wasn't that what he really was to me? Even if we hadn't really been together in years, he was here. Plus he had never left my heart.

———

The next time I awoke, Spider was at my side, the room dark and quiet.

"Morning, sunshine." His smile sent a warmth through my limbs as I woke up.

"Hey," I said.

"You did great." He kissed my cheek gently. "And you're gonna be just fine."

I nodded. He was right. The darkness had receded, and I felt a strange optimism for the future, something I'd never really allowed myself to feel before when I knew that my life would always be bound by the limitations of my disease. "Thanks for staying. I knew you were here the whole time."

He blushed and looked down. Cocky as he was, Spider didn't really like to take credit, even when it was deserved.

We sat quietly for a few minutes, Spider running his thumb over the tops of my fingers as we both watched. Finally he asked, "Tamara?"

"Yeah?"

"I need to know how you feel. I'm here. I've always been here, and I'll be here until you tell me to go. Even if you tell me to go, I probably won't, not until you're one hundred percent well again, but I need to know what you want for us. For you."

"I want you," I whispered. Gaige Spydell was the only boy I'd wanted when I was a girl, and he was the only man I wanted now. He was the only one I'd ever wanted. "I just want you."

He grinned at me and squeezed my hand, beaming, looking happier than I'd ever seen him. "Do you think it'd be okay, then, if I asked your daddy something while he's here?"

My heart picked up a quicker beat. There was only one thing a man needed to ask a girl's daddy. While I'd thought about marriage before, it had only been in abstract terms, never in a real concrete and possible way.

"Yeah," I said, the thought of becoming Spider's wife suddenly real, possible, and so good.

He let loose a holler and practically leapt to his feet. "Don't go anywhere."

I smiled as the door swung shut, the thought of spending the rest of my life with Spider settling around me like a warm blanket.

Chapter Thirty-Three

THE BAR ALWAYS WINS

Natalie

CJ and I didn't get to the hospital as early as we'd planned, both of us tired from a long night of talking and doing other things besides sleeping. Catalina was awake when we entered her room, but she looked groggy. They had kept her in intensive care overnight and moved her into another room this morning.

"That's good," I guessed. "That means you're healing well."

She nodded, trying for a smile that didn't quite reach her eyes.

We stayed with Catalina for an hour, making idle chat and trying to brighten her mood, but I wondered if being so alone through such a frightening ordeal might have worn her down. Just as we were about to leave, Tamara's brother Trask walked through the door. He towered over us all at six-foot-five and couldn't have seemed much more out of place in the small pink hospital room.

"Are you the girl who saved my little sister?" he asked Catalina, clearly thinking nothing of just appearing in the hospital room of a complete stranger.

"She is," I told him.

Trask smiled wide and sat himself down in the chair I'd just vacated. "Well, would you mind if I stay just a little bit and say hello?" he asked, already looking pretty settled.

Catalina smiled, a much more sincere smile than the one she'd worn a few minutes before, and I got the distinct impression that Trask might do a far better job of keeping her company than CJ and I had done.

———

When we got to Tamara's room, the nurse outside intercepted us. "You do know this is the intensive care unit, right?" she asked, clearly exasperated. "This place is like the Westside Highway lately!"

"Sorry," I said. "Can we see her?"

She shook her head. "One at a time. Someone's gotta enforce some rules around here. She's just had major surgery."

"I'll be quick." I dodged through Tamara's door, giving CJ's hand a quick squeeze as I went by.

Tamara lay in her bed with her eyes closed, and I paused, thinking I'd better let her sleep. Just as I turned to go, she said, "Hey Pepper," in a soft voice.

"Hey, you." I walked to her bedside. "How are you doing?"

She seemed small and frail, but there was a look on her face that I couldn't pinpoint. She appeared calm and happy... and something else.

"I'm good," she said. "Really good. When I'm better, I won't have Wilson's anymore."

"Seriously?" I was confused. I'd never heard of the disease before meeting Tamara, so I didn't really understand the specifics.

"It was in my liver. My liver is gone..."

"That's great! So your kidneys are better, too?"

"Everything is working as it should right now. Everything is amazing."

Relief washed through me, and I squeezed her hand. "I'm so glad."

"And guess what else?" Her smile widened.

I raised an eyebrow. "What?"

"Spider is out there right now, asking my father a very important question."

What very important question? I ran some possible questions through my mind and came up blank. "What?"

"The question that a man who loves you might ask your dad? Permission? You know..."

If we hadn't been in the hospital, or if Tamara and Spider had actually been an official couple before her surgery, I might have been quicker on the uptake.

"You don't mean marriage..."

"What else would I mean?"

"That's what I was trying to figure out!" I laughed. "Oh my gosh, Tamara! Did he ask you already?"

"No. Don't you watch movies? They have to ask your dad's permission first. And my dad has never been Spider's biggest fan."

"Are you worried?"

She smiled. "He's very persuasive, but it might take a while." Her voice was quiet, and she looked exhausted despite the wide smile.

"Well, I'm going to let you get some sleep while Spider works on your dad, okay?"

"Thanks, Pepper. For everything."

In the waiting room, Spider and Mr. Hunt were seated side by side in the back corner of the waiting room. Spider was showing Mr. Hunt something on his laptop, and I wondered if he was proving he was financially solvent and would be able to support Tamara. I caught his eye and smiled at him, and he flashed me a thumbs-up.

A nurse came out a few minutes later and told us that Tamara was asleep and that no one else would be allowed to see her for several hours. Tamara's brothers all stood up and formed little groups around the room.

"Statue of Liberty," Brody said.

"Empire State, man," Jeff countered.

Hal turned to me. "If you had just a couple hours to see the most important sight in New York City, what would it be?"

I thought about that for a minute.

CJ came to my side and took my hand. "That's an impossible task," he said.

I nodded. "If it was me? I'd just go for a walk. Walk through the streets and feel the energy pulse around you. This place is like nowhere else I've ever been. It's practically alive."

They all stared at me, skeptical expressions on their faces.

"Or the top of the World Trade Center," CJ said. "Plus there's a bar up there."

"World Trade Center!" they all cried, turning to head out. "You coming, Dad? Spider?"

Mr. Hunt and Spider waved them away. Adelaide pulled out a knot of yarn and some needles. She was clearly not leaving the hospital.

"Lunch?" CJ asked as we followed the Hunt boys out.

"Sure," I said, noticing that Trask hadn't rejoined his brothers. Maybe he and Catalina had found some common ground. I was just glad she wasn't alone.

CJ and I stepped out onto the sidewalk and he grabbed my hand, pulling toward lunch. It occurred to me that I wasn't alone now either, and maybe I never would be again.

Chapter Thirty-Four

CIRCLE THE WAGONS

Tamara

WHEN I WOKE UP AGAIN, Spider was back at my side, my hand in his once more, only this time, there was a weight on my finger I didn't recognize. I jerked my hand up to look at it and found a glittering diamond on my ring finger, set in a silver band.

Spider grinned at me. "Like it?"

"You're supposed to actually *ask* me." I was only doing this once. He had to do it right.

"Oh, if you're gonna get all annoying about it, fine." He pulled the ring off my finger, dropped it in his jeans pocket, and stood.

"You're supposed to kneel."

"Can you just work with me here, Tam?" he asked, faking exasperation. "I'll be right back." He disappeared out the door.

What did he have up his sleeve?

I took a swig of water, swishing it around my mouth and wondering what five days in intensive care without a toothbrush might smell like on one's breath. I patted at my hair, which was hard with the stupid IV in my arm, and pinched my cheeks. I tilted the bed up until the incision on my stomach started to ache and tilted it back down slightly.

Just then, Spider walked back in, followed by each one of my brothers, my parents, Pepper and CJ, Tom, Lulu and Andrew, Gregoire and Candace and a few nurses, including Gabe.

"Tamara Hunt." Spider stepped toward my bed. "I knew one day I would have a question to ask you. I never imagined it would be in a hospital room, but I also never imagined that I'd get to do it in front of your whole entire family and all your friends, either."

Natalie held up her cell phone. "Catalina's here, too."

Candace held up hers. "And Maggie."

"Hi, guys," I said, giggling with excitement despite the pain in my stomach.

"You've always been the girl for me, Tam. When all those other girls were busy trying on lipstick and tutus, you were running through the hills with me, gigging frogs and shooting squirrels out of trees. You've never backed down from a challenge, including that goddamned disease." He paused and shot a look at Hal, who seemed to be managing his own illness well. "You're the strongest person I know, and the most beautiful girl I've ever seen."

My mom was sniffling at this point, dabbing her eyes with a tissue.

Spider dropped to one knee. "You wanted it done right, so here it is. Tamara Hunt, I cannot imagine my life without you in it. You are literally the only star in my sky, the sun in my life. Will you marry me, Tamara?" He held out the ring he'd snatched off my finger before.

Everyone in the room seemed to catch their breath.

"Of course I will, Spider. I love you." I reached out for him. "Now give me my ring back."

Everyone laughed as he slid the ring into place on my hand. Spider kissed me, and the feeling of his soft lips on mine was a feeling I'd called up from memory and dreamed about so many times over the last few years. I'd missed him. I'd missed his kisses and everything about him. I couldn't wait to spend every day being his wife.

"Ahem," my mother interrupted as everyone else applauded and hooted loudly. "Where will y'all live? I don't want my grandbabies raised in this godawful city."

"Mom," Hal said, putting an arm over her shoulders. "Let's take things one step at a time, okay? You've got one grand baby on the way. Let's focus on that."

I raised an eyebrow at Hal. I hadn't gotten to talk to him at all.

He smiled at me. "Clarissa realized how goddamned charming I am and came back. I might've apologized for being an ass, too."

"Mistake number one," Spider yelled. "Never admit when you're wrong!"

"Oh, we have a lot of work to do," I moaned.

Chapter Thirty-Five

NEXT GIRL IN LINE

Natalie

CJ HELD my hand as Spider proposed and we smiled and laughed along with everyone as Tamara accepted. The room buzzed with a joy I hadn't often experienced, and I felt like I was vibrating with happiness.

One of the nurses shooed us all out moments later, letting Spider stay with Tamara for a few minutes longer in honor of his new status as her fiancé.

Adelaide Hunt cried good and long once we were all back out in the waiting area, and her sons took turns consoling her.

Once the excitement ended, Trask asked Spider if he planned to move in with Tamara now that they were engaged.

"Hadn't thought that far. Why?" Spider asked.

"Was just thinking it might be nice to have a place here. I think NYC has a lot to recommend it. Might want to visit from time to time." Trask grinned and looked at me. "I hope your roommate feels the same way."

I hadn't thought I could feel happier, but knowing that there was a chance Trask and Catalina might have hit it off just topped off a perfect day. I put my head on CJ's shoulder, smiling for all I was worth.

Who would ever have imagined that one of my greatest moments would be spent in a hospital waiting room in a city three thousand miles from where I grew up? I was surrounded by people who I hadn't even known two years ago, some of whom I'd met this week. Still, I had never felt more at home, or more surrounded by love than I did in that span of time.

CJ kissed my cheek and whispered in my ear, "Wanna be next?"

I stared at him, my eyes wide and my smile wider. We weren't there yet, but I could think of nothing better than becoming CJ's wife one day. "Absolutely."

I wrapped my arms around CJ's neck, kissing the man I loved and exploring the hope that the possibility of forever with him might bring.

ALSO BY DELANCEY STEWART

Want more? Get early releases, sneak peeks and freebies! Join my mailing list here or scan the QR code and get a free story!

The Kasper Ridge Series:

Only a Summer

Only a Fling

Only a Crush

Only a Secret

Only a Touch

The Singletree Series:

Happily Ever His

Happily Ever Hers

Shaking the Sleigh

Second Chance Spring

Falling Into Forever

Singletree Box Set 1

Highballs in the Hamptons

Cosmos and Commitment

The Girlfriends of Gotham Box Set

STANDALONES:

Let it Snow

Without Words

Without Promises

Mr. Big

Adagio

The PROHIBITED! Duet:

Prohibited!

The Glittering Life of Evie Mckenzie